Tiger Lily

'If it's the sex you need, Shanna, you can come to me,' said Joe. A muscle in his jaw twitched, and his lips came down hard on hers. 'I'll give you all you can handle.'

Shanna welcomed his kiss, but a part of her cringed at his words. He thought she *needed* sex, like some starved nymphomaniac. The only sex she absolutely *needed* was from him. What she'd done with Sonny and the rest of Santos's men had been for a purpose. There was a method to her madness, but he couldn't see that. He could only see that one of his agents was out of control.

Tiger Lily
Kimberly Dean

BLACK LACE

Black Lace books contain sexual fantasies.
In real life, always practise safe sex.

First published in 2002 by
Black Lace
Thames Wharf Studios
Rainville Road
London W6 9HA

Design by Smith & Gilmour, London
Printed and bound by Mackays of Chatham PLC

ISBN 0 352 33685 4

Prologue

It still smelled the same.

Shanna couldn't describe it, but it was still there. The air was heavy, pregnant with emotion. It filled her lungs with a weight she could hardly bear. Despair. Anger. Fear. They were all there, vivid in the pictures in her mind. The subtle stench had brought all the overwhelming feelings back.

Block it out, she ordered herself.

She couldn't be distracted. She had a job to do.

Her fingers tightened around the handle of her revolver. Taking a slow deep breath, she forced the thoughts to the back of her mind. She couldn't stop her memories completely, but she could use them to her advantage.

This was her turf. She knew this alleyway better than anyone suspected. She knew Giovanni's left cold pizza slices in the dumpster by their back door. The Zone wasn't as generous with its alcohol, but it was easy enough to slip inside the back exit to use the restroom. And Return to Kashmir – she knew what really went on inside that place.

Tonight, the atmosphere was nearly suffocating. She ignored it. She had her focus back, and nothing was going to stop her from her purpose.

'Move into position.'

The whispered order sent a shiver down her spine. Reaching up, she adjusted her earpiece. It was as if his hot breath had brushed the back of her neck. Just like that, her grip on her weapon became slippery. Transferring it to her other hand, she wiped the sweat from her palm on to her jeans.

Special Agent Joe Mitchell had that effect on her.

'McKay, are you set?'

Shanna quickly sidestepped an empty cardboard box and braced herself against the brick wall. The closed door was on her left, so she transferred her gun to her right hand. 'I'm at the back entrance,' she whispered into the microphone of her lightweight headset.

'Is it locked?'

Joe's voice was low and deceptively calm. The entire team was listening, but she felt as if he were standing right next to her, whispering into her ear. She swallowed hard to fight her reaction. Concentrating on the task at hand, she slowly reached out and wrapped her fingers around the doorknob. Using the slightest of pressures, she gave it a twist.

It didn't budge.

'Affirmative,' she whispered. 'Give me thirty seconds.'

Before he could respond, she was dropping to her knees and reaching for the tools in her back pocket. An ironic smile settled on her lips as she set to work on picking the lock. Funny – they hadn't had to teach this skill to her at the academy. As she used a light touch on the lock, she heard Joe quietly establish the positions of the rest of the team.

'Mustang?'

'Check.'

'Devo?'

'Check.'

'Cobra?'

'Yo.'

She'd just heard the final pin fall into place when his voice touched her again. 'Lily?'

She'd thought she was prepared, but her breath still caught. Every time he used her code name, a frisson of electricity shot down her spine. If he ever called her Shanna, her heart would likely stop.

'I'm in,' she whispered.

'Hold your positions until my command.'

Shanna pressed her back against the wall again and tried to slow her suddenly racing heartbeat. This was it! She could hardly believe it. She'd been waiting for this moment for an eternity. Tonight, Mañuel Santos was going to get what was coming to him.

Her hands began to shake out of anticipation, and she glared at them. She had to get her nerves under control. She took another deep breath. It was the wrong thing to do. The pungent air hit her nasal passages and she nearly gagged on her rage.

'Move! Go! Go! Go!'

The order burst through her earpiece and she sprung into action. In one smooth move, she kicked in the door. Dropping to a crouch, she slowly peered around the corner. Seeing the hallway empty, she entered the premises.

Her fear had vanished. In its place was cool, ruthless determination. Her gun was rock-steady in her grip as she silently moved down the hall. She placed her steps carefully, and her ears were alert for any sound, any movement.

The place was eerily silent.

It shouldn't be that way.

Shanna paused. It was way too quiet. They were walking into a trap.

Her lungs expanded with the knowledge. Her heart pounded in her ears as she considered what to do. Her training told her to back out carefully, block the exit and wait for assistance. Instinct told her to move forward.

She hadn't heard a sound. She hadn't seen a movement.

But she could feel.

Whirling around the corner, she dropped low and cocked her weapon.

She found herself face to face with the barrel of a .44 Magnum.

1

'Would somebody please explain to me why we raided an empty building last night?'

Special Agent Mitchell's words were calm, but the even staccato of the syllables made Shanna sit a little straighter. God, she hated being called into his office. It was just so small, so claustrophobic. He seemed to fill up the space until she couldn't breathe.

'It wasn't supposed to be empty.'

She threw a glance of appreciation in her partner's direction. Shawn 'Cobra' Coberley wasn't the timid sort. He wouldn't make excuses or beg forgiveness. He'd get down to brass tacks, tell things the way they were and move on. She wished she could be that way around Joe Mitchell.

Unfortunately, he tied her in knots. And to think that he was disappointed in her – well, that just made her want to cry. Given her inability to shed tears, that was saying a lot.

'Your source was solid?'

'I swear, Joe. That information was good as gold. They were there yesterday. Somehow, they must have gotten wind that we were coming.'

'It's hard to believe Santos could move that much heroin that quickly.'

'I know, but the guy's a pro. He's been doing this for so many years, he's got it down to a system.'

Shanna's stomach clenched at the mention of Santos's name, and her fingers dug into the arms of the chair. She felt more than saw Joe's gaze land on her white knuckles.

Forcing herself, she let her grip loosen. Needing something to do, she began to toy with the ring on her right hand.

'Do we have any idea where he went?'

Again, the question was directed at Cobra. Shanna swallowed hard. Lord, the walls were just pressing in on her. She focused her gaze on the bookshelf behind her boss's shoulder. Breathe in, breathe out.

'We've got a couple of ideas, but we're still working on it.'

'Well, next time, let's make sure we get the job done. We can't afford busted raids. They waste our time and our money. Worst of all, they make us look bad.' Joe's voice dropped to a growl. 'I don't like to look bad.'

Shanna's heart sank.

'No, sir,' Shawn said. Even his voice had dropped to a contrite tone. Joe Mitchell didn't chew out his employees very often. This was about as bad as it got. Somehow, the disapproval in his tone was worse than if he'd screamed.

'It won't happen again, sir,' Shanna finally whispered. They were the first words she'd managed to say since she'd stepped foot inside this closet.

Shawn pushed his chair back and stood. She began to follow suit, but Joe's words put a stop to that.

'Lily, I'm not through with you yet.'

Shanna threw a desperate look at her partner, but Shawn just shrugged. He gave her a sympathetic grimace and headed to the door. When it closed with a click behind him, she could have sworn the room shrunk to about a third of its tiny size.

'Sir?' she said. God, she didn't want to have this conversation. Joe's disapproval with last night's events hurt too much. She didn't want to hear how she'd screwed up. He had no way of knowing, but his opinions mattered to her more than they should.

'Sit down.'

With a deep breath, she followed his instructions. Her skirt hiked halfway up her thighs at the movement and she hastily pulled it back down. He said nothing, but his gaze practically scorched her legs before it skittered away. The unexpected look surprised her. Certain that she had misinterpreted his action, she focused her gaze on his desk.

It was a mistake. His elbows rested on the wooden surface and his hands were clasped together. She looked at those big, strong, masculine hands, and a vivid picture flashed into her head. She could see those hands sliding slowly up under her skirt, discovering the fact that she wore thigh-high stockings, and tugging at the clasps of her suspender belt.

Her cheeks flooded with colour and her sex clenched with excitement. She quickly glanced away, but it was too late. Moisture trickled down the inside of her thigh. Her panties had been damp from the moment he'd called her and her partner into his office. Now they were sopping.

'Are you ever going to look at me?'

They weren't the words she was expecting, and her shocked gaze collided with his. His cool green eyes were unreadable but they were compelling. They held her look. The ceiling pressed down on her and she squirmed in her chair.

Joe leaned back in his chair and it let out an ear-piercing shriek. Shanna flinched, but still she couldn't look away. His gaze moved across her face, taking in her features. She felt her breaths hitch. She waited for him to continue but he remained silent.

Helplessly, she watched him stare at her.

'You almost shot me last night.'

She forgot to breathe.

'Lily?' he said, coming out of his creaky chair in a flash and rounding the desk.

Her face must have turned white. Taking a deep breath of the diminishing oxygen supply in the room, Shanna tried to settle her whirling thoughts. It was impossible when he kneeled down beside her chair. His gaze bore into hers and she quickly shut her eyes to hide her flare of reaction.

'Are you OK?' he asked quietly.

'I'm fine,' she said, fighting to keep her voice steady.

He hovered nearby, almost as if he were hesitant to leave her side. She was relieved when he finally moved away. Instead of returning to his chair, though, he settled his lean hips against the edge of the desk directly in front of her. The position put his crotch practically at her face level. The irony struck her, and she looked away with a groaning laugh.

'You think it's funny? You almost fed me a bullet last night.'

Her gaze flashed back to his. 'I seem to recall you had me in your sights, too.'

'Lily, you're always in my sights.'

She flinched at the comment.

He quickly cleared his throat and crossed his muscular arms over his chest. 'What I mean is that I have to watch you more closely than anybody else on my team. You're a wild card. Last night proved it.'

Uncomfortable, she toyed with the ring on her finger. 'Can we not have this discussion again?'

'I don't see how we can avoid it.'

'I am not "impulsive".' He'd accused her of it so many times, she'd gotten sick of the word.

'Yes, you are. You're dangerous.'

Somehow, his inflection made a jolt of electricity shoot down her spine. 'I'm *instinctive*,' she argued.

He shifted his weight on the desk. 'I don't see the difference.'

She struggled to find the words. She searched his

handsome face, looking for signs of understanding. All she saw was an impossibly good-looking man scowling at her. 'If I were impulsive, I'd be acting without thinking.'

'Exactly.'

'But I am thinking,' she said quickly. 'I'm using more than my brains. I'm listening to my gut. It's saved me more times than I can count.'

Her tone dropped with that confession, and she bit her lower lip. She hadn't meant to say that much. His gaze focused like a laser beam on her lips, and her mouth went dry.

'As soon as you sensed something was wrong, you should have backed out of that building,' he said gruffly. 'Why didn't you follow your guts then?'

'My guts told me there was somebody around that corner.'

'How?' he said with disbelief.

To some, it might seem like an arrogant retort, but Shanna took it for what it was worth. Joe Mitchell was one of the best agents the FBI had ever had. He'd earned the nickname 'Tiger' for his ability to approach a target undetected, yet attack with a speed and agility that was stunning.

'I felt you,' she said.

'You what?'

'I felt your presence,' she said with a shrug.

She gasped when he leaned forward and gripped the arms of her chair. He trapped her with both his proximity and the fierce look in his eyes. 'You knew I was there, and you still pulled a gun on me?'

'I didn't know it was *you*,' she whispered. 'I just sensed somebody was there.'

She said the words aloud, but inside she wondered at their truth. Would she really have been able to feel anybody besides Joe Mitchell around that corner?

His green gaze burned into hers. 'You had murder in your eyes.'

She swallowed hard. 'I want Santos.'

He said nothing, but looked at her carefully. He was so close. Shanna's fingers dug into the muscles of her thighs. She was afraid that at any moment, her hands would betray her and dive into his dark hair. She wanted nothing more than to pull him close and feel those hard lips settle on hers. God, even her legs were trembling. She had visions of wrapping them around his waist, tearing open his fly and plunging on to him.

'You seem to want him a little too badly.'

'This case is important to me.'

'Why?'

She licked her lips at the direct question. He almost seemed to lean closer at the action, and she stumbled over her words. 'H-h-he's a major drug dealer.'

'Is that the only reason?'

Her backbone finally snapped into place. 'Seems like a good enough reason to me.'

He stared at her hard, but this time she held her ground.

'I think you're holding out on me,' he said softly. 'I get the feeling that something else is going on here. You're a crackerjack agent, Lily, even though you do tend to get a little impulsive at times.'

She opened her mouth to respond, but he held up his hand to stop her.

'You're riding on the edge with this Santos case, though. It's almost as if it's personal to you.'

A warning zapped through Shanna's nervous system. He was too close to the truth. 'Why did you pull your gun on me?' she asked, quickly turning the tables. 'You knew my position.'

His lips twisted up in a hard smirk. 'I knew where your position was supposed to be – outside the damn door. I heard somebody in the hallway, and I had to assume that you'd been taken out.'

'Oh, please.'

His hand suddenly left the arm of her chair and gripped her chin. 'You scared the shit out of me, Lily. I was coming to get the bastard when you spun around that corner. I was seeing red by that time. You're damn lucky I didn't pull that trigger.'

Shanna's heart jumped into her throat. He'd never touched her before. Her skin burned where his fingers held her. Unable to stop herself, she reached up and grabbed his wrist. Her palm encountered the springy black hair of his forearm, and she savoured the raspy feeling. Her nipples tightened as she considered how they'd react if they came into contact with the same sensation.

Her thumb landed on his pulse. It was pounding just as rapidly as hers. She quickly looked up into his eyes. Something hot and dangerous passed between them, but just as suddenly as it appeared, it vanished. Joe's face went deliberately blank and he pulled back as if burned.

'Next time, follow protocol,' he ordered in a clipped tone. He stood up and circled the desk back to his chair. 'One more wrong move on your part and I'll pull you off this case. Now, get out there and help Coberley figure out where that bastard Santos moved his stash.'

Shanna jerked as if he'd slapped her. There was nothing like having your hopes dashed before they even got off the ground. 'Yes, sir,' she said hoarsely.

Unsteadily, she pushed herself from the chair. She headed for the door with as much grace as she could muster. Unfortunately, his stare still bore into her back. Unable to spare a glance in his direction, she opened the door and made her escape.

Almost immediately, she began to breathe more easily.

There was air in the hallway – fresh, clean, revitalising air. She took a deep gulp and tried to get her bearings. She threw a glance towards her desk. Shawn was already entranced in his computer. Unfortunately, she knew the minute he spotted her, he'd be on her, wanting to know what had happened.

She wasn't prepared for that yet. She turned on her heel and headed to the ladies' room. Her legs were wobbly as she pushed open the door.

He'd touched her.

Quickly, she glanced under the stall doors. Thank God, she was alone. Stealing a glance in the mirror, she sighed. Her cheeks were pink. He had to have seen how his touch had affected her.

Groaning, she spun away from her reflection and began to pace the room. Her heels clicked against the linoleum floor, and the sound echoed off the walls. She'd come dangerously close to making a fool of herself back there.

Joe Mitchell was her boss, for heaven's sake. More than that, he was her idol. She knew that she'd put him on a pedestal, but in her opinion, that was where he belonged. He was just so damn perfect. And what was she? Gutter trash.

Spinning around, she began to pace in the opposite direction. Why did she let herself dream about the impossible? Hell, that was half the problem. There wasn't any hope for the two of them. She knew that as well as she knew her own name. Things might not be so bad if she could just stop fantasising.

'You idiot.'

She and Joe couldn't have been more different. He was practically the FBI poster boy. He came from the perfect background. He'd grown up in the perfect family. He'd gotten perfect grades. The Bureau had welcomed him with open arms, and he'd never disappointed them.

He'd risen through the ranks like a rocket and was now one of the youngest special agents in the department's history.

'What would he ever want with you?'

With a groan, Shanna raked a hand through her long dark hair. She knew there wasn't a chance in Hades of her ever hooking up with Joe Mitchell. Still, she couldn't get rid of her nearly debilitating attraction to the man.

He'd touched her.

She'd been waiting for that for ever.

Blowing out a long breath, she tried to slow her racing pulse. She'd had a crush on Joe Mitchell for a very long time. Her adoptive father, Robert Haynes, had been his partner when he'd first joined the Bureau. She'd heard all the stories and built up an image of The Tiger before she'd even met him. When she'd finally gotten her first look at him, she'd gone under for good.

And he'd finally laid a hand on her.

Her breath shuddered in her lungs. God. One impersonal little touch and she was ready to come.

Her sex was weeping for attention. Giving up the battle, she moved into the end stall and locked the door. Slowly, she pulled her skirt up until the material bunched around her waist. Even the friction of the material sliding across her thighs made her groan from frustration.

Quickly, she dealt with the suspender-belt clasps and reached for her panties. Hooking her thumbs under the waistband, she gently pushed them down. With a deep breath, she widened her stance and looked down at herself.

The dark curls at the juncture of her legs were glistening with her juices. Her sex was swollen and flaming red. Closing her eyes, she let her hand wander closer to that forbidden area. At the first touch of her fingers, she gasped and leaned back against the wall. Delving deeper, she parted her overly sensitive lips and searched out the bundle of nerve-endings that could bring her some relief.

A lightning bolt of sensation shot through her, and she had to reach for the stall door to brace herself. 'Joe,' she sighed.

She plucked at the responsive little button and her inner muscles fluttered. Her poor pussy was looking for something, *anything*, to grab on to. Pushing her shoulders hard against the cold wall, she reached down with her other hand. Her opening was overly sensitised, and she soothed it with the pads of her fingers before trying to penetrate.

Becoming impatient, she slid one finger deep inside her body. Her pussy latched eagerly on to the intruder and began sucking greedily. Shanna couldn't stop the cry of delight that passed her lips. Needing more, she worked another finger deep into herself.

It was good, but not as good as it could have been. She squeezed her eyes shut and imagined it was Joe finger-fucking her. Suddenly, the sensations doubled in magnitude.

Her hips bucked and she began working both her hands more aggressively. A sweat broke out on her brow and her heart pounded at a frantic pace. Still she couldn't reach that ultimate peak.

'Oh, please!' she begged. She pushed harder on her clitoris but she was hanging right on the edge. Something was holding her back. She needed more. She needed *him*!

Opening her eyes, she looked for anything that could help her. Her gaze landed on the toilet-paper roll. It might do. Diving forward, she opened the mechanism. She almost sighed in relief when she saw that the cross bar that held the roll was one solid piece of metal.

As she examined it, she felt her pussy contract. It was exactly what she needed. The metal piece was smooth and cylindrical. It was only about an inch in diameter, but it was incredibly hard. More importantly, it was about six inches long. It could reach further inside of her than any of her fingers. If she closed her eyes, she could imagine.

'You can't,' she said.

But she had to.

Leaning back against the wall, she took a deep breath. The thought of fucking herself with an inanimate object was beyond naughty. It was dirty. But that's what she was. She'd always been a bad girl. No matter how hard she tried to change things, it was what she always and forever would be.

Quickly, she disentangled her right leg from her panties. They drooped around her left shoe, creating an erotic picture. Bracing her high-heeled shoe on the toilet seat, she reached again for her core.

She spread her lips wide. They pulsed with excitement, and her shoe nearly slipped off the porcelain. Breathing hard, she settled the smooth metal piece against her opening. It was cold. She gritted her teeth until her jaw ached but she was too far gone to stop. Determinedly, she pressed the bar inside her.

'Oh, God!' she moaned. The rod was small, but its temperature made it seem much bigger. Her inner muscles contracted but they couldn't escape the icy stainless steel. She squirmed against the wall, tormented by the tiny dildo that hung halfway out of her pussy.

It hardly stretched her at all, but it was what she needed. It was hard, impossibly hard, and she began to ride it. Closing her eyes, she pictured Joe in the stall with her. He'd be bigger. He'd surely stretch her wide, and she had a thing for size. His rough hands would grab her ass, and he'd hold her in place as he pounded his big dick into her.

'Ahhh!' Shanna felt herself beginning to ascend to the

peak. She worked the bar in and out of her, slowly increasing her speed. As her excitement grew, she pressed harder and harder against her sensitive clit. Her breaths were turning ragged when suddenly the door to the bathroom swung open with a whoosh.

Shanna froze. The dildo was high inside her and her hands were between her legs. Squeezing her eyelids closed, she tried to disappear.

'Oh my, look at this.'

She nearly died of horror when she heard the elderly woman's voice. Betty Simpcox! Oh, dear God! Betty was a sweet grey-haired lady who just happened to be Joe's secretary. The woman had probably never heard the word 'masturbation'.

'Toilet paper all over the floor.'

She heard Betty lean down to pick up the mess. A movement at her feet caught her attention, and Shanna wanted to die. The line of toilet paper led directly to her stall. In her haste to get to her impromptu sex toy, she'd tossed the roll aside. It must have tumbled across the floor. Now it was pointing right at her like an accusing finger. Her face flared with colour.

'Are you OK in there, dear?'

Shanna's vocal cords froze.

'Shanna, is that you?'

Her ankles burned when she sensed the elderly woman glancing under the stall door. There was no way she could hide. 'Mm-hmm.'

'Having problems, sweetie?'

Shanna leaned her head back against the wall. The cold bar was embedded deep inside her. 'Yes.'

'Do you need any help?'

'No!' Shanna gasped aloud, but hurried to soothe any hurt feelings. 'I'll be fine.'

'Well, if you're sure.'

'I'm positive.'

'Here you go, dear.'

Shanna looked down and saw an age-spotted hand reach under the door. Automatically, she reached down to take the roll of toilet paper. Unfortunately, she forgot about the rod embedded inside her. It shifted, and she had to stifle a groan. 'Thank you,' she hissed.

'You're welcome.'

Shanna leaned against the wall and tried to get control of herself. She'd never felt so dirty. She'd been caught in the act. Worst of all, she was hotter than a pistol. She couldn't remember ever being so aroused in her life.

She waited the interminable minutes as Betty went about her business. The personal sounds that normally went by unobserved were suddenly unbearably loud. Shanna squirmed against the wall, her body begging for release. She just couldn't do it while Betty was in the room. It was too obscene.

Her pussy ached. It begged her to move that hard dildo inside of her. She was so close to coming, her toes were curling inside her shoes.

Finally, Betty's stall door opened. Being the fastidious type, the older woman not only washed and dried her hands, but also primped as she studied herself in the mirror.

Hurry up! Shanna nearly screamed. In a few seconds, she wasn't going to be able to hold back her orgasm whether she wanted to or not. At long last, she heard the clip-clop of footsteps heading to the door. They paused, though, and she nearly wept.

'Are you sure you're OK, dear?'

'Yes!'

Some of her frustration must have entered her tone, because the sweet old lady finally left. Reaching down, Shanna hurriedly began to shag herself. Closing her eyes, she concentrated on the feelings building inside of her.

With every thrust, her cunt greedily accepted the foreign intrusion. She plucked insistently at her swollen bud until the excitement peaked. Suddenly, a high-pitched whine left her throat.

'Joe,' she cried as her muscles clamped down and shudders wracked her body.

It took several minutes before the world stopped spinning. She sagged against the wall, her muscles limp with completion. After a while, the cool air from the vents became too much on her exposed skin. Opening her eyes, she took in her situation.

Her panties were still draped across her shoe. The roll of toilet paper had again been tipped on its side. Fortunately, this time the wall had stopped its momentum. Directly ahead of her, the toilet-paper holder stood barren. Her face flushed and she reached down to remove the metal bar from its slick hiding place. It slid out of her with a slurp and she groaned with embarrassment.

Her lips pressed into a straight thin line as she hurriedly cleaned herself up. She mentally detached herself as she straightened up the stall and removed all evidence of what she'd just done. Arranging her clothing, she tried to retrieve her professional front.

It wasn't working. Her panties were still wet. Resignedly, she kicked them off and stuffed them in her pocket. She'd have to stash them in her purse before anybody noticed the smell.

The door to the hallway swung open again and she knew her time was up. Even if she wanted to hide in here all day, it simply wasn't possible. Schooling her face, she unlocked the stall door.

She stepped out, intending to head to the sink, but found Joe blocking her way.

'Are you all right?' he asked.

Shanna's jaw dropped. Everything inside of her froze.

'Betty said you were having some problems.'

Her mouth worked like a fish as she searched for something to say. 'This is the ladies' room!' she gasped.

'I'm well aware of that,' he said with some discomfort. 'Everything is pink.'

The way he said the word with such distaste made her almost laugh. That, in and of itself, was surprising. She'd never felt like laughing in front of Special Agent Mitchell. Not knowing what to make of the situation, she manoeuvred around him and made her way to the sink.

Her hands were still sticky. They shook as she reached for the pink soap dispenser. She hoped he wouldn't notice, but the way he was looking at her made her feel as if he were trying to read her mind.

'Did you ... handle everything?' he asked carefully.

She glanced up and saw him looking at her in the mirror. She was glad she wasn't the only one who felt uncomfortable. Something bold overtook her in that instant. This was the ladies' room. This was supposed to be a place she could go when she needed to escape. What would have happened if he'd walked in here five minutes ago? 'Did Betty tell you what the problem was?' she snapped.

He reached up to rub the back of his neck. 'Not in so many words, but I've got an idea.'

Her cheeks flared, but she couldn't stop herself from asking, 'And you'd help me with something like that?'

He met her gaze in the mirror. 'Yes.'

Shanna's knees buckled, and she reached for the sink to support herself. No matter what his secretary had told him, his answer was enough to shake her to her core.

'I'd drive you to the hospital.'

The wind left her lungs in a rush. 'Oh.'

'But if everything is OK ...'

'It is. It is. Problem solved.' She quickly turned to the paper-towel dispenser and jerked on the handle. Her first tug nearly ripped the unit off the wall. Tempering herself, she tore off a section and wiped her hands.

'That's good.' Nodding his head, Joe looked anywhere in the room but at her. 'Good.'

'Yes, *good*.' Shanna slammed the wadded paper towel into the bin and spun on her heel. 'Excuse me, but I've got a case to get back to.'

Her heels clipped a rapid beat to the door.

'Lily?'

Frustrated beyond belief, Shanna stopped with her hand on the door handle. She considered pretending that she hadn't heard him, but he was her boss. Glancing over her shoulder, she gave him a cautious look.

'Your ... um ...' He cleared his throat and shifted his weight. 'Your panties are about ready to fall out of your jacket pocket.'

2

Three weeks later

'I hope you know what you're doing.' Shawn Coberley hissed the words as they crossed the small parking lot. 'We're supposed to blend in, Lily.'

Shanna folded her small clutch under her arm and tried not to be too self-conscious. She needed that clutch to carry her gun and her tape recorder because there certainly hadn't been any place on her body to conceal them. Surreptitiously, she pulled down on the hem of her dress. It had been at least an inch longer in the dressing room at the store when she'd bought it. Right now, it was skimming the top of her thighs. 'Believe me,' she said, 'in this place, I won't even draw a second glance.'

'No. One will be enough to grab every guy in the joint by the balls.'

Shawn's hand landed on the small of her back to guide her between two parked cars, and goose bumps popped up on Shanna's skin. With every step they took, her dress seemed to shrink. OK, so it was backless. The criss-crossing straps had given her a little too much confidence. It was her front that was causing her the most difficulty, however. It was downright impossible to wear a bra with this skimpy number. Each step in these stiletto heels made her breasts bounce all over the place. She wore a C-cup, for God's sake. She wasn't meant to go braless.

As they stepped up to the doorway, the flashing sign overhead caught her attention. *Tassels*. The neon burned its way to the back of her eyeballs. Her stomach dropped and her steps slowed.

Shawn stopped at her side. 'Second thoughts? Want to go change? I can wait.'

'No, it's all right. I was just thinking.' Thinking? God, the memories were bombarding her faster than she could assimilate them.

'Are you sure?'

'Let's do it.'

He opened the door and she stepped inside. The place hadn't changed much. She inhaled sharply. The scent of booze and sex filled her senses. No, it hadn't changed at all. She suddenly realised that the bouncer was looking at the frozen expression on her face. She tossed him a bright smile, and he let her enter without paying the cover charge.

Inside the doorway, Shanna quickly evaluated the situation. The club wasn't that crowded. Then again, it was still early. Her gaze was immediately drawn to the stage. They'd improved the lighting system. She could see that in a glance. The old spotlight used to blind her to the point where she'd see stars for hours. She dragged her gaze away from the runway and looked over the patrons. Their targets weren't here yet.

But Lenny and Squiggy were. Seeing her old fans still leering at the dancers made her laugh.

'What's so funny?' Shawn asked, his arm coming around her waist in a protective move.

'Oh, nothing. Why don't you grab us a table and I'll get us something to drink?'

He gave her a strange look but motioned to an empty table. 'That one over there looks good. We'll have a clear view of both the front and back exits.'

'If Santos's men show up, we won't miss them,' she said. She took a step towards the bar, then glanced over her shoulder. 'Coke?'

He scowled and she laughed.

'Sorry, big boy. No alcohol allowed.'

'Hell, this job is no fun at all.'

The music suddenly flared up and the lights dimmed. Shanna's grin grew wider. 'You'll just have to grin and bear it.'

A blonde dancer came on stage dressed in a nurse's uniform. Shanna gave her a considering look. She had good moves but she was young. No, things at Tassels hadn't changed at all.

She headed towards the bar. She could feel the stares attached to her body as she crossed the room. Instead of feeling self-conscious, though, the leers had the opposite effect. There was just something about this place. Almost instinctively, she began to move with a more sensuous rhythm to her steps.

'Oh, baby!'

The catcall hadn't been directed to the stage. A small grin lit Shanna's face as she sauntered up to the bar.

The bartender didn't even bother to look at her face. His gaze lasered in on her boobs and she felt their tips pucker. The gaze dropped to her legs. The man licked his lips but his gaze drifted back up to her tits. They were obviously what he liked best.

'Hey, Dooley,' she said softly.

His gaze finally sprang up to meet hers. When he recognised her, his grin took up half his face. 'Shanna McKay. As I live and breathe, I never thought I'd see you in this place again.'

She smiled back at him. 'Me, neither. I'm on a date.'

'A date?' He looked over her shoulder. 'What blockhead would bring a dame like you to a place like this?'

She followed his look and saw Shawn watching them closely. 'The blond hunk at table five.'

Dooley's eyes narrowed, but obviously Coberley measured up to his standards. His gaze turned back on her and he wiggled his eyebrows. 'He's warming you up for later.'

Shanna blushed. 'Can I get two cokes?'

'Cokes?'

'I've cleaned up my act.'

The man cocked his head. 'Well, good for you, girly.'

His gaze drifted over her again. As always, his look settled on her breasts. Her nipples peaked proudly under his stare. 'The years have been good to you, baby. Real good.'

'Thanks,' she whispered. His opinion still meant something to her.

He gave her a considering glance. 'So, where have you been? Do you know how long I've wondered what happened to you? After that cop dragged you out of here that day, I didn't know what to think.'

A soft smile crossed her lips. That 'cop' had been Robert Haynes.

The bartender leaned closer so she could hear him over the blare of the music. 'I could still kill the guy for taking away my best dancer.'

The jealousy gleaming in his eyes made her reach out to cup his cheek. 'I've missed you, Dooley.'

His dark eyes flared. Pinning her with his gaze, he asked, 'How much?'

Shanna knew what he was asking. 'A lot, but . . .'

'Come in the back with me.'

The direct order was unnerving, and she found herself responding as she always had. She glanced over her shoulder at Shawn. 'I don't know.'

'For old times' sake?'

His dark eyes filled with such wanting, her heart melted. This man had played such an integral part in her life. He was older now. The hair at his temples was greying, but his body was still taut as a prizefighter's. She told herself she'd moved on. Her life had changed so much since her time here at Tassels. Still, something pulled at her. 'OK,' she said in a low tone. 'For old times' sake. I'll just take these cokes over to our table first. Give "the blond hunk" some story.'

His eyes sparked, and he held out a hand to her. She settled her palm against his and felt his fingers wrap tightly about hers. She looked over her shoulder at Shawn. He was giving her a strange look, so she waved at him to assure him that things were all right.

Shanna carried the cokes to where Shawn was sat waiting.

'What are you doing, Lily? You're supposed to be on a date with me.'

'Don't want to lose face even on a sting, huh?' she asked.

Shawn didn't answer.

'Look, I won't be long. Old man Dooley's a prime source of information about Santos and his crew. We need all the leads we can get. You'll just have to be the blond hunk at table five for a bit longer.'

Coberley shot her a confused look as she sashayed back to the bar.

Dooley tugged her around the end of the bar and through the doorway into the back room. Shanna's stomach twittered. She'd known that the bartender would be here. She'd wondered how she would react upon seeing him, but now she knew. Excitement unfurled in her veins.

The moment the door closed behind her, he turned on her. He pushed her right up against the wooden door and settled in for a hard exotic kiss. Automatically, she opened her mouth to receive his rough tongue. She didn't have to wait. It plunged into the depths of her mouth, seemingly aiming for her throat. It slid intimately, slowly, across her tongue in one long rasp. Her groan of exhilaration was immediate.

'That's my girl,' the man said against her lips.

Shanna heard the door lock and her heart began to thud. His arms came around her and he gave her another deep, drugging kiss. God, was it possible he'd gotten even better? 'You've been practising.'

He pulled back and gave a soft laugh. 'It's hard not to practise in this place, baby.'

With a tug, he loosened the criss-crossing ties at the back of her dress. Shanna felt it sag and automatically lifted her arms to stop it from falling.

'Come on now. Let me see how you've filled out.'

She gave him a hesitant smile and dropped her arms. The dress slipped across her skin, but hung up on the curves of her breasts. Dooley reached out with one finger. He hooked it around the material in her cleavage and pulled. The dress dropped like a curtain in a magician's show.

'Shanna!' he exclaimed.

Proud of his reaction, she stood up straighter. His workman's hands cupped her breasts and pushed the soft globes upward. A thrill went straight to her core when his thumbs gently tweaked her nipples.

'Want to do a set later tonight? The boys would love to see you back in the spotlight.'

She groaned when he shifted his grip so he could pinch her sensitive peaks between his thumbs and forefingers. With every tug, they became a little stiffer and a little redder. 'I can't,' she gasped. 'I'm here with a date.'

The bartender wiggled his eyebrows suggestively. 'I'm sure he'd appreciate it as much as the rest of us.'

His hands became more aggressive on her breasts. She rolled her head against the door, trying to find some relief to the pressure building inside of her. 'He doesn't know. Nobody knows.'

One of his hands slipped behind the small of her back. With a practised tug, he arched her body so her breasts lifted suggestively. 'That's a downright shame,' he said as he lowered his head.

Shanna knew what was coming. He opened his mouth and that wicked tongue of his slithered out. Her nipple throbbed with anticipation. He lowered his head until he was only an inch away, but then stopped. Her heart thudded as she waited in agony. Then he blew.

Her breast bloomed under the hot air and she whimpered. 'Please.'

'All right, baby. Dooley's coming.'

His grey head dropped and his tongued snaked across her engorged nipple. All tongue – no mouth. The effect was astounding. Shanna's breath went ragged. With a curse, she grabbed his head. She pulled his mouth to her breast until he latched on.

The suckling he gave her was intense. With Dooley, there was no halfway. Oral stimulation was his thing. You could either take it or you couldn't. It had been a long time since she'd basked under his attention. She didn't know if she could stand it any more.

'Easy, girl. We're just getting started.' He soothed her abraded nipple with a long lick and moved to the other one. Meanwhile, his hands dropped to her hips. He pushed the material of her dress down. With a swoosh, it pooled at her feet. His hands immediately settled on her ass. In unison, he squeezed her buttocks hard and nipped at her aureole.

'Ahhh!' Shanna screeched.

'Turn around. Let me see,' he said gruffly.

Well trained, she spun around and braced her forearms against the door. She spread her palms wide on the wooden surface and waited.

'Christ almighty, look at that ass,' he said.

Once again, he put his hands on her and squeezed. She sighed with appreciation.

'And a thong. You still know how to dress up your

assets.' His finger hooked under the line of material that plunged into the crevice between her buttocks and tugged. The material popped out of its hiding place and she groaned. 'All right, all right. Patience.'

He talked about patience, but his own was slowly eroding, Shanna could tell, when he ripped the thong off her hips and pushed it halfway down her thighs. He groped her again and his orders became sharper and swifter.

'Step out of that dress.'

She kicked it aside.

'Get rid of that thong.'

She wriggled out of the confining garment and kicked it aside, too. That left her in only her blue stiletto heels.

'Spread those long legs for old Dooley.'

She widened her stance and felt the cool air rush to her heated skin.

'Now arch your back. You remember how.'

Biting her lip, she took a small step back from the door. Bending over ever so slightly, she gave him better access to her most private parts. She blushed at the lewd position and settled her forehead against the door.

Dooley dropped to his knees behind her and her hips shimmied uncontrollably. She shouldn't want this, but she did. She wanted it as badly as she wanted her next breath.

His rough hands settled on the globes of her buttocks to hold her in position. He spread the two halves like he would an orange. She could feel him leaning close, but the puff of air was unexpected. She flinched, but her sex reacted as shockingly as her nipple had. It swelled and begged for his touch.

She gave a strangled cry when his tongue finally settled on her. Once again, he used just his tongue. He licked his way slowly along one of her distended pussy lips before circling his way back along the other. He kept up the frustrating, circulating pattern until she could hardly breathe. Finally, just as she was about to beg, he curled his tongue into a velvet dagger and stabbed it into her.

Her juices were flowing and his penetration was easy. He went deep before letting his tongue slowly uncurl. The move stretched her from the inside and she moaned at the intensity of the sensation.

'Oh, God. Where did you learn that?' she sobbed.

'Stay still,' he said. His hands tightened on her hips. 'I've got more.'

His tongue was long, strong and agile. He knew it was his most effective sexual weapon, and he used it with uncanny accuracy. He toyed with her until she was nearly hyperventilating, then suddenly backed away.

'Please, don't stop!'

Her plea was too late. He'd already moved on to another sensitive region. Shanna's heart tripped over itself when he spread her buttocks wider.

'Oh, God. No!'

He'd never played around back there. She'd never ... She didn't want ...

She gave a soft yelp when his tongue rubbed firmly across her bottom hole. Before she could adjust, he was back, rooting around for more. Sharp zaps of electricity coursed through her lower abdomen, and she shifted, trying to get away from his scrutiny.

He was having none of it.

Dooley might have gotten older, but he hadn't gotten any weaker. He locked her into position with strong arms. His chin settled intimately against her, and he pressed his face firmly in the crack of her ass. His tongue renewed its assault.

Shanna's nails clawed at the door. Her pulse thundered in her temples. There was no escaping his attentions. She couldn't stop him.

She didn't want to.

That wicked tongue snaked out and swirled around the ring of her most sensitive orifice. He tried to coax it into relaxing. When it didn't, he tried a more forceful approach. The velvet sabre began poking and prodding, testing the limits of her sphincter muscle.

After several attempts, he broached her defences. Shanna whimpered as she felt his tongue move up inside her. Then he did it again. He used the same technique he'd used on her pussy. He let his tongue expand, and the sensation made her knees buckle.

With a harsh laugh, he pulled her down on to all fours in front of him. Giving her no time to prepare, he hooked an arm about her waist and lifted her hips. There was a rasp of a zipper and then he plunged into her hard.

'Yes,' Shanna sighed. It was like coming home. In effect it was; Dooley had been her first.

If there was a difference about his lovemaking now, it was that he wasn't as patient. When he'd first initiated her into the art of sex, he'd gone much slower. He'd tried different techniques to see how she responded. When she was unsure, he took his time.

This was different. He wasn't patient. He was a man dead set on screwing her brains out.

He banged into her again and again. His foreplay had been so intensive, she was close to the edge anyway. When his hand sneaked around and his fingers settled on her clit, she went off like a firecracker. Heat exploded through her body and she cried out.

Behind her, Dooley kept working. He thrust into her until he too climaxed. The fury came upon him suddenly, and he reared back. The tendons in his throat stretched tautly. He came long and hard – impressive for a man of his age.

His recovery wasn't what it used to be, though. He fell to his side, breathing heavily. Still embedded deep inside of her, he wrapped an arm around her and pulled her close.

They lay together silently on the floor until he finally found his voice. 'My stamina isn't what it used to be.'

Shanna chuckled and rubbed the arm about her waist. 'You don't need it when there's that kind of a build-up.'

His laugh joined hers. He propped himself up on one elbow and looked down at her. 'You went off kind of fast, too. Has it been a while?'

After all that had happened, she found it amazing that she could still blush. 'Yes,' she finally said.

'Why?' he asked. 'What's wrong with that big stud out in the bar?'

Shanna tucked her arm under her head. She stared at her dress, which was on the floor only a few feet away. 'He's not really a date,' she said. 'He's a co-worker.'

'Oh, come on. You can't tell me you don't have some guy in your sights.'

In your sights. It was an interesting choice of words. 'There is, but he doesn't want me,' she said quietly.

'You're crazy,' he snapped. Reaching down, he draped her top leg across his. He pushed his hips harder against her and said, 'There isn't a man in the world who wouldn't want a gorgeous thing like you.'

She stretched, enjoying the contact of his body, but shook her head. 'He doesn't. I've worked with him for five years, but there's been nothing.'

'Christ almighty. The guy's stupid, but I guarantee you that he wants a piece of this.' His hand moved up and gave her breast a firm squeeze. 'What's the matter with you, Shanna? If you want him, why don't you go get him?'

She closed her eyes. 'I've changed.'

'Yeah, I noticed. No alcohol, no dancing, and no sex from what I can tell.'

'Really, Dooley.' She looked over her shoulder at the

man who had been her protector when she'd so needed it. 'You should be proud of me.'

His voice was rough when he answered. 'I am proud, girl.'

She lifted her head and gave him a soft kiss. 'I've changed, but it's been for the better.'

His thumb flicked her nipple. 'What really happened, Shanna? You left here so suddenly. One moment you were here. The next, you were gone. I tried to find you, but it was as if you just vanished. What happened between you and that cop?'

Shanna let her memory drift back to that fateful night when she'd met Robert. Talk about a turning point in her life! 'Well, you know I tried to pick his pocket.'

'I warned you to pick your marks better.'

No matter how well things had turned out, that was still a sore point for her. Even thieves had their pride. 'How could I have known he was a Fed? He didn't look like one with his rumpled clothes and his red eyes.'

'A Fed? In my bar? God damn it!'

Shanna elbowed the bartender in the ribs. 'Don't worry. He wasn't investigating you. He was after one of your patrons.'

'So what happened? Did he arrest you?'

'No, he just talked to me.'

'Talked? Give me a break.'

'Really, we just talked. In the end, he recruited me.'

Dooley's face went harder than she'd ever seen it. 'He what?'

She laughed. 'He recruited me into his line of work. He said I was the best pickpocket he'd ever seen, and I should put my skills to better use. If you can believe it, he took me home and introduced me to his wife. They've sort of watched over me all these years.'

'You're a *Fed*?'

'Yes, and I'm a damned good one.'

'I can't believe it. I just fucked a Fed.'

She glanced over her shoulder. 'Was it better when I was a stripper?'

Dooley looked at her for a long time. When he finally spoke, his voice was gruff. 'You know the answer to that.'

'Be happy for me, Dooley.'

His voice dropped to an even more serious tone. 'I am happy for you, girl. I'm proud you made something of yourself, but something's not right. I can see it in your eyes.'

Shanna was surprised by his observation. It hit a little too close to home. Pulling away, she disconnected their bodies and stood up. Feeling his gaze on her, she crossed the office and opened the door to the small bathroom. As she was searching for a clean washcloth, he pushed himself to his feet. He grabbed a bar towel from the clean laundry stack and brought it to her. He leaned against the doorway and watched as she washed.

'What's wrong, girl? What's making you so blue? Is it this guy who won't give you the time of day?'

'No, it's not him.' Her mood was partly due to Joe, but she didn't want to discuss that part of her life with Dooley. It was too private. Her feelings went too deep. 'There's just some unfinished business that needs my attention.'

'Can I help?'

'No. I need to do this myself.'

He crossed the room and wrapped his arms around her. He settled one hand over each breast and kissed her temple. 'Well, whatever it is, I'd be happy to lend my assistance.'

'You've always been there when I needed you.'

His gaze caught hers in the mirror. She was surprised at how good they looked together even with the difference in their ages. 'I always will be,' he said.

He dropped his hands from her chest and gave her

backside a soft pat. 'Let's get you back out to your non-date. He's probably wondering where you've gone, and from the looks of him, he could tear me to bits in about two seconds flat.'

With Dooley's help, her slinky blue dress was soon back where it was supposed to be. He tied the ties at the back and intimately slid his hands around to adjust her breasts. As he did so, he pinched her nipples. 'You should let that blond stud go down on you once or twice. Maybe that would get your guy off his butt.'

Shanna shivered. How would Joe react to her and Shawn? 'It's not going to happen. Shawn is a friend, and I want to keep him that way.'

'Well, don't be such a stranger.' The old man gave her one last squeeze. Dropping a kiss to the side of her neck, he pulled back. 'This place would love to see more of you. Hell, Lenny and Squiggy will flip when they see you.'

'I did see a couple of the old regulars out there.'

Shanna slipped back into her thong. She had it pulled up to her knees before he stopped her. Leaning down, he took a whiff.

'Not bad,' he said. 'I think we got it off of you before we really got down to business.'

She blushed and pulled the underwear the rest of the way up. It had been a while since she'd experienced such close intimacies. When Dooley pulled up her skirt to make sure her thong was situated properly, she couldn't help but flinch. Resignedly, he let her dress drop back into place.

'Damn,' he said, as he took one last look at her.

Shanna crossed the room to the door and he hurried to open it for her. As she was crossing the threshold, she casually asked, 'Does Mañuel Santos come by here any more?'

She'd never been able to con Dooley. His hand

whipped out and he caught her by the wrist. 'What do you want with him?'

'It was just a question.'

'No, it wasn't.' The bartender's eyebrows drew together. 'That's the unfinished business, isn't it?'

'Stay out of it, Dooley.'

'The hell I will. After what happened to your sister, I'm not letting you go anywhere near that bastard.'

Shanna tore her arm out of the older man's grip. She pointed a sharp finger at him, and her voice shook. 'Don't talk to me about my sister.'

'You're going after him, aren't you?'

It wasn't a question. It was an accusation. 'It's business. It's a case.'

'Does the FBI know your background connection to this case?'

She didn't answer, but she knew he could read her like a book.

'Damn it, Shanna. You don't know the trouble you're asking for. That bastard is mean. Hell, his men come in here all the time.'

She took two quick steps forward. 'Who comes in here? What are their names?'

He took a step back at the ferocity in her voice.

'Answer me.'

'There's a whole group of them. They're all trouble-makers. I hate to see them coming.'

'Names. I need names.'

'Shit, Shanna.' Dooley rolled his shoulders, but then centred his look on her. 'First, there's Sonny Fuentes. That's one big, mean motherfucker. You don't want to get messed up with him. Then there's a little blond guy they call Weasel – Edwin Myers. He's a creepy little snake. There are three or four more, but I don't know their names. I don't want to know their names.'

'Well, I do.' Shanna took a deep breath and settled her nerves. 'But thanks anyway. It helps.'

'Don't thank me. I haven't done you any favours.' He rubbed the back of his neck and gave her another quick look. 'Come on, your non-boyfriend is probably chomping at the bit.'

She nodded. He was probably right. Coberley wasn't the patient type, especially when his partner disappeared during the middle of a stakeout. Hooking her arm around Dooley's, she asked, 'Can we keep my occupation confidential?'

'Like I would tell,' he said. 'The FBI isn't exactly good for business, you know.'

The music was blaring as they stepped back into the bar, and a busty redhead was now on stage. Shanna gave the girl a quick mental review, and the results weren't positive. She was about to tell Dooley he needed to improve the talent when her eyes connected with a dark gaze from across the room.

The eyes that looked back at her were nearly pure black. They were so dark, it was hard to separate the pupil from the irises. The eyes were sharply intelligent, though, and she shivered under their intensity. The dark gaze locked with hers, then wandered down her figure.

He was mentally stripping her!

Shanna gasped, and her hand went to her throat. Other men had done the same thing, but her system had never rocked like this in response. Their looks hadn't been so blatant, so intense, so devastatingly real.

The devil's gaze drifted back up until he had her full attention. He then leaned cockily back in his chair and lifted a glass in her direction. The smile that pulled at his lips was hard and cold.

Its meaning was crystal clear. He was coming after her.

'Dooley,' she asked with a rasp in her voice. 'Who's the guy in the dark suit at table thirteen?'

The bartender set two more drinks on the bar and looked in the direction she'd indicated.

'Which one?' he asked.

'The one looking at me.'

'That, my girl, is Sonny Fuentes.'

3

Sonny Fuentes.

Santos's right-hand man.

His number-one enforcer.

The man was probably closer to Mañuel than anyone else on the face of the earth, and he was looking at her as if he could eat her alive. Shanna's heart gave one solid thump and then another.

This could be useful.

Turning back to Dooley, she gave him a bright smile. 'Thanks for the drinks and the welcome back.'

'Any time, girl,' he said with a grin. 'Any time.'

Tossing her hair over her shoulder, Shanna began the long walk to her table. Her brain whirred as she considered how she could use Fuentes's obvious attraction to her advantage. The answer didn't immediately occur to her, but she knew she had to keep his interest.

That shouldn't be a problem. She'd spent enough time up on that stage to know how to work it. By her second step, all eyes had left the redheaded dancer and landed on her. She felt the looks, but she returned only one.

Her gaze connected with the dark man's at table thirteen. One of his eyebrows rose and she brazenly sent him an intimate wink. His look immediately went from interested to downright intrigued.

Shanna let her body fall into a sensuous rhythm. Her hips flowed with every step she took, and she felt his gaze drop. The hem of the short skirt suddenly seemed to catch her at a particularly sensitive spot on the tops of her thighs, but she didn't break stride. It actually felt good to bask in the attention she was getting.

The man's hot gaze slid back upward, and she held the cold drinks away from her body to give him a better look. He took full advantage of her generous offer. His gaze almost seemed to be measuring her, judging the weight of her jiggling breasts.

'Why don't you just send out an engraved invitation?'

Shawn's question jolted her back to reality. Shanna set the drinks down on the small table and slid into the tall chair. Letting her legs stretch languorously, she threw Sonny one last look. Then she did something that probably set him right on his ear.

She summarily dismissed him.

Turning her back on him, she concentrated her full attention on Coberley. She'd played this game before. If there was one thing she knew, the best way to attract a man was to ignore him. Completely.

'I'm playing the part.'

'What part? Bar tramp?'

That stung, but Shanna tried to hide her reaction from her face. 'Why else would I be here?'

'Well, tone it down. Joe wanted us to blend.'

She took a long drink. The cold liquid felt soothing going down her suddenly parched throat. 'I don't know how.'

Shawn shot her a look and then howled with laughter. 'No, I don't believe you do.'

Shanna returned her partner's smile, but she could still feel another gaze burning along the curves of her body. Purposefully, she pointed her toe and rubbed her instep along the leg of the chair.

'So what did the old man give you?' he asked.

Shanna nearly choked on her drink. 'Excuse me?'

'What did he tell you? I assume you went in the back to talk about Santos and his men.'

She patted her napkin against her lips and nodded. It was a better excuse than she could have come up with on her own. 'The barkeep didn't want anyone to overhear us. If somebody overheard him talking about Santos, it could cause problems for him.'

Coberley nodded. 'So did you get anything good?'

Shanna bit her lip to hide a smile that would have been too enthusiastic. 'He gave me a thing or two. Apparently Santos's men come in here quite often – Sonny Fuentes and Edwin Myers, aka Weasel, in particular. Fuentes is the big guy at table . . . at that table over there.'

Coberley shot a quick look over her shoulder. 'I don't get it. Even the old man warns you about Fuentes, but when you walk out into the bar and see the thug, your first inclination is to flirt with him?'

'It's a strategy,' she said with a shrug. 'Maybe he'll invite me to their table.'

'Oh, sure.' Her partner took a swig of his drink, and Shanna knew he wished it was something stronger. 'I can just picture him inviting you over and telling you all the gritty inside details of the Santos drug ring.'

'Have you got a better plan?'

'No, but Joe did. We were supposed to blend in with our surroundings, watch their movements, follow them, etc. The problem is that you decided to wear a hanky, and that plan flew right out the window.'

'A hanky?' Shanna quickly looked down at her dress. 'It's not that small, is it?'

The look on his face was almost comical. 'Lily, every time you inhale, I'm dying of suspense that you'll pop out of that dress.'

Shanna took another drink of her cola and eyed her partner carefully over the edge of the glass. 'Shawn?'

'Yeah?'

'Why didn't we ever . . .'

'Get it on?'

She nodded.

The blond hunk sat back in his chair. His gaze drifted across her body but finally came back to her face. 'Believe me, I've been tempted. There were two things that stopped me, though. One, you're my partner. I'd lose my edge if we became involved. It might work for a while, but sooner or later we'd be caught in a tight situation. If I was distracted by that body, I might miss a bullet aimed directly at my head.'

Curious, Shanna leaned forward. 'What was reason number two?'

'Joe would kill me.'

Her mind went blank. He might as well have knocked her upside the head with a two-by-four. 'What?'

His eyebrows lowered. 'You know what I'm talking about.'

She shook her head quickly. 'No, I don't.'

One side of his mouth curled upward in a smile. Then a grin worked its way on to his face. 'I'll be damned.'

Frustration gnawed at Shanna. 'If you don't stop talking in circles, I'm going to put you in a headlock.'

Suddenly, her partner became uneasy. He ran a hand through his permanently ruffled hair as if he didn't know how much he should say. 'Well,' he said, 'Joe is more than a little protective of you, if you haven't noticed.'

'Of course he is. He was Robert's partner.'

'Yeah, right. That's all there is to it.'

'He's told me on more than one occasion that he doesn't like my work tactics. That's why he watches me like a hawk.' She frowned and tried not to reveal her hurt. 'He thinks I'm dangerous.'

'To him, you are.' Shawn's relaxed posture suddenly straightened. His gaze focused somewhere behind her and his face hardened. 'Heads up. Goon at ten o'clock.'

He needn't have told her. The hairs at the back of her neck had stood on end. She didn't need to look back to see that a certain dark gaze had centred on her again. That gaze was now travelling down her bare back. She couldn't help the goose bumps that popped up on her skin.

A finger actually touched her spine, and she jumped as it leisurely travelled down to her lower back.

By the time she'd twisted in her seat, Shawn had sprung out of his chair. Sonny Fuentes stopped him with one broad hand spread against his chest. Shanna's nerves seized. She didn't want a fight.

'I wondered when you'd come over and introduce yourself,' she said with a throaty purr. She had to tilt her head back to see the giant's face.

'I've had enough of your little game. Let's get out of here.'

Her eyes widened. Well, that was blunt. Apparently, when this man saw something he wanted, he just took it. 'What makes you think that I'd leave with a man I don't even know?'

'Listen, sweet tits. I can prop you up against that table to fuck you or we can go somewhere a little more private. It's up to you.'

'You sonofabitch,' Shawn growled. He knocked aside Fuentes's hand and stepped forward. 'She's here with me.'

'Bullshit.' Fuentes didn't back down. Instead, he stepped forward until his chest nearly brushed against the smaller man's. 'If she were really with you, you wouldn't be here. You'd have her tied to a bed somewhere with her legs spread wide.'

That was it. Coberley pulled a fist back and three of Fuentes's men were on him. Shanna lunged out of her chair when she heard the first crack of a fist against her partner's face. Fuentes stopped her easily by looping an arm about her waist.

'Stop them,' she begged. Her first impulse had been to

sweep the knee of the thug nearest to her, but she held back. A bar tramp wouldn't know a move like that.

'Hey!' Dooley called from the other end of the bar. 'Take it outside.'

'Stop!' Shanna's voice rose when one of Fuentes's men caught Shawn with a right hook.

'That's enough,' Fuentes said in a low tone.

The fight immediately stopped, but Shanna was incensed. She turned in Fuentes's arms and found herself pressed tightly against his big body. It was a discovery to learn that he was all muscle. 'You didn't have to do that.'

'Are you coming with me?'

'You know that I am. You knew that I would when you first watched me walk across the bar.'

'Lily!' Shawn might have taken a few hard shots, but he wasn't incapacitated.

'Oh, come on,' she snapped at her partner. 'I just want to have some fun.'

'She needs a good hard screw,' Fuentes said. His hand slid down to her bottom and gave her an intimate squeeze.

'Get your dirty hands off of her.'

Fuentes's hand dipped under the short hem of her dress. He lifted the material and grabbed her buttocks, letting everyone see. 'I think she likes my dirty hands.'

'Hey, what's going on over there?' Dooley called.

'Where are we going?' Shanna asked, her mind working quickly. This was exactly the chance she'd been waiting for. If she could get close to Sonny Fuentes, she could get close to Mañuel Santos. Close was all she needed. If she could get anywhere near the sonofabitch, he was dead. She was a sure shot with the little pistol she kept in her purse.

'Does it matter?' the big man said. He squeezed her backside again, making her go right up on her tiptoes.

His strength sent a shot of excitement down Shanna's spine. The feel of the big brute's callused hand on her sensitive skin was downright sinful, and she wasn't kidding herself. He'd fuck her as soon as he got a chance. He'd be demanding, selfish and rough.

And big. She could feel his erection pressing against her stomach. Butterflies twittered inside of her. God, she loved a big dick.

'No,' she said. 'I don't care where we go.'

'I didn't think so.'

Shanna reached over to the table for her purse. The butterflies hadn't left. If anything, their tumbling flight within her belly had intensified. She knew she shouldn't be doing this. She shouldn't leave with these people. They were drug dealers and murderers. Her instincts, though, told her this might be the best opportunity she'd get.

'Don't do this,' Coberley warned.

She definitely, absolutely, positively shouldn't leave her partner. He was hurt and more than a little worried.

Dooley had crossed the room. 'If you guys don't break it up, I'm calling the cops.'

'Stay out of this, old man.' Fuentes's thumb sneaked into the crevice of Shanna's ass, and she flinched. 'You got a name, sweet tits?'

Her mouth opened, but immediately snapped shut. Shawn had already called her Lily, but she couldn't tell Fuentes her last name was McKay. Santos probably wouldn't recognise it after all this time, but she couldn't take a chance. 'Mitchell,' she said, without even thinking. 'Lily Mitchell. What's yours?'

He gave a bark of laughter. 'Me? I'm the big bad wolf.'

His dark head swung down, and she was unprepared for the ferocity of his kiss. With his one hand still on her ass and the other in her hair, he plastered her body against his. His lips came down hard on hers and he pried her mouth open with his insistent tongue.

He tasted of whisky and smoke. He filled her senses, depriving her of even oxygen. He consumed her mouth, taking more than giving. The hand on her bottom tightened, and she was suddenly lifted right off her feet. Thrusting his hips outward, he ground her hard against the big bulge at his crotch.

Shanna shuddered with pleasure. Fuentes finally broke the marauding kiss and gave her a look that seared her to the bone.

'You can call me Sonny.'

He gave her a knowing smile, and her eyes widened.

He knew.

She didn't know how, but he saw right through her carefully constructed façade. She'd been hiding her true nature for years, but this man had read her like an open book. She liked it wild. She liked it rough, raw and a little frightening. He knew it and was more than willing to give it to her that way.

She was two feet from the door and completely unaware of how she'd gotten there when she heard Coberley's voice. 'What about Joe, Lily?'

Shanna stumbled in her tracks.

Sonny came to a stop beside her. 'Who's Joe?' he said.

'Her husband.'

Shanna jolted at her partner's words. Thrown, she gave Shawn an uncomprehending look. How dare he say that to her? She knew she was taking a risk, but she was infiltrating the Santos organisation. They'd been working on this case too long for her not to take advantage of the situation. Now that they were finally finding a way inside, why would he decide to toss out that little improvisation? There was nothing he could have said that would have broken her concentration more.

'Husband?' Sonny gave a harsh laugh. 'Who gives a fuck?'

'Joe Mitchell.' Shawn had a deadly serious look on his

face. 'When he finds out you've been messing with Lily, he'll feed you your own dick.'

'Ooh, I'm scared.'

Shawn took a step forward. 'You should be, big man. You might think you're tough, but he'll rip you to shreds.'

'For God's sake, we're separated! He doesn't have any say in what I do or who I do it with!' Shanna said with a desperation she didn't have to fake. Oh, Lord, once Joe found out she'd left with Fuentes, there would be hell to pay. She couldn't let the chance go, though. There was too much at stake for her. In this one instance, her boss's reaction would have to take a back seat.

'Bring him on,' Sonny said cockily.

'Believe me,' Shawn said with a nod, 'I will.'

'Come on, Sonny. Let's go.' Shanna grabbed him by the arm and tugged him away from her partner. She didn't dare look back. Turning, she headed for the door with her fingers firmly clenched into the sleeve of Fuentes's jacket.

Her knees shook as she crossed the parking lot. She knew that she'd crawled way out on a limb this time. She'd ditched her partner and was now going unaccompanied into the midst of danger.

Still, this was a calculated risk. She and Coberley had been studying Mañuel Santos's drug ring for months. Although information on the group was sparse, she felt she knew enough about the gang's operation to keep herself safe. When it came right down to it, though, her safety wasn't her first priority.

Revenge. That's what she wanted the most. Whenever she thought about what Santos had done to her – how he'd forever changed her life – she was consumed with rage. She was going to pay him back for the damage he'd caused, and she didn't care what she had to do to achieve that goal.

She was even willing to play whore for his right-hand man.

'This way, sweet tits.' Sonny wrapped an arm around her waist and directed her towards an SUV.

Shanna's stomach turned as one last shot of self-doubt coursed through her system. Only an idiot would hop into a vehicle with a group of dangerous men. She didn't know where they were going or what they were planning to do. She was willing to hedge her bets, though. Fuentes was truly attracted to her, and she knew he would screw her. If she made it good for him, he might keep her around.

That was precisely what she needed. If she could gain his confidence, his defences would drop. By keeping his dick happy, she could firmly plant herself within the Santos organisation. With time, that kind of access would surely pay off.

'Where are we going?' she dared to ask.

'A party.'

'Oh, I love parties! Who's throwing it?'

Fuentes's hand crept up her side so he could brush the side of her breast with his fingertips. 'Aren't you just full of questions? It's at my boss's country house, if you must know.'

Shanna's nerve-endings tingled. Santos's home? God, this was too good to be true! They'd been searching for the man's whereabouts but it was as if he'd disappeared from the face of the earth.

That was one way that Mañuel had changed. When he was young, he'd been the biggest, loudest, in-your-face braggart ever to walk the streets. Now, though, he'd done a complete about-face. Santos was rarely seen and hardly ever heard. He led from the background. Being such a target of both law enforcement and rival gangs had forced the man to live a life of paranoia. If anything, he was now a hermit. To be led to his private home was almost unbelievable.

'Your boss? I should freshen up,' Shanna said breezily.

She reached into her purse, supposedly for her lipstick. With a quick flick of her finger, though, she turned on the mini-recorder hidden in the false bottom of her clutch. For such a small device, the microphone picked up sounds with amazing clarity. It had limited recording capability, unfortunately. Sooner or later, she'd have to find some privacy to change tapes.

'Here, let me,' Fuentes said when she pulled the tube of lipstick out of her purse.

It was a strange request, but she obligingly passed him the make-up. She came to a standstill when he pulled off the cap and turned to her. With fascination, she watched as he twisted the base of the tube and the lipstick slowly grew in length.

'It's like a little dick,' Sonny laughed. He threw her a wicked look. 'No wonder women are constantly running it over their lips. Hold still.'

Uneasily, Shanna did as she was told. She pursed her lips and waited. Sonny's gaze focused on her mouth and his hand lifted. At the first touch, her stomach did an unexpected little flip. His comparison was fresh in her mind, and it was strange how his observation changed her perception. She applied lipstick countless times a day but she'd never seen it as a sensual experience. Now she couldn't think of anything else.

His hand was steady and slow as he ran the smooth colour across her lower lip. Almost automatically, she felt herself pouting to extend the experience.

'Open.'

Her lower jaw dropped so he'd have better access. He drew a soft line along the inner, more delicate, line of her bottom lip, and she had to swallow hard. His gaze was so intent, so heated.

He switched his attention to her upper lip, and her eyelids drooped shut. The lipstick tugged at her mouth as he ran the tube from the centre of her upper lip to the right corner. Automatically, her tongue darted out to lick at the tingling sensation.

Sonny laughed softly. 'I bet you give great head.'

Instead of taking offence, Shanna's body responded to his harsh teasing. She opened her mouth wider and he obligingly ran the colour on the remaining half of her upper lip.

'Mmm,' she purred as she rubbed her freshly painted lips together in the age-old feminine ritual.

Suddenly, the hard tube of lipstick pressed against her mouth again. 'Open.'

This time the order was stricter. Fuentes's voice had gone a little rougher, and Shanna squeezed her legs tighter together to try to ease the tingling sensation at their apex. Without opening her eyes, she let her lips part. The tube of lipstick immediately slid inside.

'Suck on it.'

A little uncertain, she closed her mouth around the hard tube.

'I said suck on it!'

Cheeks working, she followed his orders and got a grunt of approval for her efforts. The little sound made Shanna proud, and she impulsively swirled her tongue around the tube. It *was* like a little dick. She ran her tongue across the smooth tip and knew that the colour was being transferred to the rough surface of her tongue. The thought excited her and she suckled harder.

Sonny's hand suddenly cupped her breast and gave it a rough squeeze. The tingling between her legs intensified and she shimmied closer to his big body. He obliged her by sliding one muscled leg between hers. Unable to help herself, Shanna began to ride his thigh.

Fuentes chuckled again. 'You are a horny one.'

He playfully slid the tube of lipstick to the corner of her mouth and her tongue eagerly followed. He squeezed her breast harder, and she whimpered in delight.

'God, you are hot! I can't wait to see if you're this eager when you're trying to swallow my cock.' He leaned closer and whispered into her ear. 'I'm big, sweet tits. Maybe even too big for you.'

Shanna shuddered.

'Hey, Sonny. Get a move on it.'

'Can't you see I'm busy, Weasel?'

Shanna flinched at the intruding voice. Edwin Myers. Her eyes immediately popped open. With Sonny still holding the lipstick between her pursed lips, she couldn't turn her head, but she could see Myers out of the corner of her eye. She cringed when she saw the man. The origin of his nickname was clear. The guy looked like a weasel. He was a thin man with slicked-back hair. His face was pinched and his beady little eyes were set just a little too close together.

'I'm not blind, Sonny, but we need to get out of here. I don't trust your little slut's friend.'

Fuentes laughed. 'What's he going to do?'

'Get in the truck, Sonny.'

'Ah, hell.' Surprisingly, Fuentes backed down. With one last squeeze to Shanna's breast, he let her go. He pulled the lipstick out from between her lips and Shanna was more than a little embarrassed when he looked at the blunt little stub of colour. His eyebrow rose and he looked at her consideringly. 'Well, well, well.'

Face flaring, she grabbed the lipstick from him and replaced the cap. She tossed the make-up back into her purse. Surreptitiously, she tried to feel how much lipstick remained on the hungry surface of her tongue.

'Come on. When Weasel gets nervous, things get unpleasant.'

Shanna's legs were wobbly as she walked to the big black SUV. Without thinking, she reached for the back door. Sonny hooked his arm around her waist and opened the front passenger door. 'The back's all full, sweet tits. You'll have to ride up front with me.'

Shanna soon found herself seated on Sonny's hard thighs. When he closed the door, the room in the front seat became somewhat cramped. There was no avoiding his touch or the gazes from the other four men in the vehicle.

'You've got to blindfold her, Sonny,' Weasel said. 'We can't let her know the way. The boss would have our heads.'

Shanna threw the driver an uneasy look. A blindfold? She was already vulnerable enough as it was. Edwin Myers returned her look with a smarmy smile. God, the man made her skin crawl.

Sonny looked to the back seat. 'Any of you have something we can use?'

'Here,' one goon said eagerly. 'Take my shirt.'

He practically tore his T-shirt off in his haste. He helpfully rolled the material into a long strip and passed it to his boss. Shanna could smell the man's sweat as the impromptu blindfold was wrapped around her head and tied. Her pulse leapt as everything went dark. She tried to calm her nerves by reminding herself she still had four other senses she could use. Without vision to assist her, those other senses would become more acute.

At the moment, the sense of touch overruled all the others. When Weasel fired up the engine, the soft vibration of the SUV rocked her ever so slightly on Sonny's lap. She fought the urge to squirm when she felt his erection prodding against her ass.

He'd awakened her arousal in the parking lot and she was having difficulty ignoring it. Now was not the time for her mind to wander. They were going to Santos's house and she had to pay attention. Sonny's hands settled on her thighs and he spread her legs until she straddled his. With his hand lower on her abdomen, he pulled her more firmly back against him. 'There, that's better, don't you think?'

'Mm,' she said. She was trying to separate her brain from her body, but it wasn't working.

Weasel backed out of the parking spot and she tried to pay attention. She might not be able to see where he was going but she could sense turns.

The SUV went over a speed bump a little too fast, though, and her thoughts were scattered in the wind. She bounced against Sonny's cock and he grunted in reaction. Her breasts shuddered as the shock absorbers on the vehicle fell far short of doing their job. Without a bra, she had no support. The harsh jiggling was unpleasant and she nearly reached for her chest. She could only imagine what the men's reaction would be to that move, though. She stopped herself and suffered in silence.

At the second speed bump, though, Sonny seemed to sense her needs. 'Here, let me be of assistance,' he said as his hands closed over her.

Shanna's back arched when he squeezed her into both palms. God, his hands were so big, he could nearly hold all of her. Everything about this man was big. She felt petite next to him and unusually submissive. When his hands began to mould and shape her breasts, she nearly whimpered.

Weasel made a right turn out of the parking lot and she tried to concentrate.

'Are your nipples sensitive?'

The question was breathed into her ear. Before she could respond, Sonny's fingers were plucking at her. She squirmed at his insistent touch. 'Yes.'

He licked the curve of her ear. 'I'll have to remember that.'

The vehicle braked and slowed to a stop. They must be at the intersection five blocks down, Shanna surmised.

She was breathing hard but she remembered her goal. *Trace the route*, she told herself. She might need to remember how to get back to Santos's house if an opportunity to kill him didn't present itself this time. Weasel drove straight ahead, so she knew they were still on Simmons Street.

One of Sonny's hands left her breast and settled on her inner thigh. She inhaled sharply but could do nothing before that curious hand slid right up under her skirt and curved around the crotch of her panties. Her hips undulated as he squeezed her mound.

'Why the hell are you wearing underwear?' he grunted into her ear.

That was a good question. She was beginning to wonder herself. First Dooley and now this. She was getting more action in one night than she'd seen in months.

'Lift,' Sonny said. Both his hands were now under her skirt. His fingers curled around the waistband of her thong and tugged it downward. There wasn't much she could do to resist. Bracing her hands against the dashboard, she lifted herself so he could work the material over her hips. Weasel took a left turn as Sonny pulled the panties down her legs.

'Let me have those,' one of the men in the back seat begged. Sonny shifted, and she could only assume that her panties were being passed to the spectators.

'God, smell that!' the man crowed.

Shanna didn't even want to think about what was going on in the back seat. She knew she was wet; her thong must be sopping with her juices. Her thighs had been sticky for quite a while. When Sonny pulled her down, she tried to pull her skirt back under her hips, but he wouldn't let her.

The vehicle made another left turn and she tried hard to concentrate. That was a right out of the parking lot and then two lefts.

'Sonofabitch, I was right.'

Sonny's body went taut at Weasel's exclamation. 'What is it?'

'That boyfriend of hers is following us.'

Shanna turned her head to the side, but the blindfold stopped her from seeing anything. Damn Shawn! She knew he would do this. He was trying to back her up, but he was jeopardising the progress she was making.

Her face flared when she realised how twisted that logic was. He was doing his job; he was trying to protect his partner. Right now, the only progress she was making was in getting herself royally screwed.

Still, sometimes the end justified the means. All five men in the vehicle might eventually fuck her, but she could handle that if they ended up at Santos's house. She'd take them any way they wanted if it meant she could get within shooting range of that bastard. One shot was all she wanted or needed.

'He's about three cars back,' Weasel said.

Shanna cringed at even the sound of the man's voice. Maybe she should revise her thinking. Screwing that creepy little guy would be above and beyond the call of duty.

'See if you can shake him.'

Weasel suddenly gunned the engine, and she was pressed hard against Sonny's body as the vehicle sped forward. She couldn't tell how far they went, but the next thing she knew, her body was being pushed towards the door as the vehicle executed a hard left turn.

This was not good. If they started using evasive tactics, she'd never remember their route. Her mind whirred. 'Left,' she whispered. She hoped it was loud enough for the microphone in her purse to catch, but low enough not to draw Sonny's attention.

The big man seemed to be engrossed in the car trailing them. 'Take a right on Highland,' he said.

Yes! she thought. Help me out, big boy.

'Damn,' Weasel hissed. 'This guy's like glue. Hold on.'

Their speed increased and Shanna reached for the dash.

'Right,' she whispered.

'Another right.'

'Straight across a big pothole.'

'Left.'

Their route became more and more entangled. With every turn, she knew that the probability of anybody deciphering her code was rapidly decreasing.

'God damn it! That's it,' Sonny finally said. 'Take care of the guy.'

Weasel braked hard and Shanna felt herself catapulting towards the windshield. Sonny's arm clamped hard around her waist and pulled her back. 'I'll stay here with her. Go get him.'

Shanna's pulse exploded at the sound of three doors opening. Oh, God! Shawn!

The SUV's occupants quickly exited. She didn't know what they had planned. All she knew was that her partner was in trouble. She was blinded and trapped, unable to help him. All thoughts of Santos disappeared, and she began to fight.

'No! Don't hurt him! Let me go!'

Fuentes wrapped both arms around her, trapping her flailing hands. 'Settle down.'

'Let go of me! I don't want to go with you any more.'

'No?' Fuentes laughed. 'That's a quick change in attitude. Seconds ago, you were squirming around on my lap like you were trying to take me pants, boxer shorts and all.'

'You sonofabitch!' She kicked her feet and was satisfied to connect solidly with his shin. 'Take your hands off me!'

He grunted with pain but his arms tightened like a vice. 'No.'

Shanna flung her head back, trying to headbutt him. 'Let me go!'

'Ow! You little wildcat!'

'If you don't turn me loose, I'll –'

Three loud echoing shots made her flinch.

'Shawn!' she screamed.

4

'What's happening? What have they done? Oh, God! Shawn!'

Shanna became unglued as Sonny continued to restrain her. 'Take it easy,' he said.

'Take it easy? My God, you have guns!' She drove her heel into the big man's shin. 'Let me go.'

'Ow! Damn it, stop doing that. He's all right.'

'I heard shots. You had them shoot him!'

'They shot out the tyres on his car.'

'Liar. What are you doing with guns, anyway? Who are you?'

'I told you, sweet tits. I'm the big bad wolf.'

He leaned forward to nuzzle her ear again and she nearly exploded. 'Get off of me, you creep. Shawn! Can you hear me? Are you OK?'

Shanna was screaming at the top of her lungs but she didn't hear a response. A sob caught in her throat. Dear Lord, she'd caused her partner's death. There was no way she could make up for this. Her impulsiveness had gotten her partner killed. 'Shawn!' she yelled.

'Quiet down,' Sonny said.

'Fuck you. Shawn!'

The men finally came back to the SUV. Three doors slammed and Shanna flinched with every one of them. Tears streamed down her face under the blindfold and sobs nearly choked her. 'Is he dead?' she cried.

'Dead?' It was Weasel. 'Hell, Sonny. What have you been telling her?'

'Is he?'

'No,' he said.

'I heard shots.'

'We blew out his tyres.'

'Why won't he answer me?' Feeling Sonny's arms loosen, Shanna burst out of his clench and yanked the blindfold from her eyes. Spinning around, she looked for any sign of her partner.

She finally spotted him lying on the road beside the car. The tyres had indeed been flattened, but she could tell that Coberlely wasn't in good shape. As she watched, though, he rolled on to his side and reached for the open door.

'You beat him.'

'He'll live,' Weasel said as he put the SUV into gear.

'You can't leave him there!' She glared at the creepy driver and then back to her partner. He was using the car door to pull himself to his feet. That gave her hope. If he could get to his cell phone, he could call for help.

'Where did that blindfold go?' Weasel asked.

Sonny found the T-shirt on the floor and snagged it. Shanna struggled as he tied the material around her head again. Soon he had her back in his lap, pressed hard against his dick. She couldn't believe that he still held such an erection. Her state of arousal had been shot all to hell by seeing her partner bruised and battered.

The sight only served to remind her how dangerous these men were. This wasn't a little sexual cat-and-mouse game she was playing. This was serious. She hated that Shawn had caught the backlash of her actions.

She'd let her partner down and she regretted it with every fibre of her being. Now, though, it was even more important that she follow through on her mission. Her sister deserved vengeance and so did Shawn. One way or the other, she was going to get it for them.

'You didn't have to do that, you know,' she said bitterly. 'It wasn't *right*. You didn't have to beat him up like that.'

Without Shawn tailing them, it was even more vital that she mark their path. They'd just turned *right* and had passed over a set of railroad tracks. The distinct sound and feel couldn't be mistaken for anything else.

'He was becoming a nuisance,' Sonny said.

'You could have just let me talk to him.'

'And lose the heat of your pussy on my lap? No way.'

He swivelled his hips underneath her and Shanna felt the flare of arousal return. The feeling made her angry. She rebelliously tightened her thigh muscles and lifted herself from his lap. His hands immediately clamped down on her waist and she landed hard against him.

'God, you're fiery,' he groaned. 'You should feel this pussy, Weasel.'

'Don't mind if I do.'

Shanna's eyes widened behind the blindfold when she heard that raspy voice. A shot of revulsion ran down her spine. In her mind's eye, she could see the man's hand leaving the steering wheel. As if in slow motion, it crossed the cab of the vehicle and headed straight for her mound. Horrified that that pale thin hand was going to touch her, she tried to shrink back.

There was no place to go. Sonny's fingers bit into her thighs as he held her splayed open wide for his friend.

She bucked when Weasel's cold fingers wove into her pubic hair. A strangled cry left her lips as those insidious fingers burrowed deeper between her legs to her most delicate skin. Her hips heaved as she tried to avoid the revolting touch, but the hand wasn't to be dismissed.

Two fingers crept along the groove outside her pussy lips and she whimpered. When he squeezed his fingers together like human scissors, she nearly came unglued.

'Make him stop!' she begged. Her mind and her body

recoiled from the clammy touch but something even more unfathomable was happening. Even as her body cringed from his touch, she was enjoying it. Whereas seconds ago, she'd been tumbling down from the sexual peak to which she'd ascended, now she was hurtling upward again. 'I'm not going to have anything *left*.'

The vehicle had just turned on to what seemed to be a dirt road. The going had become much rougher, and she reached for the dashboard to regain her balance. Myers' long fingers were still between her legs. Shanna clenched her teeth tightly. She hadn't lied. She didn't know how much more of his repulsive touch she could stand before she climaxed.

Sonny pulled her away from the dashboard so she again leaned against his chest. Before she knew what he intended to do, he pulled the spaghetti straps of her dress down her arms. Her breasts popped out, but her arms were trapped. She couldn't have covered herself if she wanted to.

'Look at them bongos!'

'Christ!'

'I can't see them. Adjust the mirror.'

The voices all came from the back seat, but Shanna could feel Sonny's hot gaze even more intimately. The road was marred with ruts. Without even the slight support of her dress, her breasts shuddered and heaved with every bump. She was blindfolded but she could feel the lust of the five men looking at her. She could sense the picture she made and her nipples tingled under the cool air of the air conditioner.

'They are sensitive, aren't they?' Suddenly Sonny's big hands were on her again, only this time it was flesh against flesh. His thumbs flicked over her already turgid nipples, and her back arched.

Weasel's fingers became more curious between her legs. With Sonny holding her breasts, her hands were free. She grabbed Myers' hand to stop his probing but she couldn't pry him away from her pussy. His fingers wormed their way deeper until he found her opening.

'No!' she gasped, but it was too late.

Two of his skinny fingers burrowed inside her. The pressure increased as he pushed them deeper and deeper. She had nowhere to go to hide from the invasion. Her mouth formed a silent 'O', but she couldn't even get out a whisper.

When those cold fingertips pressed deliberately and began an insistent rubbing, though, a shriek left her lips.

'God, that's it!' Sonny said. 'I can't take any more. She's trying to rub my dick clean off. Pull over.'

The SUV pulled off the side of the road into more uneven territory and lurched to a stop. Still blindfolded, Shanna was unable to see. She could hardly hear over the pounding in her ears, but she could feel. Her sense of touch was almost painfully alive. She could feel every centimetre of her skin – inside and out. It was as if every nerve-ending had been put on alert.

There was the sound of a back door opening. She felt the whoosh of air hit her as the door beside her opened.

'What do you want me to do?' It was the man whose shirt was tied around her head.

'Lift her off my lap so I can get my dick out.'

Sonny's voice had become gruff. He was panting hard and every breath hit her bare shoulder. A strong arm wrapped around her waist, and she was held in mid-air as he positioned himself below her.

Myers' fingers were still working hard inside her. No matter what she did, she couldn't shake his touch. When his thumb rasped against her clitoris, she flung her head back and shuddered.

'How is she?' Sonny asked.

'She's wet enough, but she's tight. I don't know if she can take you.'

Sonny grunted. 'You can't have her first, Weasel. One way or the other, she's going to squeeze me in.'

Sonny's hands brushed against her buttocks as he unbuttoned and unzipped his pants. Shanna worked her arms out of the confining straps and latched on to Myers' hand. She pulled his fingers out of her but the move only aided the man behind her. Sonny shifted ever so slightly and she felt the tip of an enormous erection prodding at her slick opening. His hands gripped her hips tightly as he held her precariously over that imposing cock.

'Spread her legs wider.'

The man standing outside grabbed her right leg and Myers took her left. Like a wishbone, they spread her legs even wider, allowing their friend unimpeded access. Shanna gasped when Sonny slowly lowered her on to his thick prick.

'Oh,' she gasped. He was bigger than she'd imagined. He'd only pressed the tip inside her and she was already stretched. Before she could accustom herself to his size, he increased the pressure and pushed further inside her.

It was like taking an elephant. She'd seen a big bull's penis flopping between his back legs during her last trip to the zoo. There hadn't been a female there whose eyes hadn't been glued to the sight. The thing had almost been as big as a fifth leg. That was how big Sonny's cock felt.

At once, Shanna was excited and more than a little alarmed. She loved being stretched but she'd never taken a man of his size. 'I don't know if I can,' she panted.

'You've got to,' he groaned. He let gravity take over, and she slowly slid down a few more inches. 'You're like a furnace.'

Oh, God! It was too much. He was pushing hard, making her accept his intrusion, but her body was fighting the penetration.

'Help her out, Weasel.'

'No!' she cried.

'No?' Sonny said. His hands crept around her body and latched on to her breasts. He gave them both a soft squeeze. 'You don't want him to make it feel better?'

No. Yes. Oh, God. She didn't want that slimy man to touch her again, but she was in acute discomfort. With a whimper, she nodded.

'Yes, you don't want him to touch you – or yes, you need him to finger you?'

'Finger me!' she said.

'Let me get the flashlight,' Myers said.

His voice was so close to her, she shivered. What did he need a flashlight for? She waited uneasily and tried to ignore her distress. She needed his touch *now*. Sonny's hands were busy with her breasts. The man standing outside the door was sliding his hand up and down the taut muscles of her thigh, but that wasn't where she needed to be touched.

She heard a soft click and felt Myers shift beside her. There was the sound of bodies shifting and a grunt or two of discomfort – her own included. When she felt Myers' skinny body press hard against her left shin, she realised what he was doing.

A soft almost unnoticeable heat warmed her inner thighs and pussy. It could only be the illumination of a flashlight. Shanna bit her lip from embarrassment. Sonny was continuing to penetrate her from below, and Weasel was watching from the floor.

She cried out when she felt a finger softly touch her strained opening. Myers rubbed her tight flesh, coaxing it to relax. Shanna turned her head to the side, unable to bear the thought of the man watching and touching her so intimately.

Admittedly, his touch did help. Sonny swivelled his hips, and she slid further on to his big dick.

'I've got to thrust,' he said. His chest heaved against her bare back. Her dress was now wrapped around her waist like a belt. It offered her no cover, and Shanna discovered she didn't want it.

What she wanted was more of his overwhelming penetration. 'Yes!'

'Not yet!' Myers warned. 'Get it inside her all the way just once.'

'She's not giving.'

'She needs to be wetter. Give me a second.'

The hand between her legs slithered to the apex of her sex. Shanna had nowhere to hide from what was surely coming next. A thumb flicked across her delicate bud and she nearly fainted.

'Oh, she liked that,' Sonny said. 'I can feel her slathering me already. Hurry up, man. I'm dying here.'

Weasel focused all his attention on her sensitive bundle of nerves and Shanna almost began hyperventilating. Her hips began moving along with the gyrations of his hand. Sonny's hands began working on her nipples, and soon she was dripping moisture like a leaky shower. 'Oh, please!' she said.

Sonny's hips lifted right up off the seat and he impaled her on his throbbing cock. Shanna let out a sharp cry and groped for the dashboard. He was so big, and she'd eaten up every last millimetre of him. His balls bumped against her, and his pubic hair scratched the base of her thighs.

She felt invaded, overwhelmed, completely filled. It felt so good. 'Can he thrust?' she asked Myers. 'Oh, please. Let him thrust.'

'She's ready.'

The man's breath was hot against her inner thigh. His face must be inches from them. Shanna was sickened by the thought, but ever so grateful.

Sonny finally began thrusting. At first, he kept it as slow as he could, but soon his impatience overtook him. The first time he plunged up into her hard, she screamed. It was too much.

Sonny was too far gone to stop. 'Lean forward,' he said. 'That way I can get at you better.'

With a whimper, Shanna settled her forehead on her arms against the dash. The position allowed him more room to thrust, and his pace increased.

Myers' fingers were suddenly touching her again. He wrapped one hand tight around her calf. The other dove between her legs and began pinching, tickling and prodding whatever flesh he could find.

Sonny pounded into her, deep and true. Myers' added stimulation was all Shanna needed to go flying right off the edge of the earth. She saw a flurry of colours behind the dark blindfold and her body pulsed with energy. She came with an urgency she'd never felt before. Her body shook in completion, then went limp in Sonny's arms.

Her orgasm seemed to trigger his, for it took only a few more thrusts before he spewed his juices into her. His ejaculation was like everything else about him. It was long and it was hard. He filled her with his come until the overflow dripped out of her.

'Oh, my God!' she gasped.

Sonny couldn't talk. He fell back against the leather cushion of the seat and fought for air.

'You did good, doll.'

The compliment was accompanied by a soft pat against her calf. Now that it was all over, Shanna squirmed against Weasel's revolting touch. She kicked out at him, but he simply caught her leg against him. She gasped when she felt his hot tongue slide up her shin.

'Christ, that was good,' Sonny said from behind her.

Shanna was fighting to catch her own breath. She couldn't deny that she'd taken extreme pleasure in their perverted sexual act. Not only had two men participated in her orgasm, three others had watched. She'd never performed before an audience before, and she was suddenly glad for the blindfold. It hid the flare in her cheeks.

'Yes, it was,' Myers said. 'But next time can we find someplace where I can have a little more room?'

Her spine stiffened at the comment. 'You won't be invited next time.'

'Oh, come on, sweet tits.' Sonny emphasised his comment by twisting her nipples between his thumbs and forefingers. 'It wouldn't have been as easy for you without him there. Admit it.'

'It will be easier the next time,' she said stubbornly.

That made her lover laugh. 'Well, at least we won't have to fight over that. You know there's going to be a next time.'

Yes, there would be a next time and probably a time after that. Shanna didn't know how long it would take for her to get close to Santos. She was willing to fuck Sonny as many times as it took.

'Aren't we supposed to be going to a party?' she asked. This was all fine and good, but now that the heat of her orgasm had passed she was ready to pursue her real goal.

'I thought this was a party.'

'I'm thinking about alcohol.'

That made Sonny laugh even harder. 'We've got a fireball this time, men. Let's find the lady something to drink.'

Myers finally moved and Shanna heard the door beside her close. Sonny gave her tender breasts one last rub before sliding her dress back up her body. He assisted her in sliding the straps up her arms and making sure the material found its home again.

The touch of the soft material against her nipples was nearly too much, but when he grabbed her hips and slowly lifted her off his soft cock, Shanna knew that wouldn't be her problem in the morning. Already, her most private parts were throbbing. She'd been well ridden and she was sure she'd be sore.

It had been worth it, though. Not only had she experienced an incredible orgasm, she was now headed to Santos's private estate. When Weasel fired up the engine again, her anticipation nearly shot through the roof.

The SUV jounced across the rough terrain until it was able to climb back up on to the comparatively smooth road. Mentally, Shanna tried to take in as much of the surroundings as she could. Sonny had said that they were going to his boss's country home. It made sense. She could tell they were on a dirt road. The sound changed briefly, and she heard the distinct, hollow, clumping noise of tyres against a wooden bridge.

They drove for a long time, taking only a few more turns. She tried to mark them on the tape recorder with her special code, but the conversation in the vehicle had gone silent. Behind her, Sonny was practically asleep. Her body rested against his as his hands leisurely caressed her curves. At long last, Myers braked.

Sonny finally roused behind her. 'We can take this off now.'

His hands left her thighs and began tugging at the knot of her blindfold. Shanna blinked when the T-shirt was tossed to the side, but it didn't take much for her eyes to adjust. It was dark enough outside now that the stars glittered against the ink-black sky. She quickly took in her surroundings and tried to commit the scene to memory.

The SUV was parked outside a gate. A big brick fence surrounded what could only be described as a compound. Barbed wire graced the top of the brick barrier and the gate looked to be controlled by advanced electronics. Beyond the gate, she could see a big, white, two-storey house surrounded by trees.

The house itself was amazingly understated. She'd expected opulence from Santos. He obviously had the money to buy something splashier. Somebody, probably his realtor, had led him in a new direction. The place was actually classy.

Shanna watched closely as Myers rolled down his window. He pressed a button on the security console for the gate and said his name. The gate clicked and swung open wide. Myers drove up the short driveway to the house.

'This is nice,' she said as the vehicle was parked. Turning, she glanced over her shoulder at Sonny. 'Who did you say you worked for?'

'I didn't.'

'Well, he's got taste. You'll have to introduce me.'

Sonny just grunted and opened the door. He gripped her by the waist and swung her off his lap. Her legs swayed as they tried to take her weight. She took one step and an ache settled at her core.

She pushed all thoughts of discomfort to the back of her mind as she looked up at the house. As she stared at the front door, her mind focused and her breaths became deeper. A new sense of purpose bloomed inside her chest and she squared her shoulders. Sonny's hand settled at the base of her bare spine but not even the touch of his callused hand against her bare skin could distract her now.

'Let's go inside and find you that drink,' he said.

Shanna's hands clenched around her purse. She wanted nothing more than to feel the cold heavy metal of her gun against her palm but she knew it was too soon. She needed the element of surprise. She'd done a good job, actually. None of these men would believe for a moment that she was a Fed.

But she wasn't here as a Fed. She was here as a sister. She didn't want to arrest Santos. She wanted vengeance for Shanille's death.

'Let's go,' she said in a steely voice.

Her jaw had hardened to the point where she could only respond to Sonny's comments with short, clipped answers. The moment he opened the door and stepped inside, her entire body went on the alert.

She had to find Santos before he saw her. She and her sister had looked a lot alike. She'd filled out in the years since she'd last seen the man, but her face, her eyes and even her hair hadn't changed that much. She knew that she'd recognise him as soon as she got within smelling distance of him.

She followed Sonny inside the front door and her gaze swept the room.

'It's kind of bare,' Sonny said. 'The boss just bought the place. He hasn't had time to move much in yet. We've been real busy at work.'

As well she knew. She'd been following these people's exploits for months. The miserable, blood-sucking leeches … She took a steadying breath and feigned interest in the house. 'I can see the possibilities. These rooms are huge.'

Her muscles were poised for action as her eyes scoured the room and its occupants. She quickly identified the people she knew were part of Santos's organisation, but she didn't see the man in question.

'Where's that drink?' she asked through clenched teeth.

With a hand on her bare back, Sonny led her to the next room. Shanna quickly oriented herself. The kitchen was the place where people always seemed to congregate, and it was packed. Sonny's hand dipped lower to give her rump a squeeze. Her toes curled, but she continued to search the room. She strained to see all the faces, but she couldn't find him.

Where was he? Where was the bastard? She was so close; she could practically feel his evil presence.

'Where is he?' she finally snapped.

'Who?' Sonny asked, coming to an abrupt stop beside her.

A warning shot through Shanna's brain. She'd lost control. She hadn't meant to say that out loud.

'Who are you looking for?' he asked again.

What the hell, she thought. She might as well go for it. 'Your boss,' she said with a smile. 'Shouldn't we say hello to our host?'

Sonny's eyebrows rose and he gave her a strange look.

Shanna did her best to look offended. 'I might be a bar tramp, but I do have manners,' she said tartly.

'Well, that's nice, sweet tits, but there's just one problem.'

'What's that?' she said, trying desperately to hold on to her patience.

'He's not here.'

5

'Not here?' The words again slipped out before Shanna could stop them. 'What do you mean he's not here?'

Sonny's eyebrows lowered. 'It was supposed to be a housewarming party, but he got called away on a family emergency or something.'

Shanna's teeth clenched together so hard it was a wonder she didn't burst a blood vessel. He'd slipped away again. She couldn't believe it. She'd managed to get herself invited to his housewarming party and the son-ofabitch didn't even show.

'What's up with you, Lily?'

Fury burned inside her veins, and Sonny was picking up on her agitation. She felt like kicking something but she had to remember her precarious position. 'I just think it's strange. I would never throw a party in my new house if I wasn't there.'

'Yeah, well, we've had a good run at work. The boss thought we all deserved a little reward.'

A reward. Revulsion shimmied down her spine. Mañuel rewarded his people for selling drugs that destroyed people's health and their lives. 'How nice of him,' she practically growled. 'Where's that drink?'

Sonny manoeuvred his way through the mass of people to the kitchen bar. An impressive display of alcohol filled the counter. 'What do you want?' he asked.

'Whisky. Straight.'

He passed her a shot glass and Shanna tossed it back. The potent liquid burned its way down her throat and into her belly. The trail of fire seeped outward but it wasn't enough. 'Hit me again,' she said as she slammed the glass back on to the counter.

'Whoa.' Sonny's eyes sparkled as he looked at her. 'You are something, lady.'

Shanna's chin came up. It was a compliment and she accepted it as it was. 'Don't you ever forget that.'

'I don't think I will,' he said with a shake of his head.

He poured two fingers of whisky into the glass and slid it towards her. Liquid sloshed over the edge and on to the counter, but Shanna didn't care. She pounded down the liquor with as much enthusiasm as she had the first time. Finally, the whisky started to take effect. The edge began to wear off. Numbness diluted her frustration and she was able to mentally take a step back.

OK, so Santos wasn't here. What had she planned to do if he was? Shoot him? There were dozens of people crowding this house. If she had managed to get to him, she never would have gotten away. The crowd would have turned on her like a pack of wolves. What would she really have done if she'd come face to face with him?

She didn't know.

You're impulsive.

Joe's words echoed in her head and she nearly reached for a third shot of whisky. She hadn't had a plan as she'd come here tonight. Her behaviour had been fuelled by emotion. She'd put herself in a dangerous situation, purely on the hope of finding Manny. She hadn't planned an exit strategy. Her partner had already been hurt. What was she supposed to do now?

Pushing her feelings aside, she began to think as she'd been trained.

She needed to call headquarters. That was her number-one priority. She needed to get help to Shawn as soon as possible. It was also way past time for her to check in. Whenever an agent missed a call, the action behind the scenes became frantic.

'Which way is the bathroom?' she asked.

'Down that hallway,' Sonny said with a nod of his head.

'I'll be right back,' she said as she began to make her way through the mob of people.

In the hallway, there were fewer guests. That was good. It helped Shanna think more clearly. Her first priority was to make that call, but other thoughts were filling her head. Mañuel might not be here but she was still in an ideal situation. She was inside his house. Nobody, FBI or DEA, had made it this far. She had the audiotape of her journey here. That should help her co-workers locate the residence. Once they found the place, they'd need to know the interior layout of the building. Entrances, exit paths, weaknesses – her brain began to document them all.

Deliberately, she began opening doors and analysing rooms. She had the perfect excuse if anybody asked; she was looking for the ladies' room.

There were four doors along the hallway. When she opened the first, she found the beginnings of a library. Books and boxes filled the room, but the thing that caught her attention the most was the window. It had curtains.

'A woman.'

Mañuel was living with a woman.

Shanna fought the urge to slam the door. She hoped the poor thing knew what she was in for. Shanille hadn't.

Her steps were crisp as she continued down the hallway. She opened the second door and found a guest bedroom.

'Oh, I'm sorry. I . . .' The words trailed off as she realised what she'd walked in on.

A blonde was on all fours on the centre of the bed. She seemed to be enjoying herself immensely as two men worked their lust out upon her. The woman didn't even look at her as she concentrated on her mouthful of cock. The man behind her paused in his vigorous thrusting as he looked over his shoulder at the interruption.

'Hey, gorgeous,' he grunted. 'Come join the party.'

'Maybe later,' Shanna said as she stepped back towards the door. She didn't recognise any of the people. She did a quick visual sweep of the rest of the room as she quickly exited. 'Have fun.'

The thing that hit her once again was the window. The curtains had already been hung in this room, too. Shanna closed the door with a soft click even as her irritation rose. Mañuel hadn't changed one bit.

She was fuming as she tried the third door. Drugs and sex; they were his manna. They always had been. She couldn't remember ever meeting a more vile person in her life. The man just oozed evil.

The door was locked.

Shanna's attention quickly focused.

The third door was locked.

She wiped her hand on her dress and tried again. The doorknob wouldn't budge.

A locked door in an otherwise open house? Why would Santos open his house to his trusted men but still keep this one door locked? Shanna felt excitement unfurl in her belly. 'What are you hiding, Manny?'

She quickly looked down the hallway. It was too crowded. Curiosity was nearly killing her. How was she going to get in that room?

The sound of a toilet flushing made her quickly move away from the door. The locked room would have to wait. She casually leaned against the wall. There was the sound of running water before the bathroom door opened. Shanna found herself face to face with a man wearing a particularly wrinkled T-shirt.

'Hey, there,' the man said with a knowing smile. 'I'm Tommy.'

'Hi, Tommy,' she said, trying to hide her impatience. The man was an underling in the organisation, and she had work to do.

'I was in the SUV.'

'I know,' she said silkily. She turned sideways and tried to brush by him.

He stopped her with a short sidestep. She was totally unprepared when he suddenly reached out and jammed his hand between her legs.

'Guess where I have your panties,' he said with a leering smile.

His big paw squeezed her tender mound, and Shanna's reaction was instinctive. Sonny's exertions had left her extremely tender, and the friction of this thug's rough hand against her swollen flesh caused a flash-fire reaction. She was a trained agent and she was pissed off enough as it was. Suddenly she had him on his knees.

A quick jab of her stiletto heel to his instep and a knee to his solar plexus was all it took. The entire sequence of events took less than five seconds. Leaning down, she whispered in his ear. 'My panties are all you're going to get, Tommy boy.'

This time he didn't try to stop her as she moved into the bathroom. Quickly, she shut and locked the door behind her. She had a very important call to make.

She pulled her cell phone out of her purse and dialled a classified number. On the second ring, she got a recorded message. Keying in her identification code, she waited for an operator to answer. A knock on the door made her jump.

'Fuck off!' she said. She should probably be nice to the man; he could have valuable information. She just didn't have time for him right now. She had to alert the FBI to Shawn's condition and make sure he was found.

'Lily, let me in.'

'Shit!' It wasn't the man from the back seat. It was

Sonny. Torn, Shanna looked back to the phone. She couldn't call in with him listening right outside the door. 'Just a minute.'

'What the hell's taking you so long?'

Hurriedly, she punched the end button on her cell phone. She shoved it into her purse and looked at the toilet. Ah, hell. 'There was a line,' she called as she lifted her skirt and squatted.

She took care of business, and Sonny was waiting when she came out. In an instant, she could see he was angry.

'What were you doing snooping in the rooms?' he asked.

Shanna stood her ground. 'You need to give better directions. All you said was that the bathroom was down this hall. Give me a break, all right?'

'Oh,' the big man said. He took a step back and looked somewhat contrite. 'Come back to the kitchen. I want to show you off.'

Like a trophy, Shanna thought. Taking a deep breath, she looped her arm through his and sauntered back to the crowd. Her eyes darted to the locked room as they passed it, and an impulse hit her. This time she knew it was an impulse, but she went with it anyway. With a bold hand, she reached out and stroked the big henchman's fly. 'I'd like to show you off sometime, too, big boy.'

Sometimes the biggest men were the easiest to control. Sonny stutter-stepped, and she slipped her other hand into his pocket. It took nothing to get his keys. She moved away quickly when his hand slid up her thigh.

'Oh, look. A poker game,' she said in delight as they walked into the kitchen. With a sensual move, she slipped into one of the open chairs. 'You'll cover me, won't you, Sonny?'

A possessive look crossed the big man's face as all his

peers looked on. 'Oh yeah, sweet tits. I'll cover you good. I'll cover you real good.'

Miles away, Joe Mitchell stalked about his office like a caged animal. He wanted to hit something. Badly. He'd already taken his frustrations out on the bin by his desk, but it hadn't been enough. If he didn't get himself under control soon, he was going to put his fist through a wall. Cursing, he turned to pace in the opposite direction.

Where the hell was she? Was she all right?

Absently, he reached up to rub his chest. An iron-like band had tightened around his ribcage when he'd first heard the news. It had been hours, but he still couldn't breathe right. He couldn't admit it to anybody, but he was scared shitless.

'Damn it, Shanna,' he whispered.

The phone caught his eye as he turned on his heel to retrace his steps, and he had to look away. He'd been putting off making that call for over an hour but he couldn't avoid it much longer. He just had to make sure he had his emotions under control first. Control wasn't coming easily.

Finally, he stopped pacing and hung his head. Robert and Annie needed to know what had happened. Still, it wasn't an easy call to make. He knew how much the Haynes cared about their adopted daughter. If they heard any sign of fear or distress in his voice, they'd be on the next plane to town. He needed to hide his own emotions to protect theirs. The trouble was, he was having a hard time donning his professional mask.

He cared too much about her – and in a way he had no business feeling. He was her boss, for God's sake. Still, if anything had happened to her ... If she was hurt ... Hell, he couldn't even let his thoughts go in that direction.

Determinedly, he lifted his head. He didn't have all the

facts yet. For all he knew, she was fine. Knowing his Lily, she'd probably somehow managed to hijack that SUV and was now leading Santos's men around by their noses.

There was a good reason why she hadn't checked in. Her cell-phone battery was dead. She wasn't near a pay phone. She was *not* somewhere lying in a ditch.

Feeling the panic start to rise again, he snatched up the phone and dialled his old partner's number.

'Hello?' a groggy voice answered.

'Robert, it's Joe.'

The voice on the other end suddenly became alert. 'What's wrong?'

'I don't want to worry you, but we've got a problem here. It's Lily.'

'What's happened? Is she hurt?'

Joe could hear Robert's wife, Annie, shuffling around on the bed. He hated that he'd had to wake them, but he knew it was what they would have wanted. 'We don't know anything yet,' he said slowly. 'She missed her regular check-in time, and we haven't heard from her since. I wondered if she might even be with you.'

'No, she's not. What aren't you telling me?'

Joe tried to take a deep breath, but that iron band wouldn't let him. He ran a hand across his tight chest. 'She was working on a case involving Mañuel Santos. The last time she was seen, she was with five of his men.'

'Damn it!' Robert said with a burst of emotion. 'Where was her partner?'

Joe tried to stay calm. 'He was trying to follow them but they caught his tail. They roughed him up pretty good. He's in the hospital right now with concussion and two broken ribs.'

There was silence on the other end of the line.

'She's probably fine, Robert,' Joe said hurriedly, although his knuckles turned white around the telephone receiver. 'Her partner said her cover was solid when she left with them.'

'She left with them? Voluntarily? Sonofa– I taught her better than that. What did she think she was doing, leaving her partner like that?'

'I don't know. You know her better than anybody. You tell me what she was thinking.'

Robert let out a sarcastic laugh. 'Nobody knows how Shanna thinks, Tiger.'

Even under the circumstances, Joe felt a small smile press at his lips. No, there was nobody on the face of the earth who thought or behaved like Lily.

But something had changed. His smile faltered as he thought about her. Something had been different over the past few months. He'd seen the changes in her, but he was the last person on earth she'd ever confide in. He knew how she felt about him. Hell, she avoided him like the plague.

'She's been unusually stressed during this latest case,' he admitted to his old partner. 'I don't know what it is, but something's been bothering her. She's pushing the limits. I've been trying to hold her back but she's nearly out of control. It's almost as if this case is personal to her.'

'Who did you say she was investigating?' Robert asked.

'Mañuel Santos. His drug ring has been growing and we know he's moving a lot of product. We've been working in conjunction with the DEA, but so far nobody's been able to get a solid lead on the guy. He's like a ghost.'

'None of this is ringing a bell,' Robert said. His voice had begun to shake, but then he took a deep controlled breath. 'Why don't you start at the beginning?'

There. That was more like it. That assured tone had come from Robert Haynes, retired FBI agent, not Robert Haynes, concerned father figure. Joe took a deep breath himself and felt his concentration sharpen. For a moment there, things had become too personal. If he looked at things logically, dispassionately, it would be much better. 'As I said, we've been working on this case for a while. Cobra and Lily learned that Santos's men tend to hang out at a strip joint. I sent them in to see if they could spot the guys, maybe follow them. Hell, we're grasping at straws here on this one. It was the best strategy we had.'

'Did you say a strip club?' Robert asked slowly.

'Yeah. It's a place called Tassels down on Lincoln. You know how rough it is down there, but I sent her down there with Cobra.'

This time, there was complete silence at the other end of the line.

'Robert?'

'Joe, you'd better sit down.'

'What?' The iron band around his chest hitched tighter.

'Just listen, and don't say anything.'

'Robert, you're worrying me.'

'I don't mean to. It's just that Shanna would kill me if she knew I was telling you this.'

Joe sat. Suddenly, his knees were the consistency of Jell-O.

'I'm not saying that lightly,' Robert continued. 'You can't ever let her know I told you, or it would crush the very light inside of her.'

'I understand,' Joe said quietly.

'Annie, could you go make us a pot of coffee, dear?' There were more sounds of rustling in the background, and then Robert's voice came back on the line. His tone was hushed but extremely serious. 'This could very well be personal for her, Joe. I don't know how everything ties together but there's a lot about Shanna that you don't know.'

Joe braced his elbows on his knees and hung his head. He didn't say a word as he held the telephone to his ear.

'She's led a tough life, Tiger.'

The older man's voice caught, but Joe couldn't get a word past his own tight throat to cover the silence.

'You know that Annie and I love her, and we consider her our daughter. I never told you how we came to know her, though. A few years before you came on the force, I was working on a case. Like this Santos guy, my target was known to hang out at Tassels.'

Joe felt his stomach turn. God, he hated where this was heading.

'My mark never showed up, but somebody else made the mistake of trying to lift my wallet.'

'Lily,' he whispered.

'Shanna,' Robert corrected. 'She was a dancer at the club – their best from all reports. She also had the lightest touch I've ever felt for a pickpocket. If she hadn't been such a looker, she might have picked me clean.

'Anyway, one thing led to another, and I ended up taking her home to Annie. We got her off the streets, Joe. It kills me to think how long she was out there, but she's a survivor. She's smart as a whip.'

'I know,' Joe said in a low tone, 'And she's got the instincts of a wild animal.'

He finally got it. Her statement about her instincts saving her more times than she could count now made sense. It had been bugging him for weeks. He just wished there had been another explanation behind it.

'That's Shanna. Anyway, that's all I know. It's all she's allowed me to know,' Robert said. 'In the years since then, she's never once spoken about anything that happened to her before that night. I don't know where she's from, how she ended up on the streets, or if she has any family. Shoot, Annie had to pry it out of her when her birthday is.'

April 28. Joe didn't have to look in her file to know. He knew the contents of that particular manila folder inside and out. He'd always been intrigued by the holes in her background, but he hadn't had the authority to dig deeper. Robert had obviously gone to great lengths to wipe out her background to even give her the chance at entering the FBI.

The Bureau had been the better off for his efforts.

Robert was still talking, and Joe tried to drag his mind away from the picture of Shanna dancing naked under a spotlight. His vivid imagination displayed every intimate detail. He could see her full, firm breasts swaying in time with the music. Her impossibly long legs wrapped around the stripper's pole as she swung round and round with her long dark hair flying.

His cock began to stiffen and he shifted uncomfortably in his chair. The creaky old thing let out a loud squawk that sent him flying to his feet like a rocket.

'Anyway, I don't know anything about this Santos character,' Robert was saying. 'I don't know if it was him or something about that strip joint that's been making her uneasy. Just know, though, that if this hadn't happened, I would never have told you any of this.'

Joe ran a hand through his already ruffled hair. 'Her secret's safe with me. So's yours. I won't let her know you told me.'

There was another silence before Robert came back on the line. 'Tiger, you've got to find her. For Annie – and for me. Please find her.'

Joe's air caught inside his lungs. Robert had always been such a stalwart of strength. As an agent, he'd always known what to do in any situation. This was the first time he'd ever sounded old.

'I'll find her, Robert,' Joe promised. 'I swear I will.'

6

Sonny's hand settled at the base of Shanna's spine. 'Let's find a room upstairs,' he said as he leaned down to whisper in her ear.

'But, Sonny, I'm winning.'

The party was still raging about them, and although Shanna did have the biggest pile of chips in front of her, that wasn't the reason she wanted to stay. She'd learned quite a bit just by sitting at the table playing poker. For one thing, she'd learned that at least two of these men had helped clean out the building she'd raided three weeks ago.

The knowledge made her grit her teeth, but she plastered a smile on her face. With a flourish, she set down a full house. Draining these thugs' wallets was a small but rewarding consolation prize.

'I said let's find a room,' Sonny said impatiently.

Weasel stood leaning against the breakfast bar, watching them. His long fingers curled around a glass of scotch. Shanna remembered the feel of those cool insistent fingers and hastily looked away. A knowing leer settled on the strange man's face.

'This way,' Sonny instructed. His fingers dipped below the low-cut back of her dress and lightly touched the crevice between her buttocks.

Shanna's toes curled. Her knees were weak as she pushed herself from the chair.

'Thanks for the winnings, boys.'

'You can't take her now, Sonny. She's got all our money,' one of the other players complained.

'She's got something else I want,' Sonny said coolly.

He was horny. Shanna felt her pussy pulse. She didn't know if she was ready to take him again. It had been good but she was so tender now. Her nerve-endings were absolutely raw.

She went with him anyway. He led her across the living room and they began to climb the stairs.

'We'll use the boss's room. He won't care. I don't think he's even slept there yet.'

Shanna froze at the mention of Santos.

'Come on, I'm already hard,' Sonny said.

Shanna gripped the handrail and forced herself to move. The thought of being in Mañuel's inner sanctum sickened her, but she needed to check out the second floor. Sonny hadn't let her out of his sight since he'd confronted her coming out of the bathroom. She didn't know if he was just being possessive or if her wanderings had worried him. Either way, this might be the only chance she got to see the rest of the house.

Her stomach turned when they reached the upper landing, but she quickly surveyed the hallway. There were five rooms. Sonny opened the first door on the right and her legs went numb. She didn't want to go into that room.

'Don't get shy on me now, sweet tits. The night's still young.'

Shanna's gaze was drawn to the bed like a magnet. Mañuel Santos's bed. She felt like retching.

Sonny reached up and squeezed her breast. 'Hey! I've got something that needs your attention here.'

He grabbed her hand and pressed her palm hard against his crotch. He was hard as iron under her fingers. Her attention was still focused on the bed but she gave his rod an obligatory squeeze. The enormous erection seemed to swell even larger under her fingers. Sonny's hips twitched and he muttered a vile curse.

'On the bed. Now!'

'No!' She wasn't doing it on that bed.

It was as if nobody had ever dared say that word to him before. Sonny's dark eyes narrowed to threatening slits. Color dotted his cheekbones and a muscle worked in his jaw. 'What did you say?' he hissed.

'I said "no".' Shanna smiled to soften the words. Mañuel's bedroom or not, she had to protect her cover.

She turned towards the angry man and reached for his waist. When she pulled down his zipper with a loud rasp, the expression on his face lightened. 'Is that OK with you, big boy?'

She slid her hand inside his fly. With a firm but gentle touch, she reached to the base of his tool and cradled his balls. Sonny let out a choked response that indicated that it was indeed OK. Smiling ingenuously, Shanna undid his belt, loosened his pants, and began working on his bulging cock with both hands.

God, he was big.

She took a deep breath as a shiver ran down her spine. She knew she shouldn't take pleasure in what was only the means to an end, but she did. She'd kept herself reined in for far too long. If keeping this man and his big banger happy improved her chances of getting close to Mañuel, she was all for it. She was more than willing to indulge in a little nasty sex to get what she wanted.

She ran her thumb around the tip of Sonny's erection and a spot of moisture appeared on his boxer shorts. She worked her thumb more firmly around the thick tip and flicked it with her thumbnail.

'Enough!' Sonny said. 'Get it in your mouth. Quick!'

His hands settled on her shoulders and forced her to her knees. He pushed her down so quickly, she knocked her knee against the floor and bumped her nose against his prick. He grunted and pushed his hips against her face. Shanna tried to back away but his hands caught her

85

head and held her in place as he rubbed himself against her.

'Pull down my shorts. Christ, I need your tongue now.'

It was difficult with him thrusting against her cheek, but she managed to grip the waistband of his underwear and pull them down. The material got caught on his erection and he let out a howl. Cursing and swearing, he pulled away from her and bent down to take care of his clothes.

Shanna couldn't help but gasp when he stood upright and that huge cock reared up at her. Good Lord! How had she ever taken that thing inside of her? If she'd seen it before he'd pushed it into her, she didn't think she would have allowed him to bring it anywhere near her.

Now he wanted to push that big stub of meat into her mouth?

On cue, her saliva began running hot and thick. She ran her tongue over her lips in anticipation, and Sonny's patience broke.

His hands dove into her hair and held her head. She cringed when the move pulled the roots of her hair taut, but he was through being gentle. He thrust the big bulbous tip at her lips and growled, 'Open.'

Shanna's sex fluttered with excitement. Kneeling as she was, she could feel the moisture dripping from her pussy. She was going to stain the carpet. There was no way around it.

'Take it,' he snapped.

Her lower abdomen clenched tight. God, this was the side of him she'd seen when he'd first kissed her at Tassels. He was demanding, urgent and not a bit compassionate. His hard cock battered the soft skin of her lips, and she felt herself melt a little inside. Obediently, she let her jaw drop open.

It wasn't enough. Forcing herself, she let her mouth relax into a big 'O'. The effort seemed to please him, because he grunted with pleasure as he slid his big cock into the hot, wet confines of her mouth.

'Oh yeah, babe. That's it. Suck it hard.'

There wasn't any room to navigate, but Shanna let her tongue wrap around the bottom of his thick penis. Her hips swayed with anticipation and she reached down between her legs.

'Hey! Get that hand up here and use it.'

The grip on her head tightened and she nearly choked when he thrust deeper into her mouth. Quickly, she lifted her hand and wrapped it around his cock. Using a motion that Dooley had taught her, she heatedly rubbed the base of the fat pole to the point where it was caught in her mouth.

'Oh yeah, sweet tits. You're good at this. You like a man between those luscious lips, don't you?'

She did. When Dooley had first aimed himself at her mouth, she'd been hesitant. He hadn't given up, though, and once she'd caught on to the pleasure in the act, he hadn't been able to stop her. For weeks, she'd gone at him like an infant rooting for milk from his mother's breast.

The hands at her head loosened their grip, then left her entirely. Shanna kept up with her work. Using what little dexterity she had, she let her suckling reflex do its job. Sonny's legs buckled but he quickly regained his balance.

'Holy hell,' he said.

There was the sound of clothing hitting the floor and then his hands were back. They gripped her head hard as his hips began to thrust. Shanna gagged when the head bumped the back of her throat. Instinctively, she tried to pull back, but he wanted her to take the whole of him. She moaned in distress and was beginning to struggle when, suddenly, she felt a presence behind her.

'Relax,' a low gravelly voice said into her left ear. 'You can do it.'

A cool hand wrapped around her body and dove below the neckline of her dress. Fingers pinched her nipple hard and she flinched.

The move was enough to distract her from Sonny's thrust. This time when he pressed inward, she took more of him than she would have believed possible. Her eyes popped open and she saw the tangle of his dark pubic hair moving towards her.

'Doesn't that feel good?' the raspy voice said.

Oh, it did. Shanna reached around Sonny and latched on to his buttocks with both hands. More. She wanted more.

His muscles clenched under her touch and he reflexively thrust harder.

Yes. He was going deeper into her throat than she'd ever taken a man before. Pride swelled in Shanna's chest.

'That's it, doll. Suck him like a big lollipop.'

That cool damp hand was mauling her breast. It squeezed, pinched, twisted and did whatever it wanted with her. She hated the touch, but she needed it desperately. When another hand flipped up her skirt and slid between her legs, she wanted to scream.

Sonny's prick stopped her from making a sound. His urgency had increased and his thrusts were becoming harder and faster. She fought to time her breaths properly. It was difficult with her own orgasm fast approaching.

The hand between her legs was devious. Three long fingers had stuffed themselves inside her and a thumb strummed her intimately. A pinky finger was doing damage of its own as it found a home for itself just outside the curve of her pussy lip. Every once in a while, it would squeeze, and waves of pleasure would course through her body.

'Fuck. Shit. Holy shit!'

Curses punctuated the air as Sonny slammed his cock

into her mouth. Shanna could feel the sweat dripping from the big man's body. A pool of moisture had gathered at the base of his spine and was dripping down on to her fingers. She braced her head against the shoulder behind her and hoped she could hold on long enough. Her body was humming at a high note.

Suddenly, Sonny stiffened. His fingers dug into her scalp, and he pressed deep. His body shook as he reared his head back and exploded into her mouth. Shanna gulped the hot salty come as fast as she could.

This time, when his legs buckled, they wouldn't support him. He dropped down to his knees and his cock slipped from her mouth.

She was close. *So close.* Shanna's body shifted and shuddered as she fought for release. The thumb on her clitoris had stopped teasing her and was now pressing hard. The three fingers inside of her had found her G-spot and were intent on stimulating her until she couldn't take any more. When that insidious pinky finger pinched again, she let out a whimper.

The whimper turned into a fully-fledged moan when a set of teeth closed over the muscle leading from her neck to her shoulder. The soft bite didn't hurt, but its eroticism was enough to send her sky-rocketing.

The hands held her tight and kept working her body to draw out the orgasm. By the time it ended, Shanna was sure she'd never be able to move again. Breathing hard, she sagged against the man behind her.

'Did you see that, Weasel?' Sonny wheezed from his spot on the floor. 'She took all of it.'

'I saw, Sonny. We've got a keeper here.'

Flinching, Shanna looked over her shoulder. To her dismay, she found herself in Edwin Myers' arms. Reaching down, she pushed at his wrist. His fingers slid out of her with a slurp, and she used her last bit of energy to scramble away from him.

Myers just laughed and wiped his sticky hand on the carpet. 'I don't think she likes me, Sonny.'

'Ah, she likes you all right,' Sonny said in a weary voice. 'She acts like a cat in heat every time you touch her. Hell, I need some sleep.'

Shanna watched as the man pushed himself to his feet. Her eyes rounded as she got her first good look at him completely nude. Everything about him was big, but there wasn't an ounce of fat on his body. He was just huge. His shoulders were wide and his chest was deep. He had thighs that looked like tree trunks. Even limp, his dick was bigger than most men's.

When he held out his hand, she willingly let him pull her to her feet. He pulled her close and grabbed the hem of her dress. The time he took to strip her was almost laughable.

His hot gaze ran down her body and her nipples perked up like good little soldiers. 'I love the sight of you in nothing but those fuck-me shoes, but I doubt the boss wants the sheets on his bed torn up by somebody else. You'd better take them off.'

'Let me,' Weasel said quickly.

'Absolutely not!' Shanna said.

No matter how much she'd gotten off by letting him touch her, she wasn't about to let it happen again. Not tonight, and not in this room.

Leaning down, she quickly untied the straps from her ankles. She knew she must look quite the sight with her breasts dangling and her butt thrust up in the air. It was better than letting that slimy man touch her. Standing upright, she kicked her feet and the shoes went tumbling in his direction.

He caught the sexy shoes and a strange smile crossed his lips. Turning, he scooped up her dress from the floor and headed towards the sofa in the sitting area of the bedroom.

Sonny turned Shanna before she could see what the pervert was going to do with her things. He pointed her towards the bed and her stomach sank. She couldn't think of one good reason or excuse to avoid touching that abhorrent piece of furniture.

'Man, am I beat,' Sonny said. 'You sucked the life right out of me, sweet tits.'

He grabbed her wrist and pulled her with him. Together, they tumbled on to the crisp white sheets.

Bile rose in Shanna's throat and she had to fight to breathe.

Dear God, she was in Mañuel Santos's bed.

For hours, Shanna lay stiff as a board. She fought off her revulsion by thinking about the case. Months of work had made her an expert on Mañuel Santos's drug cartel. She knew his territory, his targets and most of his distribution system. But she didn't have any proof to convict him of his crimes.

The locked room downstairs held the key; she could feel it.

If she could get into that room, she might find the evidence she needed. Account numbers, supplier names – anything could help. Something as insignificant as a phone number might break the case wide open, and she wanted to be the one to find it.

She owed that much to her partner, her sister and herself.

Sneaking around the house might be risky but her decision was easy. It was a risk she was willing to take.

'Weasel?' she called softly into the darkness. It was almost four o'clock in the morning.

She got no answer. Breathing slowly, she let her eyes focus on Myers. He was asleep. If she listened carefully, she could hear his soft snores.

With a gentle touch, she removed Sonny's arm from

her waist. He was dead to the world. Quietly, she slipped from the bed.

Neither man stirred as she crossed the room. Myers had her clothes, so she picked up Sonny's shirt and slipped it over her shoulders. Taking care, she picked up her purse and headed to the door.

It squeaked on its hinges when she swung it open.

Shanna went absolutely still. Holding her breath, she listened for any signs of change. Fortunately, Sonny and Edwin seemed to be deep sleepers. Gathering her nerve, she squeezed through the small opening.

'Let's hope you bozos downstairs have drunk yourselves into a stupor,' she said as she tiptoed to the top of the staircase. She was taking a chance venturing into unknown territory. She had no idea how many men were still downstairs or what condition they were in.

She crept silently down the staircase, keeping to the sides of the steps where creaking and groaning wouldn't be such a problem. Halfway down, she paused. At least three of Santos's men were passed out in the living room.

Automatically, she reached for her gun.

Her fingers wrapped around the cold metal but her heart beat out a steady pulse. It was at times like these when she was at her best. Without a sound, she slipped down the staircase and crossed the room.

'How many do you want, Smitty?'

'Give me three.'

Her heartbeat exploded when she heard voices. In one smooth motion, she spun and aimed her weapon.

'Hell, you wouldn't believe what I've got in this hand. I'm out.'

The card game was still going strong! Shanna froze in position.

What should she do?

She could almost feel her body being pulled in two directions.

Still ... The voices from the kitchen were pitched low. The players were so wrapped up in the game, they hadn't noticed her approach.

One of the men in the living room shifted in his sleep and the decision was made for her. She darted down the hallway to the locked room.

The carpet muffled the sound of her bare feet but there was nothing she could do about the sound of her heart pumping in her ears. She knew the men in the kitchen couldn't hear it, but how could they possibly not hear something so loud?

It took only seconds for her to make it to the locked door. Reaching into her purse, she pulled out Sonny's keys. She hoped to God one of them worked. She hadn't brought her tools. Muffling the set in her palm, she began trying the keys one by one.

The fourth one worked.

'Yes,' she hissed.

She slowly pushed the door open. Her luck held and, this time, there were no squeaks or groans. She slipped into the room and silently closed the door behind her.

Leaning back against the wall, she let her eyes adjust. As she'd suspected, the room was Santos's office. Excitement unfurled inside her chest. There could be information in this room that would put away the man for good.

Leaving the lights off, she crossed the room to the desk and Santos's computer. She couldn't believe her luck. She rolled the mouse on the mouse pad and the screen flickered to life.

'Damn,' she said.

It wanted a password. She swore under her breath.

First things first, though; she needed to check in with headquarters. She pulled her phone out of her purse, her mind on the computer. What would Manny use as a password?

The phone clicked and she punched in the classified number. Maybe it was something simple like his name. She reached for the keyboard as she waited for the operator to answer.

'Lily?'

Shanna lurched at the sound of the unexpected male voice. The phone slipped from her hand and fell into her lap. She hadn't known that a heart could actually stop cold at the sound of a voice.

'Lily!'

The voice called up to her from her abandoned phone and she dove for it. With a sweaty hand, she lifted it to her ear. 'Mitchell?' she said hesitantly.

'Where are you? Are you all right? Damn it, what happened?'

'I ... I ...' Suddenly, her brain didn't want to function. 'Why are you answering the phone?' she asked.

'I've been sitting here ever since you left that hang-up about five hours ago. I repeat, where are you?'

Her stalled heart suddenly jumped out of the starting blocks and began pounding as if she were running the 200-metre dash. Joe was on the phone. Things must be bad if he was waiting for her call. 'It's Cobra, isn't it,' she said tonelessly. 'He's dead.'

'No, he's in the hospital, but it's not serious. Lily, so help me, if you don't tell me where you are, I'm going to come right through this phone line after you.'

Relief made Shanna collapse on to the desk. Leaning forward, she settled her weight on to her elbows and began rubbing her aching forehead. Joe. She hadn't expected this. How was she supposed to think when *he* answered the phone?

'Lily,' he growled.

He'd asked her a question. What was it? Oh, yes. He wanted to know where she was.

'I'm at Santos's country home,' she said quickly. 'I don't know where it is because I was blindfolded on the way here. I think I can retrace the trip, though, with the tape I made. It might be difficult because we took a lot of twists and turns. Then Shawn was shot at, and I sort of lost my concentration. But . . .'

'Slow down. You're at Santos's house?'

God, she was rambling. She was reporting to her senior agent and she was rambling. 'Yes,' she said uneasily.

'Lily, come on, now. Settle down. Are you all right? Have you been hurt?'

Shock made Shanna take the phone away from her ear and look at it. He sounded almost concerned. She shook her head and brushed off the thought. Of course he was concerned. He had a rogue agent on his hands. The thought that she was acting like a fool in front of Joe Mitchell straightened her up faster than anything else could.

'I'm fine, sir. I apologise for any problems I might have caused the department by not checking in on time.'

On the other end of the line, Joe fought to keep his patience. Damn it, for a while there, she had been talking to him. *Really* talking. Yes, she'd been distraught, but there hadn't been the usual restraint she usually used when reporting to him. Now she'd reverted to that 'sir' crap. 'I don't care how it happened,' he said. 'I just want to know that you haven't been hurt.'

'No, sir. I repeat, I am fine.'

Pushing himself to his feet, Joe began to pace as far as the phone cord would allow. He wouldn't believe her until he'd checked her out for himself. He wanted to see her with his own eyes – touch her with his own hands.

His palms itched at the thought of touching her. He'd only done it once. His control had snapped the other day when he'd reached out and caught her chin. Her skin had been silky smooth, and his reaction had rocked him to the core. He wanted her back with him *now*.

'Lily, try to work with me,' he said. 'Is there any way we can locate your whereabouts?'

'No, sir.' There was a pause, and he thought he heard her take a shaky breath. 'As I was trying to explain, I don't know where I am.'

Her voice was rising in pitch again and it was making him uneasy. 'It's all right, sweetheart. What about the house itself? Is there any way we could identify it with an aerial search?'

'No, sir. It would be difficult to spot even during the daytime. It's a large compound but there are a lot of trees. They provide too much cover.'

Joe's pacing increased. They were taking too long with this phone call. It was being traced, but cellular calls were difficult to triangulate. 'Are you in danger?' he asked.

'Not right now.'

His blood pressure shot up into the red zone. It wasn't the answer he wanted to hear. 'Can you get out of there? Can you get away from the house?'

'I suppose,' she said hesitantly. 'I might be able to steal a vehicle.'

'Then do it.'

'Sir, if I did that, Santos would go back into hiding. We'd never get this close again.'

He didn't give a rat's ass about Santos or the case. He just wanted her safe. 'I don't like having you out there on your own. I'm ordering you to get out of there. Contact me when you know where you are, and I'll come get you.'

There was a long pause. 'I think they might catch me.'

The band around Joe's chest squeezed and he sat down hard. He *hated* this. He hated the idea of her being vulnerable and him not being able to help. 'Is your cover solid?' he asked.

'Yes, sir.'

He ran a hand through his hair and tried to think straight. 'Have they done anything to you?'

If they had, he was going to send out a door-to-door search party. Hidden compound, be damned.

'I'm OK.'

'Really?' he said quietly.

'Really.'

He looked at his watch. In a few hours it would be daylight. It went against every gut instinct he had, but he couldn't put her in any more danger. If she was safer staying where she was, he couldn't order her to leave. 'What do you need?' he said. 'Tell me how I can help.'

He thought he heard a sigh of relief. 'I need a place to go in the morning,' she said. 'I don't want to lead these people to my apartment. I need living arrangements.'

Joe mentally counted to ten. How could she say that she wasn't impulsive? Hell, arrangements like that took time. If she hadn't just run off with these people, she wouldn't be in this situation. 'Use the safe house out on Miller Road,' he said, thinking quickly. 'I'll get all the paperwork changed so it's under your cover name in case they do a background check on you. You're using Lily McKay, right?'

There was a long pause on the other end of the line.

'Lily!' he hissed. 'Are you still there?'

'Mitchell.'

'What?'

'They think my last name is Mitchell.'

Joe rocked back in his chair and it let out a vicious squeak. 'Why?'

'Because Shawn threw your name at me as Fuentes and Myers were dragging me out the door. When they asked who you were, he told them you were my estranged husband.'

Husband. Joe felt his cock twitch. 'Are you positive

you'll be OK until then? Are you sure you'll be able to get to the safe house?'

'I'm sure.'

How could she be sure? He hated to ask the next question, but it was out of his lips before he could stop it. 'Lily, what have you done?'

There was dead silence on the other end of the line.

'My job,' she finally said. He heard her shifting around. He thought he was going to have to ask the question again when she blurted, 'I've infiltrated the Santos organisation.'

Every muscle in his body clenched. 'How?' he growled.

'As Sonny Fuentes's new girlfriend.'

Joe felt as if somebody had just sucker-punched him. His stomach hurt and suddenly it was even harder to breathe. 'Where is he right now?'

'He's passed out.'

A flash of red appeared before Joe's eyes and he fought for control. 'Is there anybody else in the house with you?'

'Yes, I'd say there are about fifteen men still here.'

He rocked forward and his feet hit the floor. 'Where, exactly, are you?'

She cleared her throat. He knew what that sound meant. He'd heard it enough times. It meant that she'd done something that was going to give him heart palpitations.

'I managed to break into Mañuel's office.'

The thought of her breaking into Santos's office with that many men around made him light-headed. He sprang out of the chair and fought the urge to yell at her. 'Lily, this is a direct order. Get out of that office. Lay low until you get to that safe house. Do you hear me?'

'Yes.' The tone of her voice was so low, he could hardly hear her.

'Do it,' he said.

'But his computer is right here,' she said.

'Forget the fucking computer!' he roared. 'Get your pretty little butt out of that office!'

'But, sir . . .'

'Now!'

'Yes, sir,' Shanna whispered.

She lifted a shaky finger to the phone and disconnected the call. Her throat was so tight she could hardly breathe, much less speak.

She'd disappointed him again.

At first, she'd thought she'd sensed something near to concern in his voice. Hearing him revert to his special-agent tone to give orders, though, made things clear. She'd broken protocol. Hell, she'd broken nearly every rule in the book, and her partner had been injured due to her actions.

With an almost desperate longing, she looked at the computer. He'd told her to forget it, but if she came back with something, would it change his mind about her?

An unexpected noise in the hallway caught her attention and her instincts went on the alert.

Heavy footsteps approached from the kitchen.

Her gaze settled on the door. Had she locked it?

Her heart leapt up into her throat. Damn it, she should *know* if she'd locked that door.

An escape route. She needed an escape route!

She looked quickly at the windows but immediately saw the security system. There was no way out.

The footsteps were now loud outside the door. Feeling like a foolish child, Shanna dove under the desk.

The footsteps kept going.

The air left her lungs in a rush when she heard the door to the bathroom swing open. It closed, and she pushed herself to her feet.

She practically flew across the room. Joe was right. She needed to get out of here and lie low. Her hand gripped the doorknob and gave it a slight twist. Her heart nearly popped out of her chest when it gave a soft click.

It had been locked. Her head snapped to the side. Had the man in the bathroom heard that? She heard the sound of a steady stream hitting the toilet but she knew she had to move quickly.

In seconds, she was out of the room. The card game was on hold. She could hear more movement from the kitchen. She didn't have time to be cautious.

She lifted herself up on to her tiptoes and ran.

She was still breathing hard when she slipped back into Santos's bedroom. She glanced at the bed. Sonny was sleeping soundly. She looked quickly at Weasel. He'd rolled over, but he too seemed oblivious to her presence.

She didn't want that to change. She set her purse back on the floor and stripped. She slipped Sonny's keys back into his pants pocket and moved towards the bed.

It was still Santos's bed. Bracing herself, Shanna slid on to the firm mattress. She gasped when Sonny's arm wrapped around her, but he was still asleep.

It was all her nerves could take, though. Her body sagged against him. She didn't fight when his arm pulled her closer. His semi-hard erection bumped up against her backside and she shimmied against it.

She choked back a whimper and tried not to wake either of the men in the room.

'What have I done?' she whispered.

She was in way too deep. She'd risked her partner, her career, her hopes, her dreams and her life by coming here. The censure in Joe's voice had been clear.

He knew exactly how she'd infiltrated the drug ring.

She'd probably just crushed any remaining good thoughts he had about her. He'd already told her she was a risk to herself and to others. He thought she was impulsive and dangerous. Her actions tonight had done nothing to disprove that.

Now he thinks I'm a whore, she thought miserably.

Well, he was right.

Reaching back, she wrapped her fingers around Sonny's big cock. With two jerks of her hand, she had him hard enough to penetrate her. They said that people always reverted to their true colours. Sex had always been good for her. Whether slow and sensual or fast and rough, she could lose herself in the act. Right now, she needed it for comfort.

Lifting her top leg, she settled it over Sonny's thigh. She guided the big head of his cock to her opening and pushed her hips down. He was smaller and easier to take in his sleepy and half-aroused state. The danger of her escapade had given her an adrenaline rush, and for her that always meant arousal. She was wet enough to take him without too much discomfort.

Gritting her teeth, she thrust back until she had taken all of him. His balls bumped against her and his scratchy hair brushed her backside. It was only then that she could take a sigh of relief.

Her eyelids drifted shut and she tried to soothe the harsh sounds of her breaths. Her mind, unfortunately, wouldn't relax. Snippets of the conversation she'd had with Joe darted through her head.

'Lily, what have you done?'

'I'll come get you.'

She shook her head, but the words wouldn't stop.

'Are you all right?'

'Have you been hurt?'

'It's all right, sweetheart.'

The memory hit her, and Shanna's eyelids popped open. A rush of moisture coated Sonny's cock and her heart began to pound.

She scanned her memory banks, but there was no doubt about it.

Joe Mitchell had called her 'sweetheart'.

7

Shanna never did fall asleep. She spent the hours until dawn floating in that hazy, dreamy area halfway between sleep and wakefulness. The precarious state was even more taxing than staying awake the entire night. She craved sleep like a thirsty man craved water, but she couldn't make the transition.

Every time she drifted off, she'd see Shawn lying in the street beside his car. Somewhere in the distance, she would see Joe shaking his head. The visions made her sleep fitful, but they weren't the worst. Those times when Shawn would morph into Joe, she would come sharply, stunningly awake. It was hard enough to see her partner hurt. If Joe were ever hurt because of her, she simply wouldn't be able to bear it.

The sun had risen and she was verging deeper into the arena of sleep when one sharp word brought her to her senses.

'Shit!'

Her eyelids popped open to see Edwin Myers sit up quickly on the sofa. He entangled himself in the blue material of her dress and, with impatience, tossed it aside. He rubbed his eyes and looked at his watch with a scowl. 'Shit!' he repeated. 'Sonny, get up! We're late.'

Beside her, Sonny hardly stirred.

'Sonny!' Weasel barked. 'Wake him up!'

Shanna elbowed Fuentes in the ribs. He muttered under his breath but settled more deeply into the pillow.

Weasel cursed and strode over to the bed. He grabbed

Sonny by the shoulder and gave him a firm shake. 'Sonny, we're late for our meeting.'

Shanna's ears perked up at the information, and Sonny started to come to life.

'What, man?' he grumbled.

'The boss is waiting for us. Get your ass out of bed.'

Sonny shifted, but suddenly went still. Shanna felt his cock grow within her, and she rolled her hips with pleasure.

'Christ, Weasel! She's got my dick!'

Myers flipped back the covers to see. 'Well, make it quick. If we're much later, he'll have our heads.'

Sonny was already thrusting with long hard strokes. Shanna gasped when he moved, levering her top leg higher into the air. He changed angles slightly and began hitting her right at a sensitive area, close to her G-spot. She moaned when one of his arms curled around her abdomen to anchor her in place for his heavy thrusts.

'You were eager, weren't you, sweet tits?' he said into her ear. 'You couldn't even wait until I was awake.'

'No,' she said. She hadn't been able to wait. She'd needed him desperately last night for comfort. Right now, she needed him for something else. 'Oh, please. Fuck me harder.'

'On your knees,' he said.

Without breaking momentum, he rolled them both so she was on the bottom and he was stroking into her from behind. With little regard for her comfort, he spread her knees wide and placed one hand between her shoulder blades. She went down on her elbows without being told and the position allowed him free access to her.

'Give me more.'

She bent her back and assumed the submissive position that Dooley had taught her so long ago. She buried her forehead against the pillow – Santos's pillow – and felt Sonny's fingers dig into her hips.

He was impossibly huge inside her, but he was through being gentle with her. Yesterday had been her grace period. Now she was in for the full brunt of his sexual urges. He pulled back and her pussy clung to him, not wanting him to go. She didn't have long to wait before his thick rod pumped deep into her again.

The pillow muffled her scream. He'd set up such a powerful, fast rhythm, she had no time to accustom herself to it. In her submissive position, she could do nothing but accept his thrusts. He slammed in again, and she heard the slap of their bodies coming together.

'Is that hard enough, sweet tits?' he grunted.

She could only moan an answer. Reaching up, she wrapped her fingers around the headboard. Her fingers went white as Fuentes went a little wild. He was banging into her mindlessly, pulling back on her hips as his own surged forward. Now that she'd seen him, she could picture his huge cock penetrating her, disappearing into her welcoming cunny.

'Oh!' she gasped when his thrusts became shorter and faster. He was working deep within her, using her roughly. She felt the pressure building up inside of her.

The headboard banged against the wall with a quickening rhythm until it almost matched the beating of her heart. Suddenly, her excitement crested, and she screamed into the pillow.

Her quivering body set Sonny off like a firecracker. He gave a harsh yell and spurted into her. His hands held her hips so tightly, he lifted her right off her knees as he ground her on to his erupting cock. When he finally collapsed on to her, the weight of his brawny chest pushed her deep into the bedding.

Shanna fought to breathe. Talk about starting the morning off with a bang.

'Good, you're done,' Myers said. 'Let's get on the road.'

Shanna opened her eyes and saw the man sitting on the sofa. He'd watched the whole thing. Even as revulsion gripped her, an aftershock of her orgasm pulsed through her. Her muscles gripped Sonny's limp dick tightly.

'Stop that,' he said into her ear. 'You're going to get me in trouble.'

He pushed himself up on to his elbows and she took a long breath. It caught in her lungs when he slowly pulled out of her. She lay still on the bed, with her legs spread in a wide 'V'. Even with the two men looking at her, she couldn't find the energy to cover herself.

'I've got to go,' Sonny said as he pushed himself out of bed. He gave her rump a sharp slap and stood up. 'Give your address and phone number to one of the guys downstairs. They'll drive you home when you're ready.'

'Why can't I go with you?' she pouted. Whatever this meeting was about, it was important enough to drag these two vigorous men away from a willing female. They'd already said Santos was going to be there. If they left her behind, they was no way she could follow them.

'It's business, sweet tits, and you are definitely pleasure.' His hand slipped down to her buttocks again and he gave her a squeeze. 'We'll be in touch.'

Disappointed, Shanna sagged on to the pillow. She tensed when she felt another hand, this one cool and light, settle on to that same butt cheek. The inquisitive fingers dipped into her secret crevice and she tried to roll away, but the hand pressed her flat with more strength than she would have expected. Two fingers touched the tight bud of her anus and she went absolutely still.

Myers' lips settled against her ear and his raspy voice sent shivers down her spine. 'One of these times, doll, it will just be you and me.'

The fingers brushed her intimately, and then both men were gone.

* * *

A little over an hour later, Shanna thanked the man who'd driven her 'home' and stepped out of the car. She closed the door behind her and walked around the block to the safe house. She hoped to God that Joe had been able to get things arranged. She needed to keep her cover intact now that she was under the microscope with Santos's men.

Feeling ridiculously self-conscious in her skimpy blue dress and high heels, she walked up the front sidewalk to the house. Out of the corner of her eye, she saw the window shade on a nearby house move. Looking more closely, she saw an elderly man giving her a dour stare.

No doubt they didn't see the likes of her in this sedate neighbourhood very often.

Glancing over her shoulder, she saw that the car hadn't moved. The driver was obviously trying to be a gentleman and make sure she arrived home safely.

'Gentleman, my ass,' she said. It was nine o'clock on a sunshine-filled morning. The thug was catching one last long look at her ass before he went back to his job of dealing drugs and enforcing territory.

She just hoped that Joe had left the door open. She didn't have a key and he hadn't told her where he would leave one. It would be a bitch if her cover were blown because she couldn't find the key for her own 'home'.

She reached for the doorknob and swallowed a gasp when it turned of its own volition. The door swung open and there, filling the doorway, was her boss.

Shanna's jaw dropped, and she went mute.

Oh God, she wasn't prepared for this. Not now. She hadn't had time to go over what she wanted to say to him. She wasn't ready for another speech about her impulsiveness.

Her heart thudded in her chest. What was he going to do to her? There had to be repercussions. He looked angry enough to do anything. His eyes flashed green fire and energy radiated from his tense body. He wouldn't stop staring, and it made her nervous.

'Ti–,' she began.

He moved so quickly, she wasn't able to get the rest of his code name out. His hand jutted out and caught her at the nape of the neck. His lips came down hard on hers, silencing what she'd intended to say.

Shock paralysed Shanna. Joe Mitchell was kissing her.

His other arm wrapped around her waist and pulled her close. An almost electrical jolt of energy zapped through her at the contact of their bodies, and her eyelids drifted shut.

Five years of wanting bubbled up inside her. His body was warm and hard against her soft curves. His lips ate at hers, and his hands ... Lord, his touch was like fire.

Her body started shaking with need. Almost hesitantly, she ran her hands up his arms. His muscles clenched under her touch.

This wasn't a fantasy. He was real, and he was kissing her as if his life depended on it.

She wasn't about to question why. With a groan, she wrapped her arms about his neck and hung on for dear life. When his tongue pressed at the seam of her lips, her body melted. She clung to him, letting his body take her weight.

'Joe,' she said, her voice full of need.

His knees seemed to buckle at the sound of his name on her lips.

'Lily,' he said in a ragged tone.

His touch became more urgent as he tried to touch all of her at once. Shanna squirmed under his wandering hands. Her skin burned wherever his fingers brushed against her.

One of his hands dove into the dark waterfall of her

hair. The other one sneaked under the hem of her dress to her buttocks. His jaw went tight when he discovered she wasn't wearing any panties.

'Lord help me,' he said.

Urgency seemed to hit him then. With his hand firmly on her bare ass, he pulled her across the room with him. They tumbled down on to the couch and his lips found hers again.

His kisses jumbled Shanna's thought processes. She didn't know why he was here, and she didn't care. She didn't want to think about why he was touching her. She just wanted to touch him.

With frantic hands, she pulled his T-shirt out of the waistband of his jeans. She'd always seen him in suits and ties. These casual clothes were driving her wild. Her hands skimmed up his body and she shivered with desire.

Each and every muscle was clearly delineated. She couldn't stop her fingers from reaching out and tracing every line. His stomach shuddered when her fingernail skimmed along his six-pack.

'Please,' she said on a high note. 'Oh, please.'

She reached for the zipper of his jeans and he let out a harsh curse. He pulled away far enough for her to work and ran a line of kisses up to her ear. 'We're being watched,' he whispered.

She didn't understand, and she didn't want to.

'Santos's men have bugged the place. There's a camera in the corner of the room.'

This time the words got through. Her hands stilled, and a sabre of pain lashed through her.

He'd been putting on a show for the cameras.

Mortification set in, and Shanna wanted to sink into the cushions and disappear. She'd been making love to him, and he'd been putting on a show.

His hands moved on her ass and he dipped his head to kiss the side of her neck.

'No!' she said. She pushed him away and hurriedly arranged her clothes.

'Lily?'

The confusion in his green eyes was too real to be faked. She didn't care. She batted his hands away and quickly crawled over him. Her legs almost wouldn't take her weight but she forced them into action. She walked to the centre of the room and stood with her back to him.

Her brain and her body were still whirling but she tried to concentrate. 'Why are you here?' she asked.

She heard him sit up on the couch, but she still couldn't look at him. 'I'm still your husband, baby.'

Things began falling into the place. The case. Coberley. Her cover. Inside her chest, her heart had begun pounding the rhythm of a big bass drum. She wasn't up for this. After everything she'd gone through last night, both the highs and the lows, she just couldn't handle playing house with Joe Mitchell. She didn't know if she could handle that on the best of days.

She turned quickly on her heel to face him. 'I threw you out for a reason. Don't think you can just waltz back in here and have me accept you with open arms.'

'Your arms were pretty open just a few seconds ago,' he said sarcastically.

His green eyes watched her like a hawk's. Shanna felt the room begin to press in on her, and she snapped. She couldn't do this. 'I've got to take a shower and get to work,' she said tonelessly. 'Stay or go, I don't really care.'

Joe saw her turn, but she was quick as lightning. He reached for her but she was gone before he could catch her.

'Damn!' he swore. He sagged back on the couch and inhaled deep gulps of air. He'd always known she was a live wire, but he hadn't been prepared for the voltage they set off together when they touched. His dick was straining to get out of his pants and his skin still simmered wherever she'd touched.

He'd just lost all control of his cognitive processes when he'd opened the door and found her in that skimpy dress. He'd handled it all wrong. He'd meant to signal to her that the house was bugged. He'd planned on working with her to establish his cover.

Instead, she'd started to say his code name, and he'd done the one thing he could think of to stop her. He'd kissed her, and they'd nearly gone up in flames.

Then she'd shut down completely. What had gone wrong? Was it the cameras? What had happened last night? She seemed OK physically, but had she been hurt emotionally? Was that why she'd clung to him so tightly? Had she been happy to see a safe, familiar face?

Oh, to hell with it. He couldn't let her just go like that. He needed to make sure that she was all right.

'Lily,' he called as he pushed himself off the couch.

He heard the shower running as he strode down the hallway. Perfect. He could talk to her without having to worry about the listening devices. He lifted his hand to knock on the bathroom door, but reconsidered. Hell, he was supposed to be her husband.

'Lily, we need to talk,' he said as he burst into the room.

He had to give her credit. She gasped in surprise but her reflexes were sharp. She reached out and grabbed a towel to cover herself, but not before he'd caught an eyeful of smooth white skin. His zipper bulged but he fought off the need to touch her again. They really did need to talk.

'Santos's men have the place under surveillance,' he said without preamble.

He saw her glance quickly at the shower.

'It should drown out the microphones, but they've got video cameras in the house, too.'

Her jaw dropped. 'I only gave them my address an hour ago. Why didn't you stop them?'

'I couldn't without arousing their suspicion.'

She nodded and pulled the towel more tightly around her. 'OK. I guess we'll have to debrief back at HQ, sir.'

Sir. Joe's teeth ground together. They'd just been rolling around on the couch together. 'You'd better drop the "sir" routine. They think I'm your husband.'

Her dark eyes flashed. Watching her closely, he took a step further into the room and turned to lean against the counter top. Her gaze flew to the door and then back to him. When she got the point that he wasn't leaving, she took great care in making sure the knot on her towel was tight.

'They'll never believe it,' she said nervously.

'Why not?' Joe cocked an eyebrow. This was interesting. He was getting more out of her here in this tiny humid bathroom than he'd ever gotten in his office. There, she was always tense and guarded. Here, she was showing more of her true nature. He liked seeing her vulnerability. He liked it a lot. 'I thought we were pretty convincing. We work well together.'

Her eyes rounded. 'That wasn't working!'

A fire leapt in his belly. He hadn't been thinking about work, either. 'Then what was it?'

'It . . .' Her hands gestured wildly. 'It . . .'

'It what?' he pressed.

'You're my boss,' she said.

'I'm also your partner.'

'My partner?' she gasped. 'What about Cobra?'

Her face went white and she took a step towards him. 'Oh, my God, did he take a turn for the worse?'

He held up a hand to comfort her. 'He's fine, but he's in no shape to back you up. That's why I'm stepping in.'

The colour still hadn't returned to her face. 'As my husband,' she said quietly.

'The two of you inadvertently created the perfect alibi for me.'

She wrapped her arms tightly around her chest as if the idea made her extremely uneasy. 'But we aren't prepared for this. We haven't made any plans.'

The irony of her words made him lift one eyebrow, but when her towel dipped he became distracted. His gaze zeroed in on her breasts and he shifted his hips uncomfortably. Something caught his attention, though, and everything inside him went still.

'Come here,' he said on a low note.

She blinked at his sudden change in attitude. She took a cautious step back, but he caught her wrist and pulled her to him. She inhaled sharply when he lifted his hand and gently trailed his fingers over a faint blue mark.

It was a bruise.

Rage was unleashed inside Joe's chest like a crazed beast. He reached for the knot of her towel and gave it a yank. The towel came undone and she reached for it. He tossed it towards the corner of the room and caught her by the waist.

His gaze dropped to her breasts and acid burned in his gut. Gently, he trailed his thumb along the faint marks. She'd been manhandled.

'Sonofabitch,' he hissed.

He gently cupped his hand over her soft flesh. Her nipple prodded at the centre of his palm and she let out a soft groan.

Using his free hand, he brushed her hair back over her shoulder so he had a better view of her other breast. The marks there were more apparent, and fury lashed through his system.

With shaking fingertips, he brushed the bruise. 'Shanna, who did this to you?'

* * *

Shanna jerked. He'd said her name. She didn't know what he'd said after that, but he'd said her name. Moisture collected between her legs, but she stared at him silently.

'Honey,' he said softly, 'who did this to you? Who hurt you?'

She looked down at where his fingers were brushing her swollen breast. The sight of his strong hand against her flesh was almost too erotic to look at. She'd never allowed herself to dream it could be this good.

His callused fingers brushed against a red spot close to her nipple, and a coldness shot through her veins. Sonny had left that.

Oh, God, and Joe had found it. Her throat tightened and she pressed her lips tightly together. If he'd been looking for a sign as to why she wasn't good enough for him, he'd just found it.

She pulled back but he didn't let her get far. He held her at arms' length, and suddenly she felt more exposed than she'd ever felt in her life. Even when she'd been dancing stark naked under that glaring spotlight, she hadn't felt this vulnerable.

Her boss was giving her the most intimate of inspections, and she squirmed with a sudden need to cover herself from his prying eyes.

'Stay still,' he said.

He caught her hands and lifted them away from her body. His intense gaze was now on her hips. He let one of her hands go so he could brush his fingers across her skin. With the slightest of pressures, he turned her so he could get a better look.

Shanna felt as if she was on the auction block, but that just went to show how classy a dame she was. His attention was turning her on.

'Oh, sweetheart,' he said softly.

Unwillingly, she looked down. Already, slight bruises

were showing on her buttocks. They didn't hurt but they showed exactly what she'd let Sonny do.

Joe turned her back towards him and she gave up on the fight to cover herself from his view. He was having none of it, and she knew he'd never let her out of this room until he'd inspected her from head to toe.

Shanna swallowed hard and looked somewhere over his shoulder. She'd wanted this man for ever. Now she was standing butt-naked in front of him. His touch, though, could best be described as clinical. Here she was squirming with overwhelming lust, while he was giving her a physical. God, she couldn't take much more of this. She couldn't take him looking at her, touching her.

His hand moved unexpectedly and she couldn't stop her harsh cry when he slipped his hand between her legs and cupped her mound.

'I'm still in the room, Lily. Don't act like I'm not.'

She was still sore down there after Sonny's vigorous thrusting, and seeing Joe Mitchell's hand cupping her most intimate flesh was nearly unbearable.

'Are you hurt?' he asked, immediately gentling his touch.

'No,' she said.

He gave her a hard look, and she tried to explain.

'I'm just . . .' She had to look away. 'Sensitive.'

He caught her chin and made her look back at him. As he held her gaze, she felt his hand move. Instead of cupping her, his fingers began gently exploring. She tried to back away from the intimate probing, but he wouldn't let her budge.

His dark gaze held concern, arousal and a tempered fury. The emotions were clear in his eyes and he didn't try to hide them. Shanna's mouth went dry.

'Open your legs, sweetheart,' he said in a low tone.

She could do nothing but obey. The look in his eyes held her captive.

The tip of his middle finger rimmed her opening, and she bit her tongue to keep from groaning.

'Tender?' he asked.

She could only nod her head.

He wrapped an arm around her to hold her in place and opened the drawer beside his hip. He rummaged around and finally found what he was looking for. 'This should help,' he said.

Shanna's eyes widened when he pulled out a tube of salve. 'No, it's all right.'

'Stay put,' he said, as he took off the cap and squeezed a good portion of the salve into his palm.

Her breaths shortened as she watched him lube up his fingers. He looked up at her then. His green eyes glittered with an emotion she couldn't quite read, but she couldn't look away. She bit her lip when his hand moved towards her again. It seemed natural to reach out and brace her hands on his strong shoulders.

'Easy,' he said softly, as his finger again went to her tender opening.

One determined finger penetrated slightly, and she flinched. The finger immediately pulled out and changed directions. It moved forward and brushed her clit. Her hips jumped but he wasn't diverted from his task. He circled the bud again and his eyebrows lowered as he caught her almost exaggerated response.

'You are sensitive,' he whispered.

His fingers reversed direction and Shanna prepared herself to be penetrated. She was shocked when his fingers moved right past her opening. His wrist pressed against her soft curls as he reached further between her legs and into the crevice between her buttocks.

'No!' she gasped.

His finger lay against her anus, and he watched her closely.

'No,' she whispered again and shook her head.

He took her at her word. His hand retreated, and she knew what was coming next. That insidious middle finger of his circled her opening, moving in unending loops until she thought she'd faint. Just when she thought she couldn't take it any more, he slid his slick finger into her. He used a steady and gentle pressure, but she knew he wouldn't be deterred.

Colour dotted her face. He was checking to see if she'd been fucked. She didn't know how he'd be able to tell; she just knew he would. If the marks on her breasts and hips weren't enough to convince him, her swollen cunt surely would. She could hardly take his long hard finger.

Closing her eyes, Shanna resigned herself to her shame. She couldn't have been more surprised when his lips covered hers in a soft kiss.

It was gentle, warm and understanding. She hadn't been prepared for it, and she couldn't fight it. She relaxed against him once more and her embarrassment disappeared.

'Were you raped?' he asked against her lips.

'No,' she said honestly.

'I don't expect you to go to those extremes,' he said before kissing her again. 'Not even with me.'

'I'll do what I have to do.'

'So will I,' he said with a dangerous edge to his voice. 'If I ever catch Sonny Fuentes, I won't be held responsible for my actions.'

Shanna pulled back to look at him. He was dead serious. His eyes had darkened to the point where the green was nearly black.

Joe Mitchell was mad, and everybody knew what happened when you caught a tiger by the tail. In a million years, she'd never expected him to be with her like this. Maybe he was angry that somebody had taken advantage of one of his agents. She didn't know. She just knew she preferred to think that he was angry because it had happened to her.

She'd never intended for this to happen, for them to have to take on this intimate cover of a husband and wife, but she wasn't above taking advantage of it. She'd been hot after this man for five years, but she'd never had the guts or self-confidence to do something about her feelings.

Now here she was, standing in a steamy bathroom, with his finger burrowing deep into her pussy.

She leaned forward to kiss him.

The ringing of a cellular phone made them both jump.

'Ah, hell,' Joe said. He reached for his back pocket and pulled out his phone. Gently, watching her every reaction, he pulled his other hand away from her.

Shanna went red with embarrassment and reached for her towel. When she saw Joe wipe his wet finger on his jeans, she turned away.

'This better be good,' he snapped at whoever was on the other end of the line.

Shanna ran a hand through her damp hair and took a deep breath. She nearly coughed at the humidity in the room. She could hardly see through the haze. The mirror had fogged over long ago, and her skin was clammy.

Out of the corner of her eye, she saw Joe nod. 'We'll be right there.'

He ended the call and pushed the phone back into his pocket. 'That was the hospital. We need to get there right away.'

8

The phone call destroyed the intimate mood, and Shanna quickly excused herself from the cramped quarters of the bathroom. She heard Joe turn off the shower as she opened the closet in the bedroom. She hadn't really needed a shower anyway; she'd cleaned up at Santos's house. She'd just been using it as an escape.

She was still stunned that she'd walked into this house and found him waiting for her. She hadn't been prepared for that. She'd been even less prepared for his kiss and his touch. Her body shivered in remembered delight, and she shook her head to clear her mind.

This turn of events wasn't good. In fact, it was the worst thing that could have happened. She was finally getting closer to Santos. Her mind needed to be clear and focused if she was going to achieve the goal that she'd set for herself years ago. Joe's presence would distract her.

She had absolutely no idea how she was going to deal with him.

He was waiting when she came out of the bedroom dressed in a very conservative blue suit. His eyes raked her figure and her face flared. 'I'm ready,' she said, not meeting his eyes.

'Let's go.'

Those words were almost all he said during the entire trip to the hospital. Their erotic encounter had changed everything. Their relationship had just moved to an entirely different plane, and neither of them seemed to know how to deal with it. Sitting in the close quarters of the pick-up only increased the tension between them. Finally, Shanna had to roll down the window just to find air to breathe.

'Don't be surprised when you see Shawn,' Joe said when they pulled into the hospital parking lot. 'He's got a lot of bruising.'

'How is he doing?' she asked. Her guilt became greater when she stepped out of the truck and looked up at the big white building.

'The doctors are most concerned about the concussion,' Joe said. He threw a glance at her as they walked to the front entrance. 'His broken ribs are painful, but they'll heal.'

Shanna bit her lip. Her partner was suffering because of her actions. 'I'm sorry,' she said quietly.

'We'll talk about it later,' he said in a clipped tone.

He'd tried to prepare her, but she couldn't help but gasp when she walked into Coberley's room and saw the colourful bruises on his face. She quickly walked to his bedside. 'Oh, Shawn. I'm so sorry,' she said. 'This is all my fault.'

'Shanna!' he said with relief. He reached out and covered her hand. 'Where were you? Are you OK? I've been going out of my mind worrying about you.'

'You're the one in the hospital,' she said, feeling even worse. 'How can you be worried about me?'

'What happened? Did they hurt you? Where did they take you?'

'Take it easy,' she said. She lifted a hand and gently smoothed back his hair. 'I'm fine. They just took me to a party.'

Her partner gave her a disbelieving look. She could feel Joe's stare boring into her, but she refused to look at him. It had been a party, just not the kind he was envisioning in his head. She sighed. His impression of her must be getting better and better with each passing moment.

'They took me to Santos's country home.'

'Holy shit!' Coberley exclaimed. 'We've been looking for that bastard for months. Where has he been hiding?'

'We're still not sure,' Joe said. 'She wasn't allowed to see the way.'

'But I might be able to retrace it,' Shanna said quickly. She smoothed the sheet across Shawn's chest. She didn't want him to feel that any of this was his fault.

Joe threw her a look from the other side of the bed but addressed his question to the man lying on the bed. 'Cobra, on the phone you said that you'd remembered something.'

'Yeah, I did,' Shawn said with a little more energy. He turned his head too quickly and let out a groan of pain. 'Sonofabitch, I keep doing that.'

'Take your time.'

'I'm all right,' he said, even though he reached for his head. 'It's not as bad as it was a few hours ago.'

'What did you remember?' Joe asked again.

'I think I got the first three letters of the licence plate on that SUV.'

Joe was reaching for his back pocket before his agent even finished talking. He pulled out a notebook and pen. 'Give it to me,' he said as he flipped to a blank page.

Shawn told him the letters and continued with a description of the vehicle. Shanna verified the make and the colour, but she couldn't corroborate the licence number. She'd been dealing with a lot of other things at the time.

'Good work,' Joe said as he tucked the notebook away again.

He stood with both hands tucked in his back pockets, and Shanna's thoughts scattered. Only a few minutes ago, she'd been trying to rip those jeans off of him. Suddenly, she felt Shawn's gaze upon her and she started guiltily. She turned away and poured him a glass of water.

'So what's our next move?' he asked.

She handed the glass to him and he gave her a questioning look.

'I'm taking over for you as her back-up,' Joe said.

'Really? How's that going to work?'

'I'm her jealous husband.'

The questions in Shawn's eyes disappeared. A smirk appeared on his face as he looked at her, and Shanna fought the urge to punch him in the shoulder. Only his injured state saved him.

'That should be pretty solid,' he said. 'What am I supposed to do?'

'Follow the doctor's orders.'

The smile faded from his face and he looked quickly at his boss. 'Joe, I've got to get back to work. Now that the case is starting to break open, I should be there.'

'When your doctor says the concussion isn't affecting you, I'll think about it.' Joe's tone brooked no room for argument. 'Let's get going, Lily. We've got a lot of work to do today, and this guy needs his rest.'

'Can I just have a moment alone with my partner?' she asked.

The look Joe threw at her was inscrutable, and for the slightest of seconds he hesitated. Then he nodded his head. 'I'll be waiting in the hall.'

Shawn watched him go before he turned to look at her. 'What the hell is going on between you two? It's gotten worse.'

He didn't have to explain what 'it' was.

Shanna shrugged uneasily. Her partner knew her better than most people. 'He's not happy with the tactics I used.'

'There's more to it than that. Hell, the tension in this room was thicker than molasses.'

'We're having some difficulties adjusting to our new status,' she said. She ran her finger along the edge of the bed rail. That was an understatement if she'd ever heard one.

'Hell, the two of you should be able to ease into your roles without much of a problem.'

'Without a problem?' Shanna blurted. Her hand fluttered helplessly in mid-air. 'Shawn, I can't breathe whenever I'm in a room with him.'

Her partner started to laugh but he stopped on a sharp inhale of breath. 'Damn ribs,' he groaned.

'Oh, God. I'm sorry.'

'Would you stop apologising? It's not your fault.'

'Yes, it is. Joe's not in here any more, so don't deny it.'

Shawn settled back against the cushions and gave her a steady look. 'You were just being yourself, Lily. You can't help your nature.'

'I know. I'm impulsive.'

'You're a damn good agent,' he said firmly. 'You just need to promise me something.'

'Anything,' she said, leaning towards him. 'You name it.'

'I'm not going to be there to cover your back. Promise me that you'll work with Joe, not against him.' He caught her fidgeting hand and held it tight. 'You need him.'

Shanna nodded. It would be difficult, given her feelings, but she would do her best to keep everything on the utmost professional level. Her face flared when she realised how ludicrous the thought was. Their encounter at the safe house had been anything but professional.

'What else?' she asked, hoping he'd change the topic.

'Promise me you'll get this bastard Santos.'

That she could promise. There wasn't a chance in hell that Mañuel was going to get away from her this time. 'You've got it,' she said determinedly.

'Good. I'm sick of that slimeball making us look bad.'

She was sick because of a lot more than that, but she held her tongue.

'Now get out of here. I need to heal up so I can get back to my desk job,' said Shawn.

Shanna stood from her chair and bent over the bed. 'Is there anything I can bring you?'

'How about a six-pack and a blonde?'

She couldn't help but laugh. Now that was more like the Shawn she knew and loved. 'I'll see what I can do,' she said as she placed a soft kiss on his cheek.

When she left the room, she found Joe leaning against the wall in the hallway. He still had that look on his face. She couldn't quite figure out what it was. He looked agitated, as if he was ready to rip somebody's head off. At the same time, he looked almost hurt. She couldn't figure out what she'd done to put such a look on his face.

'Ready to go?' she asked, not really wanting to know why he was upset with her this time.

He nodded and spun on his heel. The walk down the hallway and the ride in the elevator were very quiet. Shanna began to become even more uneasy. Things weren't good when he was this quiet. The trip to head-quarters was even worse. By the time they arrived, she was a bundle of nerves.

'Drop that tape off with the lab technicians and come straight to my office,' he said as he slammed the door to his truck. 'You need to be debriefed about your little adventure.'

'Yes, sir,' she said quietly as she fell into step with him.

'And stop that damn "sir" crap!' he snapped. He pivoted sharply on the ball of his foot. 'The name is Joe. If you forget that while we're under surveillance, it could blow the entire case.'

'Yes, s . . . I understand,' she said, unconsciously taking a step back.

He was so mad at her, and she didn't understand why.

At the house, he'd been much more understanding, much more approachable. Of course, he'd had his tongue down her throat and his finger up her pussy at the time.

Shanna's face flamed with colour, and she almost stumbled.

She finally got it. God, how could she have been so naïve?

He'd been playing a part. Mortification settled in her chest. That had been Special Agent Mitchell back in that steamy bathroom. He was just so smooth, so good at his work. Even she hadn't picked up on the fact that it had all been for the benefit of the cameras. Instead, she'd let her stupid daydreams overtake her. She'd let herself believe that he might actually be attracted to her.

Her head hung low when she realised what a fool she'd made of herself. The moment they'd set foot outside that house, his entire attitude had changed. He was upset at her for running off and leaving her partner stranded. He was probably also counting every single rule she'd broken.

This debriefing session was going to be pure hell.

'I'll be right up,' she whispered as they entered the building. She made a quick right to head down the hall. By the time she walked into the lab, she was a walking mass of misery.

'Hi, Shanna,' one of the technicians said. 'Can I do something for you?'

Shanna looked up and saw Melanie, one of the lab's best researchers.

'Oh, my God, what's wrong?' the woman said in a hushed voice. 'Is it Shawn?'

Shanna's eyes closed. Her impulsiveness had put everybody on the alert last night, even the lab techs. Gossip travelled quickly around the place, and she was just about to add fuel to the fire. 'No,' she said in a subdued voice. 'He's doing all right. I just saw him at the hospital.'

'Then what is it?' Melanie asked. 'You look like some-body ran over your dog.'

Shanna ran a hand through her hair. 'I'm having a really bad day.'

A concerned expression crossed Melanie's face, and she looked across the room. 'The conference room is open. Why don't we go talk?'

Shanna was surprised when the little lab technician took her by the arm. They'd worked together for a while, but she didn't really consider the woman a friend. Still, the opportunity to talk to somebody was tempting.

Melanie closed the door behind them and sat down. 'What's wrong?' she asked.

Shanna looked at her closely. Could she trust her? With her big black-rimmed glasses, the woman didn't look like a threat. She was a quiet, hardworking scientist who always seemed to fade into the background. Would she keep their conversation confidential?

'I think I'm about to be fired,' Shanna said in a quiet voice.

'But why?' Melanie asked. Her eyebrows lifted so high they appeared above the rims of her glasses. 'The rumour around here is that you infiltrated the Santos drug organisation.'

Shanna hooked her hair around her ear. News trav-elled like wildfire. She thought of the tape. If anybody were ever to hear what was on it, she'd never be able to show her face again.

'I did,' she said, 'but Special Agent Mitchell isn't happy with the methods I used. After I get done here, I have to meet with him to be debriefed.'

'Oh, I understand,' Melanie said. She folded her hands together primly on her lap. 'He can be very intimidating.'

Shanna looked up quickly and caught the other

woman's gaze. She saw empathy, and something inside her chest eased. 'That's why I need your help. I don't know who else I can trust.'

Melanie's eyes went wide. 'What do you need me to do?'

'I need you to analyse this,' Shanna said as she reached in her purse. She pulled out the tape and carefully set it on the table.

The technician adjusted her glasses on her nose and reached for the cassette. She looked carefully at the label and flipped it over to examine the other side. 'What kind of an analysis do you need?'

'I recorded my trip from Tassels strip club to Mañuel Santos's country home last night,' Shanna said. 'The problem is that I was blindfolded.'

Melanie's jaw dropped, and her eyes flashed towards Shanna's face. 'Oh my goodness, weren't you scared?'

'My adrenaline was pumping pretty hard, but I tried to trace my path using verbal clues. I'm hoping that by using a map, my signals, and the background noise, you can find Santos's hideout.'

The scientist's nose crinkled, and Shanna could almost see the wheels turning in her head.

'That's very creative,' she said. 'I'd love to tackle that kind of a challenge, but George is much more advanced in audio technology than I am. We should bring him in on this.'

'No!' Shanna said. She quickly reached out and caught Melanie by the arm. 'This needs a female touch.'

Melanie had started to stand, but she sat down slowly. 'What's on this tape, Lily?'

Shanna bit her lower lip. How could she ever explain the sounds on that tape to a shy, reserved woman like this? 'Have you ever had any experience with undercover work?'

'Shawn's told me a little about his undercover work,'

Melanie said, her eyes brightening. 'It always sounds so exciting.'

'It can be, but sometimes undercover agents are put in situations where they have to do things they normally wouldn't do.' Shanna lifted her hand and rubbed her temple. This was very difficult to explain. 'There are things on that tape that I don't want George to hear. In fact, I don't want anybody including Joe Mitchell to ever hear that tape.'

'But why?'

'I'm having *sex* on that tape,' Shanna said bluntly. She might as well quit circling around it. As soon as the woman listened to it, she'd know.

'Oh!' Melanie gasped. A nervous hand reached up to tuck a stray blonde hair back into the tight bun at the back of her head. 'Oh, my!'

'I did what I had to do to keep my cover.'

'Well, I ... I don't know if I understand, but I can certainly do my best to keep this tape confidential.'

The woman's gaze was darting about the room as if she were looking for a safe place to hide. Their discussion was obviously embarrassing her, but Shanna couldn't help it. She needed the technician's help. 'Thank you,' she said sincerely.

Suddenly, Melanie's eyes widened. When she looked at Shanna, there was horror in her eyes. 'Am I going to hear Shawn being beaten?'

The question surprised Shanna, and she felt as if she'd just been socked in the chest. She hadn't thought of that. 'Yes,' she said hoarsely.

Melanie bit her lower lip and dropped the tape like a hot potato. Her eyes blinked rapidly and her hands clenched together tightly in her lap. 'I don't know if I can do this.'

Shanna finally saw the truth that was dangling right in front of her eyes. 'You have feelings for him.'

A blush crept up the woman's neck. 'No, it's not that. I just ... I don't like violence.'

'Have you told him?'

The blush became brighter.

'You should go visit him in the hospital,' Shanna said softly. 'He's going to go crazy there with nothing to do.'

Melanie looked at her with wide eyes. 'I couldn't do that. He doesn't even know who I am.'

Shanna paused and reconsidered the woman. Under that white lab coat and those glasses, she was actually quite pretty. And her hair was blonde ... Shanna leaned back in her chair and let out a puff of air. Shawn had been spending a lot of time in the lab lately, and he always, always insisted that Melanie do their work.

A knock on the conference-room door derailed her train of thought. She glanced at the door as George opened it. 'Joe's on the phone, Lily,' he said. 'He's looking for you.'

Her stomach sank when she remembered what was in store for her. 'Tell him I'll be right there.'

She pushed back her chair but hesitated when she looked at Melanie. 'Are you doing anything on Saturday?'

The woman looked surprised. 'No. Why?'

'Why don't you and I make a day of it? We'll do a little shopping, stop by the salon, and then – if you feel like it – drop by the hospital.'

Melanie's mouth dropped open. 'Why would you do something like that for me?'

'You're doing me a favour. I'm simply returning the gesture.' Shanna turned and walked out of the room before Melanie could refuse.

'Besides,' she said quietly, 'I owe my partner.'

A sense of doom weighed heavily on Shanna's shoulders as she rode up in the lift. This meeting with Joe was not going to go well. Still, when it came right down to it, her sister was more important than her job. If she had to do it all over again, she'd make the same decisions.

Knowing that didn't help as she walked into the open bay of desks. She could feel the stares of her fellow agents as she walked across the room. Most of them had probably put in some overtime last night looking for her. She couldn't face them now, not with Joe Mitchell bearing down on her. Bracing herself, she walked into his office. The ceiling immediately began to press down on her.

His green gaze flashed to hers. 'Close the door,' he said in a cool tone.

She quickly obeyed his order.

'Sit,' he said, pointing a finger at the chair in front of his desk.

She was more than happy to take her weight off her shaky legs, but the position put her at a distinct disadvantage. Joe Mitchell didn't seem inclined to sit. He was more intent on pacing back and forth in his office, much like his namesake.

'I want to hear a recount of last night's events,' he said. 'You're going to tell me everything that happened, and you're not going to leave out one single detail. Do you understand?'

'Yes, sir.'

The pacing stopped, and he turned to glare at her.

'Yes, Special Agent Mitchell,' she corrected.

He spun on his heel and ran a hand through his hair. It took two more trips around the room before he spoke. 'Let's start with Tassels. Were Santos's men there when you arrived?'

'No, sir . . . No.'

'When did they show up?'

'It couldn't have been long after we got there.'

'You don't know?'

'I was in the back talking to Dool– a man named

Dooley. He's the bartender there. I asked him about Santos and his men. When we stepped back out into the bar area, he pointed them out to me.'

'So what happened next? How did you end up leaving with them?'

'Well, one of the men started hitting on me.'

'Which one?' Joe snapped.

'Sonny Fuentes,' she said quickly. His impatient attitude was making her uneasy.

'Your new "boyfriend",' he practically growled. He snatched an 8x10 photo off his desk and pointed at a grainy picture of the man.

'Yes,' she said quietly. 'That's him.'

He glared at the picture before slapping it back down on the desktop. 'If I remember correctly, my instructions to you and your partner were to go to Tassels and observe. You weren't supposed to make contact. Then again, considering the dress that you wore, I can see how that plan was shot all to hell.'

'There was nothing wrong with that dress,' she said. She toyed with the ring on her finger nervously.

'Nothing that a few more yards of material wouldn't fix.'

Suddenly, Shanna just couldn't sit meekly in the hard wooden chair. She came to her feet with a flurry and planted both hands on his desk. 'Have you ever been to a strip joint? Have you seen the women in the audience? Well, they aren't quiet, church-going, Betty Simpcox types. They're either lesbians or women who like the wild side. I didn't think I could pull off the lesbian role, so I chose to show a little skin. If I'd worn something that covered me from neck to toe, our cover would have been blown before we even stepped inside the door.'

Joe had stopped pacing but the muscles in his forearms bulged when he crossed his arms over his chest. 'All right.

I'll give you that one, but what did you do when you caught Fuentes's eye?

'I flirted back.'

His lips pressed together in a straight line, and the room pulsed with energy. 'Why?'

'I wasn't going to pass up on a chance like that. He's a high-ranking associate in the Santos crime ring.'

'So that was reason enough to let him fuck you.'

The words lashed at her from across the room, and Shanna took a step back. He made it sound so dirty, so trashy. Well, it had been, and she'd gotten off on it. 'At that point, I didn't have any back-up. It was either have sex with him or blow my cover and risk my safety.'

'How many men did you accommodate to protect your cover, Shanna?'

'One,' she said hoarsely.

His eyes flashed fire. 'You told Shawn there was a party. It doesn't take much for a guy to picture what could happen if you showed up at a party wearing that tiny dress.'

'Fuentes was the only one,' she said defiantly. She'd known he'd taken that comment the wrong way. She'd *known* it! 'It was a party, Joe. You know – drinks, food and poker games. It wasn't an orgy! My God, what do you think I am? I hadn't had sex in six months until last night!'

The words were out before she could stop them. Horrified, Shanna slapped a hand over her mouth and spun away. She heard a sound behind her, and she glanced back to see Joe closing the blinds to the windows that overlooked the sea of desks. Work had stopped outside and every single agent was watching them through the plate-glass windows.

Damn it. Why, *why*, had she told him that?

'They can't hear us,' he said as he closed the last shade.

The fact didn't make her feel much better. With the shades drawn, the room seemed tinier than it had ever been. The walls pushed in on her, and he took up all her breathing room.

'I only had sex with one man last night,' she said in a tight voice. Weasel didn't count, and Dooley had been personal. 'I did it to protect myself and my cover.'

'I should take you off this case right now.'

The threat brought her head up with a snap. 'You can't do that.'

One of his dark eyebrows rose. 'I can.'

Panic started to bubble up inside Shanna's chest. He couldn't pull her off the case – not when she was getting so close. She'd vowed vengeance for her sister, and she'd waited for years to follow through on that promise. He couldn't take that away from her now.

'Please don't,' she said, her voice catching.

She took a step towards him. Her hands were clasped tightly in front of her. 'I know I made some serious mistakes last night. Let me make up for them. Please.'

Joe was taken aback by the pleading tone in Shanna's voice. He'd never seen her beg for anything. The hairs on the back of his neck stood on end.

This was exactly the kind of behaviour he'd tried to describe to Robert. Something about this case had definitely gotten under her skin. He still couldn't quite figure out what that was. 'Give me a good reason to keep you on it,' he said.

Her tongue darted out to lick her dry lips, and his gaze zeroed in on the movement. 'I've been studying the Santos organisation for months. I know it better than anybody.'

She moved a step closer and Joe felt his body automatically respond. Mentally, he took a step back to distance himself. He was still her boss. 'There's Shawn, and you've kept good files. Somebody should be able to get up to speed in a relatively short amount of time.'

She ran a shaky hand through her long silky hair and he clenched his hands to stop himself from reaching for her. When her dark eyes lifted and met his, he was stopped dead in his tracks.

'But I'm already in,' she whispered.

It was the wrong thing to say to him. He'd stared at that picture of Sonny Fuentes the entire time she'd been down in the lab. In that short amount of time, he'd had several creative ideas on what he'd like to do to the sonofabitch.

The thought of Fuentes or any other man touching her made him see red. He knew he'd reacted a little strongly at the hospital, but he'd even been jealous of her relationship with Shawn, and he was pretty sure they weren't involved. They were just close.

He wanted some of that closeness for himself.

She stepped forward until she was nearly toe-to-toe with him, and his body practically started to hum with electricity. 'I know you don't like the way I got there, but I'm in,' she said. 'Nobody else has gotten this far.'

His pulse was pounding in his ears. At the moment, he didn't give a damn about the case. All he cared about was her and the way she made him feel. 'You broke almost every rule in the book,' he said.

'I'm sorry.'

'Why, Shanna?' he finally asked. 'Why is this case so important to you?'

Her eyes lowered and she wouldn't look at him. It was a telltale sign that he wasn't going to get the whole truth. 'Santos is a notorious drug dealer. Does there have to be any more reason than that?'

Her pulse pounded at the base of her neck, and he had to fight the urge to pull her close and run his tongue across it. 'No,' he said softly, 'But I think there is. Tell me what you're hiding. It will stay between you and me, I swear.'

She hesitated for a second but then shook her head. 'Just give me another chance. I swear I won't screw up again.'

Everything inside Joe rebelled at the idea. Hell, he just wanted to pick her up and carry her away. The instinct to protect her was strong, but she was asking him to let her put herself in the middle of danger.

'I'll work with you any way you want,' she said softly. 'I'll play the part of your wife if that's the way it has to be.'

Damn. She'd gone right for his Achilles' heel. The idea of living with her under the same roof was beyond tempting. 'We'd be partners, in nearly every sense of the word. I need to know I can count on you.'

Her keen ears picked up on the fact that he was wavering, and her eyes flashed. 'I won't let you down.'

Their relationship had always been strained. He knew she didn't like him, but the dynamic between them had changed this morning when he'd put his hands on her. 'They have cameras and microphones on us. We'd have to behave like a normal couple.'

She nodded in understanding but he wanted to make sure they were both perfectly clear. 'We're going to have to have sex, Shanna.'

She shifted her weight nervously, but her gaze was steady on his. 'I know.'

The admission nearly sent him off like a rocket. Every muscle in his body pulled tight, but he fought to keep his head clear. 'Are you sure? Are you listening to what I'm saying? I'm going to have to touch you, Shanna.'

He reached out and caught her by the waist. 'You're going to have to touch me.'

Her hands had come up to brace herself when he'd pulled her close. Her palms were splayed across his chest.

She looked at them and silently lifted her gaze to meet his.

'We can fake it if that's what you want,' he said in a raspy voice. 'We can hide under the sheets and pretend.'

She swallowed hard and finally looked away. 'We're supposed to be a married couple getting back together. It has to look natural. I don't want modesty to give away our cover.'

Joe didn't even want to analyse that statement. He couldn't let himself think about what she must have done with Sonny Fuentes last night. It would drive him stark raving mad.

'You pulled away from me this morning when you learned about the cameras,' he pressed. 'Do you think you can go through with it?'

She looked everywhere in the room but at him. 'We seemed compatible.'

Compatible? She called that compatible? The top of his head had nearly exploded when her anxious hands had gone to his zipper.

'I need to know things,' he said in a whisper. 'I need to know what you like, what your favourite position is . . . I need to know you intimately, Shanna.'

Dots of colour appeared on her cheekbones and she tried to back away. 'Do we have to talk about this? Can't we just let nature take its course?'

That tactic had worked well enough this morning. More than well enough, in fact. There was one other thing to consider, though. Reaching down to his chest, Joe caught her hand. She'd been toying with the ring on her finger ever since she'd stepped into his office. 'Is there a boyfriend out there who might get upset about this?'

She looked down at her hand with surprise. He ran a finger across the ring and she quickly pulled away as if his touch burned her. 'It was my mother's.'

A different kind of alertness caught him. It was the

first time she'd ever told him anything that personal about herself. Even Robert had said that she never talked about her family. 'Has she passed away?' he asked.

She inhaled sharply, but nodded. 'My parents were killed in an accident when I was twelve.'

'I'm sorry.'

She stared at the ring for a while, but then snapped out of whatever memory had caught her. 'What about you?' she asked, looking up at him. 'Is some woman going to dislike the fact that you're ... working ... with me?'

'No,' he said.

As he watched, she straightened her shoulders and lifted her chin. 'Does this mean that you're willing to keep me on the case?'

It was time for a decision. Did he pull her off the case, or did he go undercover to protect her? His brain told him that the first option was the better choice. She'd be safe that way.

If he went undercover as her husband, though, he could watch over her. He could protect her and make love to her all at once. The opportunity to get closer to her was too intriguing. He couldn't pass up the chance. 'You've made more progress in one day than we've made in months. If you promise to keep yourself safe, I'm willing to give this a shot.'

Her face brightened, and her relief was apparent. 'Thank you, sir,' she said.

'The name's Joe,' he told her. He couldn't wait until saying his name seemed natural to her.

She started to pull away but he quickly stopped her. 'There's just one more thing.'

'What's that?' she asked.

He let her go. She watched him closely as he rounded his desk and opened a drawer. When he pulled out the tiny jewellery box, her jaw dropped. She reached for the chair and sat down hard.

'We need to firm up our cover stories,' he said as he pulled out a set of rings.

She stared at him in complete silence as he walked towards her. He reached for her left hand and had to lift it out of her lap. Watching her closely, he slid the diamond engagement ring and matching gold band on to her finger.

'Now you're officially Lily Mitchell,' he said softly.

She still didn't say a word. She simply stared at the rings as they glittered up at her.

He'd hoped for more of a reaction than that. Sighing, Joe reached for his own ring. That was when she finally broke out of her stunned silence. Her hand flashed out suddenly to stop him. Surprised, he looked up her.

'May I?' she asked.

9

The morning passed in an absolute daze for Shanna. She worked on sketching the layout of Mañuel's house, but she did it subconsciously. Once Joe had slipped that diamond ring on her finger, her brain had gone numb.

Her gaze dropped to her left hand once again. It still shocked her to see it there, and she'd been wearing it for hours. She took a deep, calming breath, but nothing could stop the excitement that gurgled in her veins.

She knew it was all an act. The ring was for Lily Mitchell, not her. Still, that didn't stop her heart from jumping every time she looked at it. Other parts of her body weren't so subtle in their reactions, and she had to squeeze her thighs together to ease the tingling between her legs.

'Why does it have to be him?' she whispered.

If it had been anybody, *anybody* else, she could go into this with more detached feelings. She could embark on a phoney affair, but keep her concentration on her real target. With Joe, it wasn't so simple.

She was going to have sex with him.

They were going to play house, and she'd never been so nervous in her life. She'd certainly never been so nervous about sex. She'd always enjoyed physical intimacy. Some psychologist would probably analyse her and conclude that her strong sexual drive was a result of losing her parents' love at such an early age.

She didn't think so. She just loved screwing. She liked it soft and slow, rough and rowdy, rude and crude.

How could she ever show that side of herself to her boss?

Her problem tonight wouldn't be awkwardness; it would be hiding her enthusiasm.

'Lord help me,' she said as she returned to her blueprints.

The lunch hour finally rolled around, and Shanna escaped from the building. Between answering her co-workers' questions and worrying about exposing her feelings for Joe, she was mentally exhausted. She checked out a car from the carpool and just started to drive.

She cranked up the radio and, once her tension eased, realised that she was famished. She hadn't eaten since before she and Coberley had gone to Tassels last night.

'No wonder I'm in such a daze,' she said.

A deli in the strip mall on her right caught her eye, and she turned into the parking lot. A turkey sandwich filled her stomach, and the food was the fuel she needed. Her head cleared and she felt much better as she thought about her situation.

She could actually kill two birds with one stone. Not only was she in a position to bring Mañuel Santos down, she might also find herself in a position to go down on Joe Mitchell. The thought made her laugh out loud. Patrons at the deli looked at her strangely, but she didn't care.

As she left the restaurant, the boutique next door caught her eye. It was a lingerie store.

'Oh, that's too perfect,' she chuckled, still feeling the effects of her good mood.

She had to go in; there was no way around it. She stepped into the store and let her eyes adjust to the dimmed lighting. The saleswoman politely greeted her, and Shanna began to explore.

The thought of buying something special for Joe sent a shiver down her spine. She'd had fantasies, but nothing compared to this.

Life seemed to have come about in a full circle. Here she was again coming face to face with Mañuel Santos. In the process, her sexual nature was refusing to be repressed. She'd fought back that part of herself for years. Now, not only was she involved in a sexual ménage à trois with two of Santos's men, she was about to embark on an undercover romp with her boss.

She'd never thought this would happen to her.

'Are you looking for something in particular?' the saleswoman asked.

Shanna glanced at the striking woman and felt better about herself. It was nice to know that a woman could be sophisticated and sexual at the same time. 'Yes, I am,' she said. 'I'm just not sure what I want.'

She lifted her hand to run her fingers through her hair, and the saleswoman let out a gasp. 'Look at your ring!' she exclaimed. 'That's gorgeous.'

The woman took a closer look and Shanna hid her smile. She knew the ring was fake.

'Are you a newlywed?'

Well, that thought hadn't occurred to her. 'I suppose I am.'

The woman glanced up and her eyes glittered. 'I have just the thing for you. It just came in with the shipment today. Come with me.'

Shanna was surprised when the woman grabbed her hand and took her into the back room of the store. She watched with curiosity as the woman dug into an open box. When she lifted up a white lace teddy, Shanna's eyes went round.

'That's beautiful,' she said.

'Isn't it?' the woman absolutely cooed. 'It's form-fitted with underwire cups. I think it looks sexy and virginal at the same time.'

She turned the teddy around, and Shanna saw the sheer lace back and the skinny thong. 'I love it.'

The woman winked. 'You haven't seen the best part yet. It's crotchless.'

Shanna's stomach twittered. Endless erotic images flashed through her mind. 'Can I try it on?'

'Absolutely. With your body, this will look amazing. What size do you wear?'

'I'm a six.'

A smile tugged at the woman's lush lips. She passed Shanna a size six, but then reached down and grabbed another one. 'Might I suggest you try a four, too?'

Shanna took the smaller size and went into a dressing room. She stripped down to her panties and shimmied into the larger teddy. It fit her perfectly. As she stepped back and looked into the full-length mirror, she felt a familiar twinge between her legs.

The saleswoman was right. It was as if the lingerie had been designed with her in mind. The padded cups lifted her full breasts high. She turned and tried to imagine what her ass would look like without her blue panties in the way. It would be perfect, she decided. The cut of the material would frame the twin moons, leaving them free for wandering hands.

She felt her panties getting wet, so she quickly took off the lingerie before she soiled it. She put the teddy aside and was about to get dressed when the size four caught her eye. Why had the saleswoman smiled?

Shanna had never handled curiosity well, and she quickly reached for the smaller lace creation. She pulled it up her legs, and the moment the thong slid into place, she felt different. She tugged the bodice up and slid her arms through the spaghetti straps.

'Oh, my God,' she gasped.

The virginal teddy had turned into an exotic bondage outfit. The stretchy lace pulled tight across her stomach, and her breasts were locked into a high pouting position. The material conformed to her curves, allowing very little give. The thong pulled tight, sharply dividing her buttocks and creating a snug fit in the crotch at the same time.

Her body quivered with sexual excitement, and Shanna bit her lower lip. This was the one.

She quickly stripped off the teddy and removed her panties. She wanted to feel the full effects. She tugged the white garment back over her naked hips. The effect was staggering.

'Yes,' she said, sighing as the lace once again embraced her.

The tight fit pulled open the crotch, giving clear access to her pussy. The thong was pulled almost to the point of being uncomfortable, but she loved the naughty feeling. Every time she moved, she could feel the hot touch of lace against her anus.

The lingerie caressed her body with every breath she took, and she leaned back against the dressing-room wall. She stared at herself in the mirror. She had never looked so sinful and angelic at the same time. Her eyelids drooped and her hand wandered to her naked crotch.

A phone rang, jarring her from her erotic haze. The noise left her body in shock and she looked around the small room in confusion. When she realised that the call was for her, she quickly dove for her purse. The bent-over position tugged the thong tight into the crevice of her ass, and she gasped. She was breathless when she answered.

'Hello?'

'Hey there, sweet tits.'

It was Sonny.

A hard jolt of sexual awareness rocked her. 'Sonny,' she said, letting the name melt from her lips.

'How you feeling today, baby?'

'I feel wonderful.'

'Yeah? Your pussy's not too sore?'

Shanna glanced down. Her pussy was pulsing with excitement. 'I'm aching in places I haven't felt for a long, long time.'

'That's good,' he said. 'Means you'll remember me.'

'Oh, I don't think I could ever forget you, Sonny,' she said. Or his connection to Mañuel.

'Feel like going another round tonight?'

Her thoughts immediately flashed to her plans with Joe, and disappointment caught her. The teddy would have to wait for another night. She sighed softly but let her brain focus. Her whole set-up with Joe was meant to bring in offers like this. He hadn't been happy about the way she'd handled events last night, but this time she would tell him beforehand. 'What do you have in mind, big boy?'

'Why don't you meet me at Tassels?'

'Can't we go back to your boss's house?' she asked innocently. 'I had such a good time there.'

'Nah, the boss is back home. We'll have to go to the strip club. Hey, maybe the old man will let you get up on stage and show those sweet tits to everybody.'

The thought made Shanna uneasy. Not only was the idea too close to home, there were other things to consider. That stage had been hers for a few years. There were still regulars who would remember her, and her stage name hadn't been Lily back then.

'I don't know, Sonny. I'd rather just show them to you.'

'And Weasel.'

A shiver of revulsion ran down her spine. 'And Weasel.'

'When you gonna let him get a piece? He's dying to do you.'

The thought of screwing that skinny pervert made her sick. 'I like you, Sonny. Your ... equipment ... is so satisfying.'

'Do you like my big dick, sweet tits?'

'You know I do.'

He laughed. 'Yeah, I could tell by the way you were moaning and grabbing that headboard this morning.'

Shanna looked at herself in the mirror. She'd thought he'd been rough this morning. How would he react if he caught her in this get-up? The possibilities made her toes curl. 'I like the way you fuck,' she said in a sultry voice.

'You, too, sweet tits. You're a natural slut.'

'Thanks, I guess.'

'Hell, you know what you are, so enjoy it. Meet me at Tassels tonight. Eight o'clock.'

'All right.'

'And wear something sexy. Don't bother with a bra, but make sure you wear some panties. Tommy's enjoying the pair you gave him last night.'

Her stomach rolled. The guy from the back seat. Was she expected to pleasure him, too? 'I'll find something nice and frilly.'

'Great. See ya tonight, Lily.'

The line went dead, and Shanna returned her phone to her purse. She looked with mild regret at her teddy. It was going to have to wait. Resignedly, she pulled off the tight lingerie. Her mind, though, was cranking with adrenaline.

She was looking forward to this. Not only was her body already oiling up for Sonny's big cock, but she had a plan. While she was entertaining him and his band of thugs, Joe could look for Santos's house. She had solid information that Mañuel was going to be there tonight, and there wouldn't be a better time to get to him. He'd be vulnerable without his bodyguards.

There was a sense of purpose to her stride as she walked back out to the sales area. 'I'll take the size four,' she said with a wink at the saleswoman. 'And I'll need a nice pair of panties. Red, I think.'

* * *

When Shanna strode into Tassels that night, she was actually upset. She and Joe had had a good old row of it. He'd been adamant that she wasn't to meet Santos's men. She'd been just as insistent that he search out Mañuel's home. They'd gone round and round in his office until Betty had finally come in and made them seek a compromise.

The problem was that the compromise hadn't made Shanna happy. Joe hadn't been willing to let her go to the strip club without a back-up. She didn't know where he was right now, but he was watching her. If anything went wrong, he was bound and determined to step in.

That was where she got nervous. Shawn had been put in the hospital as a result of trying to protect her against Sonny and his men. If Joe were hurt because of her, she simply wouldn't be able to handle it.

She'd finally agreed with the arrangement because it was the only way Joe was willing to work. When it came right down to it, all she wanted was for Mañuel to be caught. If she could distract Sonny while the search team found his home, then so be it. It wasn't the vengeance she'd always pictured, but she'd take what she could get.

Suddenly, wolf-whistles permeated the air, and Shanna cocked her hip to acknowledge the men's calls of approval. She winked at the bouncer and obediently gave a slow twirl to show off her assets from every angle.

It was this bar, she swore. She could do things in this place and not feel the slightest bit of modesty.

'Come over here, sweet tits,' Sonny yelled.

OK, being called 'sweet tits' from across the bar did bother her. *Slimeball*, she thought, as she crossed the room.

'Hold it there,' he said when he got to their table. 'Give us another twirl.'

She threw him a cocky smile and stepped back in a

seductive pose. She'd been a pro on that stage behind her. If there was one thing she knew, it was how to work it.

She'd extended her shopping spree this afternoon to look for something appropriate to wear. As she'd explained to Joe, she couldn't wear suits or Sunday dresses to this place. Unfortunately, that was all the FBI had thought to put in her closet.

She wore a crisp, white, wrap-around blouse, tied at her side, which displayed a good two inches of her tight belly. She'd matched the top with a leather mini-skirt and knee-high boots. A dainty gold waist chain and a pair of lacy red bikini panties for Tommy completed the ensemble.

From the looks on the men's faces, she'd achieved the effect she was looking for.

'Sit by me, doll.'

She strove to keep the sexual smirk in place as Weasel and another man stood up to make room for her. Soon, she found herself seated between two familiar bodies. Myers was on her left and Sonny was on her right. She could only imagine what devilish delights they had in store for her.

'Somebody get me a beer,' she said. She had a feeling she was going to need it.

Joe walked in the front door of the strip club and let his eyes adjust. For a moment, he couldn't find Shanna and panic ran cold through his veins. She'd given him the slip. She'd gone to find Santos. A rowdy crowd to his left caught his attention, and he saw a flash of white.

There she was.

His edginess didn't ease. Four men. He shook his head and turned towards the bar. She claimed she could handle them. Well, he couldn't.

He'd done everything he could short of pulling her off the case to stop her from coming here tonight. There was no telling what could happen, but he had a gut feeling it wouldn't be good.

She'd been right about the opportunities the situation presented, though. This was the best shot they'd ever had at getting to Santos. He was vulnerable without his bodyguards. Joe had had to rein in his feelings and think as an agent, not a man. If Shanna could stall Mañuel's henchmen, the search team might be able to make an arrest. He'd had to agree to the compromise, no matter how much he hated it.

'What can I get you?' the grey-haired barkeep asked.

'Whisky,' Joe said. Definitely whisky.

The old man poured him a shot and left him to his own devices. Joe twirled the liquid in the glass and tossed it back. He heard the tinkle of Shanna's laughter, and the glass came down to the bar with a slam.

He leaned his elbow on the spotless counter top and turned to watch her. Seeing her flirt with that crowd was giving his blood pressure fits. It was going to be one hell of a long night.

The bartender returned and filled his glass. The old man followed his line of sight and nodded. 'Now, that's a real looker.'

'Isn't she?' Joe agreed.

'And classy, at that. I don't know what she's thinking hanging around with that crowd.'

'Me neither,' Joe said. He fingered the shot glass and watched the liquid swirl around inside. Hell, he might as well set up his background story now. He had a feeling he was going to crack a few heads tonight. He might as well plant the story of the jealous husband early. 'She should be home with her husband.'

He showed the man his fist and the ring on his finger. Funny how he'd adjusted to the thing so quickly. He wasn't a jewellery sort of guy, but Shanna had put that ring there. It felt right.

'Bullshit.'

Joe was taken aback when the bartender started laughing at him.

'You're not her husband,' the old man cackled.

'The hell I'm not.'

'Shanna's not married.'

Joe's head whipped around. He'd been trying to keep an eye on her, but with that one little word, he knew he had bigger problems. 'Her name's Lily. Lily Mitchell.'

'I've known that girl more than half her life. Her name's Shanna McKay.'

Joe felt pressure building inside of him. If he didn't shut this guy up, Lily or Shanna or whatever her name was at the moment could get hurt. 'Shut up, old man. Her name is Lily.'

The bartender's jaw hardened and his eyes narrowed. 'What's your name?'

'Joe Mitchell.'

'You work with her?'

'I'm *married* to her.'

'What happened to the guy who was in here with her last night? Sonny got in a few good shots before they all left.'

Joe gnawed on the side of his cheek. He hated to break his cover but this guy knew just enough information to be dangerous. 'That was her friend. I heard he's in the hospital.'

'Yeah, I'd have to say I saw that one coming. You guys should have sent more back-up for them.'

Joe's jaw hardened, but before he could say anything, the lights dimmed and an announcer's voice came over the PA system. 'Ladies and gentleman, for your dancing pleasure, let's welcome Tatiana.'

There was a roar of applause before a bluesy number started pulsing through the air. Joe glanced over his shoulder and saw a sweet-looking young thing step out on to the stage. For a moment, he was caught. She looked innocent, but she could grind with the best of them. Hell, he wasn't a saint. His dick started to swell before she even got her top off.

'That's one of my best girls. Reminds me a lot of Shanna. Have you ever seen her moves? She was the best dancer I ever had.'

The trance was broken. Joe's head snapped back towards the man so hard he nearly gave himself whiplash. Fury built up inside his chest and he nearly went over the counter after the man. 'You sick bastard.'

'Ah, so now you admit her name is Shanna.'

'Shut up, you old freak. I should grab your ass and take you downtown right now. How old is that girl, anyway? Seventeen?'

'She's twenty-one, a junior in college, and a diver on the women's swim team. She's legal, Mr Fed.'

Fuck! Joe realised he'd walked right into that one. Hell, he'd never blown his cover before, but all it had taken was one or two cagey moves out of this guy, and his cover was lying in bits and pieces on the floor.

'Relax,' the bartender said. 'I won't tell anyone.'

Joe ran a hand through his hair and tried to think straight. What should he do? Could he pay the guy off? Would that keep him quiet?

'I'm not going to do anything to hurt your "Lily",' the old man said. He stuck out his hand. 'The name's Dooley.'

As much as it pained him, Joe accepted the handshake. He'd rather rip the man's arm out of his socket, but he couldn't very well do that at the moment.

'Get that sour look off your face, boy. I'm not going to blow your story. If you say you're her "husband", I'll play along. Just know that I know better.'

Joe nodded, still too furious to get a word past his tight throat.

'You really should do your homework before you go

into these things,' Dooley said as he picked up a shot glass and polished it.

'We didn't have time,' Joe said. 'Her partner was put out of commission yesterday, so I had to step in.'

'And how do you usually fit in?'

'I'm her boss.'

One of Dooley's eyebrows lifted. 'How long have you worked together?'

Joe glanced over at the table, but with the lights dimmed, it was hard to see. 'Five years,' he muttered.

The shot glass came down on the bar with a bang. 'You're the one!'

Joe looked at the old man sharply. 'What the hell are you talking about?'

A sly smile settled on to the old man's face. He took a step back and Joe had the distinct feeling he was getting a once-over. 'I'll be damned. You don't look stupid.'

'Listen, old man . . .'

'Dooley.'

'Listen, Dooley. I've had about all I can take off of you. I've got a job to do here, and you're not making it easy.'

'Hell, what's the matter with my girl? I taught her to pick up on the signs better than that.'

'She's not "your girl",' Joe growled. He was fighting the impulse, but he couldn't stop his hands from clenching into fists. It wouldn't be a fair fight, what with the guy being so much older and all, but he was begging for it.

'She used to be,' Dooley snapped. 'She was my girl before your guy came and took her away.'

Robert. He could only be talking about Robert. 'He saved her the day he took her out of this place.'

'Bullshit. I saved her when I pulled her off the streets. I gave her a place to stay, warm meals and protection. I gave her everything else she needed, too. She was mine.'

Joe knew he could drill this guy for more answers

about Shanna's past, but he didn't want to hear it, not out of this man's mouth. He wanted her to tell him. Voluntarily – because she trusted him.

'Well, she's mine now.'

'She's not, but she could be if you'd get off your lazy ass and do something about it,' the old man snapped. 'Hell, take off the blinders, boy. I thought federal agents were supposed to be smarter than that.'

The lights dropped, the music started pulsing, and Shanna was taken back to a different place and a different time. The announcer called the dancer's name, and she walked confidently on to the stage.

In those four steps, Shanna knew that this girl was special. She didn't prance out on stage trying to draw attention, nor did she slink as if she were demeaning herself by showing her body. Shanna understood the difference, and so did this Tatiana.

The girl strode down the stage like a catwalk model, swung twice around the pole, and tugged the rubber band out of her hair. Her ponytail collapsed into a beautiful flow of light-brown hair, and beside Shanna, Weasel sighed.

She couldn't help but agree. The girl was mesmerising. The entire table, including herself, watched in a trance as the girl worked her magic. Sonny's hand settled on to her thigh, and Shanna couldn't help the swaying of her hips. Her tempo matched the music and the girl on stage.

The dancer had on a schoolgirl outfit, including a top much like her own. It was the first piece of clothing to go. Her high, firm breasts were held in lacy white cups, and Shanna felt an almost unbearable need to see them swing free.

Shaking her head, she reached for the glass of water beside her beer. She took a long drink, but still she couldn't tear her eyes from the girl.

'Is she making you hot?' a raspy voice said into her ear.

Shanna turned, and her nose bumped against Weasel's. His narrow eyes were glazed with desire, and she shivered. Was that for the girl or for her? 'Yes,' she whispered, unable to stop her gaze from dropping to his thin lips.

'Maybe I can help you cool down,' he said.

His clammy lips brushed against her cheek as he looked back to the table. Reaching out, he put two long bony fingers into her glass of water. Drops of the liquid splashed on to the table and her thighs as his fingers came towards her. Shanna squirmed against the padded backrest of the booth but she had no escape. With wide eyes, she watched as those fingers headed for her chest and deliberately landed on her right nipple.

'There,' he said with his nose brushing against her ear. 'Is that better?'

Her traitorous body was responding to his foul touch. Looking down, she saw her red nipple tighten and lift towards the wet, pricking fingers. The wet spot on her shirt grew as he massaged the water into the material, and her body came into stark relief.

'Maybe some more will help,' he said, almost daring her to say no.

'Maybe,' she agreed.

God, she hated this man, but he could do things to her that made her pussy cry. Even the sight of his hands touching her skin was repellent, but she craved that dark pleasure that only he could bring.

'That's a good girl,' he said.

Again, two fingers dipped into her drink. When they headed back towards her, her breast practically bloomed like a flower begging for sustenance. The water was cold and the fabric was already sopping. It couldn't absorb any more liquid, and the cool sensation had her skin tightening.

'Oh, that's pretty,' Sonny said. His arm wrapped around her shoulders to hold her in place for Weasel's attentions. 'Hey, Tommy, I think that Lily brought a present for you.'

'Yeah? What's that?' the thug asked, unable to tear his eyes away from the dancer on the stage.

The girl's breasts were now free, and they were beautiful. Shanna stared at them as Weasel pinched and prodded at her own responsive flesh. Would that girl enjoy these men's attention as much as she did?

'Try looking under the table,' Sonny said with a chuckle.

His arm slipped away from her shoulder. It squeezed between her back and the seat cushion until his hand clamped on to her ass. He pushed her forward until her hips balanced at the very edge of the seat. Tommy had disappeared under the table, and soon, Shanna felt the stranger's hands land on her knees.

'Let's try this one,' Weasel whispered into her ear. His cold wet fingers landed on her other nipple, and she gasped when he gave it a hard pinch.

'Whatever you just did, she liked it,' came a muffled voice from beneath the table. 'I can smell her from here.'

Callused hands slipped up the outside of Shanna's thighs, pushing her leather skirt up. Her thighs were splayed wide as the man squeezed not only his head, but also his wide shoulders between her legs. 'Oh man, you guys should see this!' he said in eager delight.

Before she could prepare herself, rough hands slipped under her hips and a hard mouth came down on her. The man was trying to eat her, panties and all. Shanna let out a sharp cry as his face, lips and clumsy tongue pushed against her.

His forehead banged against her clit, and her hips came right off the bench at the intense pleasure/pain. God, the man needed lessons. He was trying to press his tongue into her, but her panties were in his way. Shanna started to struggle. Reaching down, she slid her fingers into the man's hair and pulled.

'Get him off of me!' she cried. 'He doesn't know what he's doing!'

'So give him the practise he needs,' Sonny said.

His concentration was on her wet breast. His head dipped down and his mouth clamped on tight. Shanna knew he would be of no help to her.

'Oh, Weasel, help me,' she begged.

She pushed hard on Tommy's head as she squirmed in discomfort. At that moment, she felt a tug on her panties. The waistband slipped over her buttocks, allowing more give in the crotch. It let the Neanderthal between her legs finally push his thick tongue into her cunt, silk panties and all. He used his teeth to nip at her, and her eyes closed in tortured delight.

'Ahhh.'

Her cry was cut off when Weasel's mouth clamped down over her own. He tasted of whisky and nicotine. He had a long tongue, and she nearly gagged when he pressed it towards her throat.

His hand tired of playing with her through the wet material of her top, and he jerked it to the side. He seized her naked breast and began kneading it for all it was worth. She squirmed, but was pinned between the three men.

Weasel began to squeeze her breast, strategically pinching her nipple between two fingers. His tongue was working in the same cadence, and soon she couldn't help but kiss him back.

Sonny had practically her whole breast in his mouth as he suckled her like a starving baby. The man between her legs was the clumsiest fool on earth, but her hand was no longer pulling at his hair. She cupped the back of his head, and her hips twisted under his special kind of treatment.

She felt her passion rising.

It was coming closer . . .

Closer . . .

So close . . .

The music came to an abrupt end, and silence permeated the air.

Shanna didn't care. She was intent on finding the pleasure that so fiendishly avoided her.

There was the sound of a table crashing, and footsteps rushing to get out of somebody's way.

Oh God, she couldn't believe she liked the way Weasel kissed.

The harsh sounds came closer, but she didn't pay attention until one of the goons at her own table was plucked up and tossed aside. Weasel's mouth tore away from hers as he looked to find the source of the interruption.

Glancing sideways, Shanna saw a big angry figure.

It was Joe.

'Get your fucking hands off my wife,' he hissed in a low but deadly voice.

10

Joe saw the whole scene through a haze of red. Two of Santos's men had their stinking paws all over his Shanna – and one of them ... One of them was that bastard Sonny Fuentes.

Rage pumped through his veins and he went straight for the big man. He didn't care that the count was four against one. His response was primitive.

'She's mine, you sonofabitch,' he growled.

He let loose a right cross that completely knocked the smirk off Fuentes's face. The man sagged back against the seat, but Joe didn't let up. He threw a left hook and the thug crumbled like a house of cards. For such a big, tough bastard, he had a chin of clay.

'Joe!'

Shanna's voice reached him through his violent haze and he turned to look at her. She was pushing a freaky little guy off of her. The man was reaching under his jacket, but he was too far away to respond. For the first time, he saw Shanna use her training. She jammed an elbow into the skinny guy's solar plexus. With a shuddering gasp, he doubled over.

Joe knew he couldn't give him time to recover. Reaching down, he grabbed the edge of the table and threw it to the side. It went tumbling across the room, forcing people to scramble to get out of its way.

A roar of rage erupted from the very centre of his chest when he found the guy between her legs.

Shanna pushed frantically at the man's shoulders, but

Joe wasn't about to be so polite. He grabbed the bastard by the roots of his hair and gave a solid yank.

'I should kill you,' he said as he dragged the man halfway across the room.

The fourth thug followed them, but that was a mistake. The fury within Joe wasn't about to be contained, and he used the two men as punching bags. It was only when they were on their backs that he remembered he'd left Shanna alone with the other two.

'Lily!' he yelled as he spun around.

He found her standing uncertainly behind him. Her blouse was wet, and her skirt had ridden high up her thighs.

'I'm sorry,' she said in a voice that was hardly louder than a whisper.

He didn't want to hear it. He grabbed her by the wrist and pulled her towards the door. A noise behind them caught his attention and he turned to find the little guy again. He was a persistent little pest. Before he could make any sort of a move, Joe grabbed him by the throat and slammed him against the wall.

'If I catch any of you touching her again, I won't be so nice,' he spat into the freak's face. The man clawed at his arm to try to get him to release the pressure on his windpipe. Joe didn't ease up. 'Stay away from her.'

Shanna finally pulled him off and guided him to the front door. One glare at the bouncer had the guy holding his hands up in defeat. Joe stomped by the man, and the cool night air hit him in the face.

He gulped down the oxygen. His breath wheezed in and out of his chest as he tried to get his temper under control. Beside him, Shanna's quick breaths sounded close to the point of panic. Gravel crunched under their shoes as he led her to his truck.

'My car,' she said timidly.

'We're leaving it.' Without any ceremony, he yanked

open the truck's door, caught her about the waist and lifted her into the seat. He slammed the door shut with a conclusive bang.

Shanna's pulse pounded in her ears. Her breaths were so close, she was on the point of hyperventilating. Oh God! Where had her brain been? She'd forgotten that he was even there!

'Joe,' she said on a weak note as he climbed into the driver's seat.

'Not now.'

Dear Lord, she'd never seen him so angry. His face was red and the pulse at his temple was pounding wildly. She couldn't bear to see him so upset with her. Turning away, she curled into a miserable ball.

The wet spots on her shirt rubbed against her nipples and she looked down. The evidence of Sonny and Weasel's work was apparent.

Oh God, she couldn't bear to know what Joe must be thinking right now.

The drive to the safe house was agonising. His anger and her misery filled the cab of the pick-up until she could hardly breathe. By the time they pulled into the driveway, she was ready to pull her hair out.

Why didn't he yell at her? Why didn't he pound his fist on the steering wheel? The way he was keeping everything inside made her nervous. He was like a volcano ready to blow.

'Joe,' she said, trying again.

'I'm too angry to talk to you right now,' he said in a tone that sent shivers down her spine. 'Get in the house.'

Shanna's knees felt weak as she walked up the steps to the door. It was only then that she looked down for her purse. Oh, thank God! She'd subconsciously remembered it. If she'd left it there, and they'd searched it ... Her cover would have been blown, and that would have made things worse than they already were. With shaky hands, she opened the clasp and reached for her keys.

'I've got it,' he said in a flat tone.

She moved sideways on the step, and her heel slipped off the edge. She grabbed for the railing but his arm whipped out and caught her around the waist. She looked at him, and for the first time, looked into his eyes.

She'd expected to see anger, but the hurt in his dark brown eyes caught her right in the middle of the chest. Her breath caught on a sudden hitch, and her lips trembled.

Why would he possibly feel hurt by what had just happened?

Before she could ask, he turned away and dealt with the door lock. As he turned the handle, he pulled her close. 'Remember your cover,' he said tonelessly.

Pain rippled through Shanna's chest where that slight glimmer of hope had just appeared. Of course. The cover. He was a jilted husband. That was why the sheen of pain was in his eyes.

She stumbled into the house on legs that were suddenly too weak to hold her. Joe walked by her with his hands planted solidly on his trim hips. He turned to look at her, and she hoped he wouldn't put on a show for the cameras right now. She wasn't up for a pretend fight. Anything he said right now would cut her to the bone.

Gritting her teeth, she waited for him to let loose. He didn't. Instead, he shook his head and turned away. He walked to the door that led to the back yard.

'Joe, please,' she called out to him. Watching him walk away was harder than bearing his disapproval.

He disappeared out the door, and she spun on her heel. She'd just lost the respect of the one man whose respect really mattered to her.

Suddenly, Shanna couldn't bear to be in her own skin. She ripped off her wet blouse and dropped it on the floor as she ran to the bathroom. A trail of clothes was left in her path. Turning the water nozzle on high, she stepped into the stream of freezing cold water. Her skin shrivelled under the cold spray but she didn't care. She needed to get clean.

She scoured her body with soap and shampoo until her skin was pink. Finally, she could scrub no more. She dropped the soap and stood under the spray of water. The temperature had warmed, and the room was beginning to fog. The hot muggy air joined with her sorrow and threatened to suffocate her.

'Why?' she asked herself quietly. Why did Santos have to show up again? Why were her sexual urges resurfacing so strongly? Why had Joe had to catch her like that?

Suddenly, the door to the bathroom sprang open and the shower curtain was ripped away. Shanna gasped and instinctively reached to cover herself. Spinning around, she found Joe staring at her.

He was still angry, but there was now a sense of purpose in his eyes.

Oh, God, he was going to fire her.

His gaze raked down her body, and her eyes went wide when he reached for his belt buckle.

'I might as well get some of what you're so willing to offer to everybody else,' he said.

His belt snapped as he whipped it out of the loops and it went sailing. Shanna swallowed hard and took a step back. The shower wall stopped her.

This was a side to Joe she'd never seen before. She knew his patient side. God knows, she'd tested it enough times. With one look into his eyes, she could see that his patience was gone. It unnerved her, even as a tinge of excitement swirled low in her belly.

She'd always wondered what Joe Mitchell would be like if he lost control.

He whipped his T-shirt over his head, and her mouth

went bone dry. Lord help her, he was gorgeous. Muscles rippled across his chest and down his belly. Each and every one was honed by hours of physical exertion, and she now understood how he'd so easily tossed Tommy by the wayside.

Her fingers itched, and she ran a tongue across her dry lips. She wanted to test the strength in those hard muscles. She wanted to kiss her way across that smooth tanned skin. Her tongue practically begged to have a go at his tiny brown nipples.

She wanted him. She'd wanted him for years.

'Why did you let that trash crawl all over you? Is this the tactic you use in all your cases? Have you and Shawn been going at it all this time?'

He tugged off the rest of his clothes and stepped into the shower with her. Shanna gave a frantic sideways glance, wondering if the bugs were picking up their conversation.

He caught her chin and made her look at him. 'I smashed the microphone,' he said, 'but the camera is still on.'

'Should we take this somewhere else?'

'No. We're taking it right here. Right now. I want an answer.'

Water was sluicing down both their bodies, but he didn't blink as he stared at her. Shanna watched as water ran like a river off his chin, and she could hardly stop herself from leaning forward to take a drink.

This was nearly unbearable. He was naked. She was naked. How could he expect her to have a rational discussion with him? She was having to fight her own body to stay off of him.

'No,' she said through her tight throat. 'I don't usually use sex to break a case.'

'Why this time?' he pressed.

'I didn't see any other way.'

'Damn it, we could have found another way, Shanna.'

Her knees nearly buckled at the sound of her name on his lips.

'You know, I thought it was my fault,' he said. 'With the low lights and the music, I thought I'd missed your signal. I thought it was my fault those slimeballs had their hands on you. I cut off that old bartender mid-speech just to get to you.'

Dooley? He'd met Dooley?

'When I got to your table, though, you weren't fighting them off. You were just letting them do whatever the hell they wanted to you. Why?'

Shanna swallowed hard. 'I was trying to keep my cover.'

'And Lily Mitchell is a slut? Hell, you could have fought them. What woman wouldn't fight three guys who tried to do that to her in public?'

Shanna wished she could slip right down the drain. She'd enjoyed it. She couldn't deny that she'd enjoyed being at the mercy of three men intent on taking their pleasure from her. Still, a white knight like Joe Mitchell would never understand that.

She'd never want him to.

'I'm trying to find a way to Santos. Isn't that what's most important?'

For a moment, Joe said nothing. When she dared look into his eyes again, she saw shock. He looked like he'd been taken aback, but then his eyebrows lowered and he leaned close.

'No, that's not what's most important. *You're* what's most important. If anything ever happened to you, I don't know what I'd do. What would I tell Robert and Annie?'

Shanna's hopes crashed hard back into reality. Of course, that was the source of his concern. He was Robert's old partner. He was just watching out for his old friend. Water from the shower splattered her face, and she closed her eyes.

'Why would you lower yourself to that level, Shanna?' Joe whispered. He dipped his head and brushed his lips against her ear. 'You're so much better than that.'

'No, I'm not,' she said hoarsely. He didn't even know the half of it.

He caught her chin. 'Look at me.'

She didn't want to, but he made her.

His serious gaze captured her miserable one. He shook his head as if he couldn't believe what he saw in her eyes. 'You're everything,' he said.

His head dipped low, and she gasped when his lips covered hers. Before she could react, he'd caught her wrists. He pulled her hands away from her body and lifted them high over her head. When he pressed them tight against the slick shower wall, something inside her melted. She felt like the ultimate sacrifice.

His gaze travelled leisurely across her naked curves, and her body shook with repressed desire. She didn't know what to think. Was this all a part of the act? Were the cameras supposed to be seeing a reconciliation scene?

He leaned down to kiss her again, and his touch captured every ounce of her attention. His lips were hard against her own, but his tongue was gentle as it invaded her mouth.

'You're smart,' he said as he pulled back to change angles.

'You're brave.'

He kissed his way under her chin, and she craned her neck to give him better access.

'You're loyal.'

Her fingers curled into fists when he licked his tongue across the pulse at the base of her neck.

'And you're drop-dead gorgeous.'

Her breath hitched when he crowded her against the wall. His hard chest pressed against her breasts, and her nipples tightened at the contact with his hot body. They itched for friction, and she struggled not to squirm against him.

She still wasn't sure what was happening. Was this for real or was it for show?

His erection was caught tight between their bodies, and her eyes widened when she felt it twitch. Its message wasn't hard to miss. He wanted to fuck her. But why? She was more than willing to do whatever he wanted, but what was the reason behind it?

With Joe, it mattered.

His voice went gravelly as he looked down at her. 'If it's the sex you need, Shanna, you can come to me.'

A muscle in his jaw twitched, and his lips came down hard on hers. 'I'll give you all you can handle.'

Shanna welcomed his kiss, but a part of her cringed at his words. He thought she needed sex, like some starved nymphomaniac. The only sex she absolutely needed was from him. What she'd done with Sonny and the rest of Santos's men had been for a purpose. There was a method to her madness, but he couldn't see that. He could only see that one of his agents was out of control.

She hated the thought of him coming on to her just to save the case. Still, this was probably the only opportunity she'd ever get with him. Once this case was over, she'd never get this close to him again.

'Fuck me, Joe,' she whispered.

His green eyes flared and his face became hard with intent. The hand at her wrist flexed, and suddenly Shanna found him tugging her arm down. With his eyes dead centre on hers, he guided her hand between their bodies. He pulled back slightly to give her better access, and she wrapped her trembling fingers around his hard cock.

'Christ,' he hissed. His hips bucked softly at her touch.

Timidly, she pumped him. He was hard as steel and hot as a poker. Her breath shuddered from her lips, and she gave in to temptation. Ever so gently, she brushed her thumb across his tip. His groan echoed off the walls of the small room and her control shattered. She launched herself at him and his lips came crashing down on hers.

'Joe,' she said on a high note.

She squirmed to get closer to him, and he let loose of the wrist he still had pinioned over her head. She wrapped it around his neck and rubbed her breasts against his rock-hard chest. Her breasts nearly went up in flames at the hot contact.

'Baby,' he groaned. 'Do that again.'

Shanna shimmied against him like an animal in heat. The tight beads of her nipples dragged against his upper abdomen. The sensation made her head spin. She'd denied herself for so long. She'd dreamed of what it would be like with him, but she'd never thought it would be like this.

So intense. So wild.

'Let me at 'em,' he said. He caught her by the hips and lifted her until her breasts were at face level. Leveraging her against the wall, he went in for the prize.

His lips latched on to one pouting tip, and Shanna fought for air. Her peak swelled under his tongue and he gave it a soft nip with his teeth. She nearly came unglued. He held her tight, and her fingers went white against his shoulders.

Opening his mouth wider, he took more of her softly bobbing breast into his mouth. He closed his eyes and began suckling her with an intensity that had her shrieking and writhing in his arms. It was as if he wanted her milk.

'Oh, God . . . Please,' she begged.

She still hadn't let go of his prick, and she tried to get his attention by pulling harder on it. His cock swelled.

'Hurry,' she said. Her legs wrapped around his waist like a boa constrictor as she tried to guide him to her. 'Put it in. Please!'

'Not yet,' he said.

He swirled his tongue around her nipple and lifted her an inch higher. Her hips swivelled in their limited range of motion as she searched for him. Her hand led him to her wet opening, and she literally tried to push him inside of her.

'Fuck me. Please fuck me,' she begged.

'Easy, baby,' he said.

He let his tongue rasp across her already overworked nipple before going back in for more suckling. Her breast was hardening under his mouth. She could feel it.

Twisting his hips, he found better purchase. She guided him to her, giving him words of encouragement. With a deliberate slow movement, he finally pushed into her.

Shanna nearly came right then and there.

Her hands ran desperately down his back. The strong muscles were pulled taut. Her fingers settled against his hot skin and she tried to pull him even closer. God, she wanted all of him.

He stopped to catch his breath but her need was overwhelming. Her body was writhing with anticipation. She pushed her hips towards him but he pulled back. 'I can't,' he said in a rough tone. 'I'm too close to the edge.'

She didn't care. He could come without her. She just needed him deep inside her. 'Now!' she demanded.

Her fingernails bit into the base of his spine and his body jerked. The move broke his steel-hard control, and he thrust recklessly up into her.

'Yes!' she screamed. Her heart pounded as he pulled back and thrust again.

Oh, God, she'd never imagined it would be so good.

Her shoulder blades pressed hard against the shower

wall as she lifted her hips towards him. His hands bit into her ass, but she was too out of control for him to guide her. She met his every thrust as he pounded into her again and again.

Shanna felt the heat rising in her veins.

This was Joe Mitchell. He was making love to her like a wild man, and she was clawing at him for more. Her breasts were on fire, and her pussy was red hot. Every time their bodies slapped together, she let out a moan. Soon, it was one continuous sound.

With desperate hands, she reached for him. She threaded her fingers through his hair, and her other hand went to his pumping buttocks. Water splashed against them, and too soon the orgasm was upon her.

'Joe!' she cried. Her back arched against the fibreglass wall and a soundless scream left her lips. Her entire body went tight as pure energy streaked through her veins.

Shanna didn't know how long she was caught in the grips of ecstasy, but when the world righted itself, she found herself still in Joe's arms. His thrusts had slowed, but he hadn't joined her. His lips had left her breast, and he was looking at her with an intensity that was unnerving.

He'd watched her come.

The thought was incredibly intimate – especially with this man. Shanna's breath caught when he ground into her. He stilled at the deepest point, and a muscle worked in his jaw.

'Again,' he said harshly.

Her eyes fluttered closed, and her fingers caught his shoulders in a death grip. Dear God, he'd held back! He'd held back, and she'd literally come apart in his arms.

'I don't know if I can,' she said. He'd wrung every response out of her body the first time.

'You can, and you will.'

He worked his arms under her legs and grabbed her

ass with both hands. Shanna was disconcerted until she felt the pressure against the back of her thighs. Using his arms, he spread her legs wider and pressed her knees back towards her chest. She let her muscles go lax, and he spread her legs into a wide 'V'. With her legs draped over his arms, she was at his complete mercy.

'You're mine,' he said, looking her straight in the eye.

He plunged into her and the move took her breath from her lungs. The position he'd manoeuvred her into left her no defences. She was totally vulnerable to him, and his thrusts penetrated her to the core.

Shanna felt herself quickly rising to her peak again. She tried to pull back but she couldn't move. It was too fast – too intense. 'It's too much,' she cried.

'It's not enough,' he said in a raspy voice. Water poured across his tight features, but he paid it no mind as he focused on her.

His thick cock began working hard and deep within her. His thrusts were rough, and her body shuddered as she accepted each and every one. This was the true Tiger, the true animalistic appetite of the man.

'You're mine,' he said again.

Her muscles tightened at the possessive statement. She was his.

The heat inside her began to burn out of control. Shanna felt her climax coming but she didn't want to leave him behind. This time, he was coming with her.

He thrust deep, and her toes curled. Her fingernails clawed down his back, but some tiny part of her brain knew he wasn't ready yet.

No. Not this time.

'Come with me,' she begged.

His concentration was centred on fucking her brains out, and she couldn't tell if he'd heard her or not. Her inner muscles began fluttering, and her eyes closed tightly as she felt the waves of exhilaration sweep over her.

'No.' She whimpered as she fought the orgasm.

Frantically, she reached out for the showerhead. She ripped the nozzle off its holder and reached down. Deliberately, she aimed the pulsing water right at the point where their bodies connected. The spray caught Joe between the legs, and he went up on to his toes.

'Christ almighty. Shanna!'

He jerked hard and went a fraction of an inch deeper into her. That was all it took for her to go off. With a shriek, her body clamped down hard. Her reaction pulled a corresponding eruption out of him. His teeth ground together, and the veins in his neck bulged as he came into her.

The shower nozzle clattered to the floor.

'Good God, sweetheart,' Joe said against her temple.

Shanna couldn't talk. She was too overwhelmed by what had just happened. In her dreams, she never imagined it would be like that.

She didn't know how long they stayed frozen in the erotic position. The sounds of splashing water and harsh breaths filled the foggy room. Joe leaned his head against the shower wall, and she could feel his breaths hitting her bare shoulder. Her own air was still coming hard into her lungs.

Her body felt heavy, but he held her high in his arms. An aftershock of her orgasm caught her body, and he raised his head when the pulses squeezed his softened cock.

'Well, that took the edge off,' he said. His gaze dropped to her lips. 'Now let's get down to business.'

He gently disconnected their bodies and turned off the shower. With an ease that was almost frightening, he lifted her firmly into his arms. He carried her to the bedroom and they tumbled on to the bed. The sheets clung to their wet bodies.

Joe rolled himself firmly on top of her and Shanna looked up at him. His body pressed hers deeply into the mattress, and she felt a familiar twinge between her legs. They regarded each other carefully, but neither said a word. She wished she could read what was going on behind those fascinating green eyes.

His gaze swept over her face, and she knew she must look wanton with her hair spreading wildly across the bed sheets and her breasts pointing up at him. He slowly wrapped a long strand of her hair tight around his fist. He watched her closely, and with one smooth thrust, penetrated her.

'Oh!' she gasped. She hadn't realised he was hard again already. With Sonny, it took hours. She quickly tossed the thought from her mind. She was with Joe. *Her* Joe.

'Too soon?' he asked.

'No,' she sighed. She spread her legs wider to accommodate him. His hips settled against the cradle of hers, and she shivered with pleasure. Giving in to the feeling, she ran her toe gently up the back of his calf.

A muscle in his jaw flexed. 'I'm going to fuck you until you realise it's true. You're mine. Only mine.'

His hand came up to cup her breast, and Shanna's breath caught sharply. 'And you're mine,' she said back, daring him.

He accepted the challenge with a long hard kiss. His tongue danced with hers, and she groaned when his hips thrust gently against hers.

It was almost as if his hot cock had been made for her. Their fit was too perfect. She flexed her inner muscles to hold him deep within her. She wanted to savour the feeling of their connection.

'If I ever catch one of those goons pawing you again, I'll kill him.'

The words had an edge to them, and Shanna realised he wasn't talking to her. He was talking to the ears on the other end of the microphones in the room. She shrank back, remembering that there were people watching them, listening to them.

'No more Tassels,' he said.

'But Joe...' The case hinged on her relationship with Santos's men.

'I said "no".' He emphasised his words with a firm squeeze to her breast. 'I won't be responsible if I catch them on you again.'

His green eyes went cold, and she realised he was serious. Case or no case, he didn't like Santos's men touching her. A tiny thrill ran through her, and she reached up to brush his hair off his forehead. 'All right,' she said. 'I won't go there again.'

Something close to relief crossed his face, and the touch on her breast gentled. His fingers began toying with her stiff peak, and he flicked it with his fingernail. 'I went a little crazy when I saw what was happening,' he admitted.

'Yes, you did.'

'But I held back.'

Her breath caught, and she was sure that whoever was listening to them sat up and paid attention. Four of Santos's men hadn't been able to lay a hand on him – and he'd been holding back.

'You're my wife,' he said firmly. 'I'm the only one who gets to touch you.'

He bent down and nipped at her earlobe. 'I'm the only one who gets to screw you.'

His leisurely thrusts became more intense, and Shanna wrapped her long legs around his waist. 'Yes,' she sighed. 'Fuck me, Joe.'

He took her request seriously. He fucked her from the front, then flipped her on to her stomach and took her from behind. Seeing that she liked that, he dragged her over to the dresser at the side of the room. He bent her over it, spread her legs wide, and pumped into her as she watched their reflections in the mirror.

The night went on and on as he screwed her endlessly in every position imaginable. Pillows and sheets slipped off the bed and cluttered the floor. They used them for padding there.

Eventually, the room became too trashed and the sheets were too wet against their drying skin. The sky was turning pink with the morning sun when Joe picked her up and carried her to the guest room. He pulled back the covers on the bed and carefully laid her on the crisp sheets. He slid in beside her and pulled her into his arms.

'You belong with me, Lily,' he whispered against her hair.

Shanna ran her fingers down his arm and entwined her fingers with his. In this fake world, it was easy to pretend.

'Always,' she said as she finally let sleep overcome her.

11

The sun was high when Shanna awoke. For a moment, she was disconcerted, but her memory slowly pieced together the events of the previous night.

She and Joe had made love all night long. Her body quickened, and she hurriedly glanced over her shoulder. She was alone in the bed. Disappointment caught her, but then the scent of fresh coffee infiltrated her senses.

'Mm,' she sighed. Reaching her arms overhead, she stretched luxuriously. She'd never felt so thoroughly sated. Her body felt absolutely alive. Her nerve endings were sensitive to the slightest touch. Even the sheet rubbing against her breasts made her wet between the legs.

Reaching under the sheet, she touched herself there. It was amazing. She thought he'd ridden her until she was dry, but here her body was, oiling itself up for more. Experimentally, she slid a finger inside herself. Her inner muscles greedily latched on. It felt almost wrong to be empty. He'd spent more time inside her last night than not, and her body had accustomed itself to his presence.

It wanted him still.

The scent of coffee and the promise of seeing him finally lured her away from the crisp sheets. Why play with herself when she could play with him?

A silly smile settled on Shanna's lips as she got up. Her nakedness should have embarrassed her, but the cameras had been on them all night long. It was almost impossible to have any modesty left after some of the things she'd done last night.

'Joe?' she called as she wandered into the kitchen. He was still nowhere to be found.

Taking a deep breath, she headed to the coffee maker. She poured herself a cup and looked out the kitchen window. That was when she spotted him. He was standing in the back yard, dressed only in his jeans. Her eyes focused on his tight ass, but gradually she realised he was talking on his cell phone.

The case! How could she have forgotten? A search team had been sent to look for Mañuel while they had been at Tassels last night.

Shanna set down her cup of coffee and hurried back to the bedroom. The disaster area surprised her, but she tiptoed through the rumpled bedding on the floor and opened the closet. She found a short silk robe and pulled it on to her shoulders. She was still tying the sash when she darted out the back door.

Joe heard the screen door slam and glanced her way. His gaze quickly ran down her figure and then back to the door. He jerked his head towards it, and she realised she'd left it open.

'Betty, patch me through to Devo,' he said.

The tone in his voice made Shanna pause. The voice was distinctly that of her boss, Special Agent Mitchell. Uncertainty gripped her, and she hurried back to close the door so the microphones wouldn't pick up his discussion.

Once the door was closed, she didn't know what to do. She stood cautiously on the step. Even from this distance, she could see the change in him. He stood a little straighter, as if the weight of the world was carried on his broad shoulders.

Sudden doubts assaulted her. Would he change again when he set foot back inside the house? Was he that good at playing his role?

He waved for her to come closer. Shanna swallowed

hard. She wanted nothing more than to hear that Santos had been arrested, but suddenly she didn't know how to act around Joe. Was he her tireless lover from last night or was he her boss?

'Did you do a cross-pattern search?' she heard him ask.

She searched his face for a sign. Had they arrested Santos? Was this nightmare about to be over?

'Nothing?' He looked at her and shook his head.

The disappointment she felt was too familiar. Every damn time they got close to Mañuel, he managed to slip through their fingers. This time, it was even worse, because of what had happened at Tassels. She'd hoped that if Mañuel had been caught, Joe might have been able to overlook her indiscretions.

She couldn't be so lucky. She ran a hand through her hair and turned away.

'Do the lab techs know where they might have gone wrong?'

Shanna heard the question as she walked back to the house, and she cringed. The last thing she wanted was for Melanie to get in trouble.

'That's OK,' Joe said into the phone. 'We're zeroing in on the bastard. One of these days, we'll catch a break.'

His voice sounded close behind her, but she was surprised when he caught her by the arm. He pulled her to a stop and looked into her eyes. Her disappointment must have been apparent, because he hooked a finger under her chin and lifted her face up to him.

In the bright morning sunlight, Shanna felt amazingly shy. It was surprising, considering all they'd done last night. But then it had been dark. She could pretend. It wasn't as easy in the harsh light of day. Here, she found herself facing Joe Mitchell, FBI golden boy.

'Devo, we'll have to go over the details later,' he said. 'I've got something else that needs my attention right now.'

He signed off on the call and tucked the phone in his back pocket. 'Hey,' he said softly.

Shanna bit her lower lip. 'They didn't find Mañuel, did they?'

'No, but we're making progress.'

She wrapped her arms around her waist. 'I'm sorry about another failed mission. I know how you hate those.'

A small smile lifted the corners of his mouth. 'I wouldn't call last night a failure.'

He dipped his head to kiss her. Shanna was so surprised, she literally jumped.

'What's wrong?' he asked, pulling back.

She looked up at him blankly. 'You don't have to do that.'

'What?'

'There aren't any . . .' Embarrassment made her tongue feel thick. 'We're not under surveillance out here.'

She pointed back to the house, but he caught her hand. Stark red blotches appeared on his cheeks and the fierceness in his gaze shocked her.

'I just thought . . .' she said weakly.

'That we were play-acting for Santos's goons? Jesus, Shanna,' he barked. 'Is that why you spread your legs for me?'

'No!' she said quickly. Confusion and uncertainty almost paralysed her. 'I just thought that you'd forgotten where you were.'

'Where I am? You think my dick cares? Sorry, sweetheart, but I haven't got that much control over it.'

Shanna's heart gave one solid thump and then threatened to stop. 'Then last night was real?' she asked. The question was out before she could stop it.

He looked at her as if he couldn't believe she was serious. 'What the hell kind of a question is that?'

Colour heated her cheeks and she quickly stepped back.

She was absolutely horrified that she'd asked. 'Never mind.'

She moved quickly, but he was even faster. She hadn't taken two steps before he'd caught her. His arm wrapped around her waist and jerked her back against him. The silk robe pulled tight, making her sensitive nipples come to life.

The bulge of his erection rubbed against her buttocks and his free hand settled low on her belly. He pulled her snug against him and rolled his hips. 'Feel that? It seems pretty real to me.'

He caught one of her breasts in a tight grip. 'What was it for you, Shanna?' he asked, his lips moving against her ear. 'Were you banging me for the cameras or because you liked having me between your legs?'

Shanna squirmed against him, trying to get away from his probing questions. She wished she'd never even brought up the subject.

'Damn it, answer me,' he growled. The hand on her belly parted the slick material of her robe. It slid between her legs and cupped her intimately. One of his big fingers penetrated her, and her hips rolled forward to give him better access.

'I wanted you,' she said.

Some of the tenseness left his body, and his touch gentled. The finger inside her began searching for sensitive spots. He found one, and her body arched. He zeroed in on the delicate region and set up a persistent caress. 'That's what I thought,' he murmured. He nipped her ear. 'You were too responsive last night. I didn't think you were faking it.'

He ran kisses down the side of her neck, but eventually came back to whisper in her ear. 'Why did you think I was?'

'I didn't know,' she whispered. He pushed another

finger into her, and her head dropped back against his shoulder.

'Damn, I thought I was pretty obvious.'

'You're famous for your undercover work,' she said softly. His cock was rubbing hard against her backside and his hands were driving her to distraction.

'So you thought I was working? Literally?' he said. 'Are you insane?'

Shanna's breath was coming in pants, and she rolled her head back and forth against his shoulder. Her body was humming, and she could feel the uneven breaths coming in and out of his chest behind her.

'Honey,' he said softly. 'I've been hard for you for years.'

The admission cut through the erotic haze in her head, and her knees went weak. She leaned against him for support. Warmth filled her chest and her heart pounded a little faster. 'Why haven't you ever done or said anything?' she asked.

He dipped his head and kissed her shoulder where the robe had slipped and bared her soft skin. 'First there was Robert to consider,' he said in a low tone. 'I didn't think he'd appreciate what I wanted to do to his daughter.'

At the mention of Robert, Shanna stiffened. She didn't want to bring him into this. She didn't want to hear that she'd been a charity case.

Joe wouldn't let her go. The hand between her legs anchored her in place. 'Then there was you.'

'Me?' she said with surprise. His fingers were circling around her delicate opening, and she had to concentrate to ignore the electricity that shot straight to her core.

'You ran out of my office every chance you got. I couldn't even talk to you without you skittering away. You made it clear that you didn't want anything to do with me.'

Nothing to do with him? Shanna almost groaned with

frustration. 'You're my boss. My fantasies about you weren't appropriate.'

He went still. 'Fantasies?'

Her breath worked hard in her lungs. She couldn't believe she'd just told him that. She writhed with need under his still hands, but he wouldn't give her what she needed until she confessed her deepest darkest secret. 'I wanted to crawl over your desk and ride you until that squeaky chair fell apart.'

His groan originated from somewhere deep within his chest. 'Show me,' he said in a voice that sounded like sandpaper.

'What?'

'Show me,' he said with more determination.

The world suddenly tilted. Shanna shrieked, but caught his shoulders as he picked her up high in his arms. He moved quickly to a lounger on the patio. He sat down, leaned back, and hauled her right up on top of him.

'Joe,' she gasped. She levered herself up from him, but his hands were already loosening the sash of her robe. He parted the material and his big hands cupped her naked breasts. She could feel them getting heavier at his touch.

'Ride me,' he said, daring her.

Quickly, she looked around at the neighbours' houses. His hands began working her breasts more adeptly, and she bit her lip with longing. When he lifted his hips and ground the bulge of his erection against her wet pussy, she felt her control slip a notch. 'What if somebody sees us?'

'We've had an audience all night,' he growled. 'Fuck me, damn it.'

The order gelled both sides of his personality together for her, and Shanna shivered. She reached for his zipper. The denim around it was pulled taut. Slowly, she pulled the tab down. The moment the confining material loosened, his big cock sprang upward.

'I can't believe you thought I could fake that,' he said.

Shanna looked down at his raring cock, and urgency gripped her. God, she needed him inside her now. She spread her legs to straddle his hips and found his thick prick aiming straight up at her. The tip brushed against her clit and her body liquefied.

She quickly lowered herself on her haunches. His big cock burned a passage into her, stretching her wide, and she had to stop halfway. It was too hot, too intense. They'd fucked long into the night, and her soreness was new and sharp.

'What's wrong?' he asked, immediately stopping.

'It hurts,' she panted.

His hands came back to her breasts, and he began pinching her nipples. Each little jolt of pain shot straight down to that secret place between her legs. Heat seared her, and she forced herself to accept more of him.

'Better?' he asked.

'Oh, God,' she groaned.

Slowly, inch by inch, her burning pussy ate him. When her pubic hair tangled with his, the eroticism of the picture hit her. She was impaled on Joe Mitchell's cock. Moisture gathered between her legs, slathering him. The burning pain went away, but the heat of her passion only increased.

'Let me see you,' he said.

At his urgent request, she shrugged out of the robe. She let the silk slide down her back and pool across his thighs. The look in his eyes made her feel like the sexiest woman on the face of the planet.

'God, you are gorgeous,' he whispered in awe. 'How could you think that I wouldn't want you?'

His hands swept across her body and Shanna luxuriated under his touch. His fingers bit into her thighs and she sighed. She pulled her hair off her neck and piled it on to the top of her head. His thumbs settled into the crease where her legs met her torso, and her breath shuddered in her lungs. 'I'm not in your league, Tiger.'

'Bullshit.'

She settled her palms on to his shoulders. Ever so slowly, she ran her hands down his body. His muscles were rock hard under her touch, but they quivered wherever she touched him. The power excited her.

'I'm a bad girl,' she said. 'You're a good boy.'

'And together we're fucking incredible,' he said stubbornly. The determined light in his eyes warned her not to argue with him.

She didn't want to fight.

She wanted to explore him. Her fingers wandered across his chest to his dark nipples. She flicked them and was delighted when they stiffened. Gently, she traced his ribs and found a small scar.

It distressed her more than she wanted to admit.

Deliberately, she lifted her hips high and disconnected them. Joe called out, but she shimmied down his body. She gently paid homage to his scar, and his hand tangled in her hair. 'I hate that you were hurt,' she whispered.

'Baby, I am feeling no pain.'

His erection stood straight up next to her, nearly begging for attention. Shanna gave his scar one last kiss before laying her head on his hip. His cock was beautiful. Reaching out, she gently cupped his balls. They were drawn up tight, and the slightest touch from her drew an almost exaggerated groan from him. She petted the soft hair and massaged him lightly.

His hips arched right up off the lounger. 'Are you trying to kill me?' he choked out.

His hand fisted tightly in her hair when she moved closer to his throbbing erection. The dark strands brushed against his hips and cocooned them in intimacy.

'God, baby, I don't know if I can,' he said on a note of panic.

She didn't give him time to finish. His cock was twitching in front of her face. Her mouth begged to taste him. Leaning down, she licked her tongue slowly across the bulbous tip.

'Fuck!'

He wasn't able to stop himself from thrusting up at her, and Shanna eagerly took a mouthful of his cock. A litany of curses and prayers hit her ears as she suckled him. He was hot and salty under her tongue.

He tasted of them.

The thought made her pussy tremble. She lifted her ass higher into the air and felt the warm breeze brush against her.

Joe's hand pulled tighter on her hair, and the pinpricks hurt her scalp, but the pain was a good pain. She moved back down to the base of his cock and swirled her tongue against him.

'That's it!' he said. He moved as quickly as his namesake and caught her under the arms. He pulled her up his body and, as soon as her pussy was in range, he hammered up into her. Shanna inhaled sharply at the sudden penetration.

'Joe,' she said.

He felt so wonderful inside her and she began pumping against him. She could fuck like this for ever. She kept her movements slow and relaxed, drawing out the pleasure of having him fill her. His hips lifted every time she dropped down, and they fell into a seductive rhythm.

'Oh, baby,' he groaned.

His teeth clenched tight. He wanted to go faster, she could tell, but she was experienced enough to know the benefits of going slow. She rewarded him by sinking down hard and grinding herself in a leisurely circle.

'Christ!' he muttered on an expulsion of air. His neck arched against the mattress as she did it again.

He was close.

She rode him, still slowly, but with more power. Sweat broke out on his brow, and his hands bit into her hips. 'Shanna!'

He hadn't called her that all night while the cameras were on them. Shanna's body shuddered with pleasure, and she began to thrust in earnest.

They were coming together hard when Joe gave a sudden curse. His body began to go tight, and he thrust a hand between her legs. His finger found her clit and he pressed it hard as he began spurting into her. Shanna cried out and threw her head back as rapture overtook her. Hard shudders shook them both until they collapsed together.

They lay there for a long time with their skin clinging to each other. When Joe moved, it was to kiss the top of her head. 'This is real, sweetheart. Don't convince yourself otherwise.'

She nodded against his chest because she didn't trust her voice. She'd dreamed about this for so long, it was hard to believe it had finally happened.

His fingers combed through her hair, fanning it out across her back. 'You should go back to bed,' he said gently. 'I didn't let you get much rest last night.'

'I have to work,' she said.

'It's Saturday,' he said. 'I have to go in, but you should take the day off.'

'Saturday?' she said, her head snapping up. 'What time is it?'

Quickly, she twisted his arm so she could read his watch. Her eyes widened when she saw what time it was. 'I'm going to be late!'

'Late for what?' he said. His arms tightened around her and his eyebrows lowered.

The proprietary tone in his voice rekindled the flame of happiness in Shanna's chest. He was jealous. 'I'm going shopping with Melanie,' she said.

'Melanie? From the lab?'

For once, she'd surprised him. 'Yes. I'm giving her a make-over.'

Bemusement settled on his handsome features. 'I didn't realise you were friends.'

'She's got a crush on Shawn.' Shanna blushed when she realised how childish it all sounded. 'I thought I'd try to help them.'

'You're playing matchmaker.'

She felt her cheeks heat.

'Have fun, baby,' Joe said. He reached down and patted her bottom. 'Spread the wealth.'

Shanna did have fun. In fact, she hadn't had this much fun since ... Well, since her sister had been around. After Joe had dropped her off at Tassels to pick up her car, she and Melanie had gone to the mall. They'd hit each and every store in the place, and they'd had a ball.

With the life she'd led, Shanna hadn't had the chance to partake in the normal habits of teenage girls. She'd been dancing on stage or helping Dooley count the take from the cash registers. She'd never played dress-up, unless she counted the outfits she'd worn under the hot lights of the strip club.

The outfits she helped Melanie pick out weren't of such an erotic nature, but it was interesting for her to see how much their tastes varied. The little technician seemed afraid to show any skin whatsoever, whereas she was used to baring a lot of it. They finally settled on a casual pink dress with skinny spaghetti straps.

'Stop tugging,' Shanna said.

'I've never worn a strapless bra before!' Melanie said in a stage whisper. She glanced quickly around the store to see if anybody had heard her scandalous words.

'It will be fine if you stop trying to pull it up to your chin.'

'I'm afraid I'm going to fall out of it.'

The pretty blonde had a nice shape. In fact, she was perfectly proportioned. Shanna had been somewhat surprised at that. The white lab coat hid her figure well. 'Your boobs aren't that big,' she said.

Melanie's eyes widened, and she looked around in horror. 'Shhh!'

'Well, they're not. You're not going to pop out, if that's what you're afraid of. Let's go find some make-up.'

With a bright smile on her face, Shanna looped her arm through her new friend's. They hit the make-up stand, the shoe store, and the beauty salon. When the stylist finished the trim, Melanie sat staring at her reflection in shock.

'You're beautiful,' Shanna said.

It was true. Getting Melanie's hair out of that horrible bun allowed more of the rich blonde colour to show. The stylist hadn't had to do much. Just a trim of the split ends and some shaping around the face were all it took to make a dramatic change.

Best of all, those terrible, terrible glasses were nowhere to be found. When Melanie had confessed she just needed them for working in the lab, Shanna had confiscated them.

'I can't do it,' Melanie said in a tight voice.

Shanna didn't have to ask what 'it' was. Their next stop was the hospital to see Shawn. 'Yes, you can. We didn't go through all this just so you could go home and hide.'

Melanie swallowed hard. 'I don't know what to say to him. What if he laughs?'

Shanna took one glance at the mirror. 'If there's one thing he's not going to do, it's laugh. Believe me. He'll be lucky if he doesn't crack another rib when he pulls you on to that hospital bed with him.'

The timid blonde went bright red and didn't answer.

'Come on, let's go.'

Shanna had to pull Melanie out of the stylist's chair. She footed the bill herself and nearly had to drag her new pal out to the parking lot. Melanie's hand gripped hers tightly.

'Stop,' she said weakly.

'No.'

'No, really. Stop. I need to talk to you about the tape. That was my half of the deal.'

Shanna's steps slowed, and she turned to look at the lab tech. 'I heard that Devo's team wasn't able to find Santos's house.'

'That's because I'm not done!' Melanie said in a huff. It was obvious that she was taking the failed mission personally. 'I'm only three-quarters of the way through my analysis. I gave them the information that I know is correct, but it wasn't enough.'

'That's all right. I understand,' Shanna said. Melanie didn't look convinced. 'Is there anything I can do to help you interpret what you're hearing?'

Melanie bit her lower lip and looked away. 'I've managed to suppress the male voices so I can concentrate on your verbal clues. I know you crossed a set of railroad tracks and a bridge. I'm trying to ascertain which bridge it was. I'm not quite there yet, but I'm making progress.'

'That's good.'

'I just . . .'

Melanie stopped, and Shanna looked down at the shorter woman.

'Did they hurt you?' Melanie whispered.

Shanna's breath caught in her chest, and embarrassment hit her hard. 'No,' she said slowly.

'Because . . . Well . . . I'm sorry. It just sounded as if they were rather rough with you. I was worried.'

Shanna could feel her own cheeks flushing. She wished

nobody at the Bureau had had to know about that tape, but it was a vital clue as to the whereabouts of Mañuel's hideout. The embarrassment was hard to avoid, but she was glad that Melanie was the one analysing the tape. 'I was a consenting adult,' she said.

'It sounded as if you ... *liked* it.'

Shanna couldn't look her new friend in the eye. She ran a hand through her hair and took a deep breath. 'I did.'

'But I don't understand. Those men are dangerous. You're investigating them. You know what they've done. You know what they can do!'

'Danger can be exciting,' Shanna tried to explain. 'It's a powerful aphrodisiac for some people. I happen to be one of them.'

'Oh.' The scientist obviously didn't understand.

'Some people can separate the physical act from the emotional.' Even as she said the words, Shanna wondered if she was capable of that any more. 'I don't think you're one of those people, so you probably can't appreciate that.'

'I'm not judging you, Shanna. You probably think I'm a prude.'

'No, I think you're very sweet.'

The blonde didn't seem to take the comment for the compliment it was. 'I don't think I'd fit in with your world. Or Shawn's.'

'Is that what this is about?' Shanna turned and opened the car door. With a grand gesture, she hurried the blonde inside. 'Why don't you let him decide?'

By the time they got to the hospital, Shanna didn't know who was more excited, her or Melanie. Still, the blonde's excitement was nearly drowned out by her nervousness. Shanna nearly had to drag her into her partner's room.

'Hey, partner,' she said as she pushed open the door. 'Your doctor vetoed the six-pack, but I found you a blonde.'

'Thank God, *company*,' Shawn said. He lifted his hand to turn off the TV. 'I'm going out my mind with bore –'

Shanna had never seen such a transformation come over her partner. The moment he saw the woman behind her, the television remote dropped out of his hand. It clattered to the floor. Smiling, she crouched to pick it up for him.

'Hi, Melanie,' he said softly.

'Hi,' the blonde said in a whisper.

'Melanie and I were out shopping, and we decided to drop by and see you,' Shanna said.

'That's great.'

Shanna had a feeling she could do jumping jacks and her partner wouldn't notice her. All his attention was focused on the shy woman standing beside her.

'Oh, Shawn, your poor face.' Melanie started to reach for him, but pulled back before she could touch him.

Something flickered in Shawn's eyes, and Shanna was fascinated.

'Ah hell, they couldn't do much damage to this ugly mug.'

Melanie's lips tightened into a flat line. This time when she reached out, she let one finger lightly trace the bruise on his cheekbone. 'You're not ugly,' she said firmly.

Shawn swallowed hard. When he looked at Melanie, Shanna realised that she was no longer in the room for the couple.

Wow. If she'd only known, she would have done something about this sooner.

Shawn reached up, and Melanie went absolutely still when he caught a tendril of her hair. 'You look different today.'

Melanie didn't respond, and Shanna thought she might have to step in.

'Shanna helped me make myself over.'

'You look great, but you didn't need to do that.'

A lump formed in Shanna's throat. Good Lord, she thought this only happened in fairy tales. 'I think I'm going to leave,' she said.

'Yeah, get out of here,' her partner said.

'Oh, if you want your rest . . .' Melanie said uncertainly.

'You stay,' Shawn said as he caught her wrist.

Shanna's heart was twittering as she slipped out of the room. Oh God, that was so sweet. She felt almost ashamed at having witnessed such intimacy. She fanned herself as she walked down the hallway to the elevator. They were so cute together.

That was one thing she'd never been – cute.

No, she'd been a wild child. So had her sister. They'd grabbed life by the balls and refused to let go. Looking back, she supposed they weren't the types of girls a guy could take home to his mother. To bed, yes. To Mom, hell no.

Shanna opened the door to her car, sat down, and slammed it shut. She'd managed to pull her life out of the gutter, but she'd never be as pure and innocent as her new friend. She didn't begrudge Melanie her life, but it made her open her eyes.

She'd fallen into the dream Joe had created for her last night, and she'd blissfully spent the day shopping and playing dress-up. It was time to get back to reality, and with the events of the past day, her resolve was only stronger. Mañuel Santos had taken away any chance her sister had had for a normal life.

It was time he paid.

Reaching into her purse, Shanna pulled out her cell phone. Determinedly, she flipped through her caller ID list and found Sonny's number. She'd already tried to trace it, but cell phones were a bitch. His was secure, and she'd never be able to get to him through it. She could do it the old-fashioned way, though. She dialled and waited as the phone rang.

'Hi, big boy,' she said breathlessly when he answered. 'Wanna play?'

12

Shanna considered her actions as she drove across town to a seedy motel on the West Side. Technically, she wasn't breaking her promise. She wasn't going to Tassels. Still, that was splitting hairs.

She was meeting Sonny.

And they were going to screw like rabbits.

If Joe ever found out . . . Her blood froze in her veins at the very thought.

She couldn't let that stop her, though.

She had a lot of making up to do. Last night things with Joe had definitely taken a turn for the better, but her relationship with Mañuel's men had been severely damaged. She hoped she could salvage the situation. It was the only shot she had of getting close to the drug lord.

And she'd been dreaming about that even longer than she'd been dreaming about Joe.

Determination settled in Shanna's gut like a rock. She wasn't going to back off now.

She turned into the parking lot of the motel. Almost immediately, she spotted the familiar SUV. Sonny hopped out of the driver's seat, but Weasel wasn't with him. Instead, her eyes landed on the man named Tommy.

'What's he doing here?' she asked, as she got out of her car and slammed the door.

'He wanted to come, and he paid the price last night when your husband kicked his ass across the floor,' Sonny said. His dark gaze ran down her body. 'I figure you owe him a bit of pussy.'

A shiver ran down Shanna's spine. She didn't like the look in Sonny's eyes. He'd been embarrassed last night. From the looks of it, he didn't take embarrassment well.

'Where's Weasel?' she asked.

'He's got a meeting with the boss. Why? Ya gonna miss him?'

'Not one bit,' she snapped. Myers made her skin crawl, but something about his absence made her uneasy. Why was *he* meeting with Manny? Why not Sonny? Had she been targeting the wrong man this whole time? Come to think of it, Weasel did seem to be the brains of the motley bunch.

Sonny placed one hand at the base of her spine and directed her to the room he'd rented. Tommy opened the door, and the smell of the place hit her. It reeked of sex. She just hoped the sheets were clean. 'Nice place, guys. Is this the best you can do?'

Sonny had the decency to look discomfited. 'Yeah, well, it's close.'

'Close to what?'

'We're on call.' As if he'd reminded himself, he looked down at his watch.

'On call? Are you doctors?' Shanna had to bite her cheek to keep from laughing.

'We've got a job going down tonight,' Tommy said, piping in.

'Shut up, Tommy!' Sonny snapped. 'We're not supposed to talk about that. She doesn't need to know what we do.'

'I don't really care,' Shanna said in a bored tone, even though every muscle in her body was tensed. 'I just wondered where Weasel was. He always seems to be lurking somewhere. The guy makes me nervous.'

'We don't need him,' Sonny growled. 'I brought Tommy instead. Now shut up and take off those damn clothes.'

Well, that was direct and to the point. So Sonny had a

kink. She wondered if he couldn't get it up without an audience. That would be a pity. With that nice big cock, it shouldn't take more than two people. 'How romantic,' she snapped, suddenly irritated with her role of a slut.

Joe was right. A real woman wouldn't let these creeps treat her this way.

Joe.

Shanna swallowed hard. Suddenly, she felt dirty.

'Strip, Lily. We've got to make this fast.'

Even as her mind rebelled, that naughty little part deep inside of her responded to the crisp order. She liked it dirty. She liked it rough, nasty and on the edge. No matter how erotic her night with Joe had been, he couldn't do that for her. 'What if I don't want to?' she asked, heightening her arousal.

'Then I'll have Tommy do it for you.'

Tommy. She looked at the eagerness on his face. He was a low-level thug, but after last night's encounter she had a long way to go to secure her position with this group of men. If she had to start at the bottom, so be it. 'I think I'd like that,' she said.

'Yeah, yeah. Me, too,' Tommy panted.

'Maybe I can teach him to do it right.' Shanna set her purse on the nearby table. With an unseen flick of her fingers, she turned on the tape recorder. She wasn't through asking questions about Weasel or the job that was going down tonight.

Actually, with Myers not here, she might be able to squeeze more information out of these two brain trusts.

'Have at her, Tom,' Sonny said, rubbing his chin consideringly. 'She wants you bad.'

A broad smile split Tommy's face, and he hurried towards her. Shanna stopped him with a hand to his chest. His eagerness was somewhat alarming. 'Slow down,' she said. 'It's better that way.'

The man wasn't as big as Sonny, but he was twice Weasel's size. He stood so close, Shanna had to crane her neck to look at his face.

'I want to rip those fucking clothes off of you,' he snarled.

'Such enthusiasm,' she cooed, even as a part of her signalled a warning. This was a foot-to-the-floor kind of guy. It was going to be hard to keep him under control, and she had two of them in the room. Suddenly, a small part of her yearned for Weasel's presence.

'Let me at her, Sonny,' Tommy practically begged. He thrust his hips at her aggressively.

'These are the only clothes I brought. I'd like to have something to wear when I go home to my husband.' Shanna flipped her hair over her shoulder as if she didn't have a care in the world. 'You remember him, don't you?'

'Take it easy,' Sonny grumbled. 'With a deal going down, the last thing we need is problems from some jealous prick.'

'That's right,' Shanna said. 'Take it nice and easy.'

'I'll take it any way I want it,' growled Tommy.

She'd dressed casually for her outing with Melanie, and the man went straight for her tight T-shirt. He yanked it out of the waistband of her shorts and jerked it up. Obligingly, she lifted her arms over her head. The T-shirt went sailing, and Tommy ogled her breasts in her black bra. She began to let her arms drop, but he stopped her. 'Leave them up there. I like the way it makes your tits look.'

With a leering smile, he reached for the clasp on the waistband of her shorts. It popped open easily, and he slowly slid the zipper downward.

He's learning, Shanna thought just before he thrust his hand down her shorts and between her legs. Her air left her lungs on a gasp as he squeezed her pussy tightly in his clumsy paw.

'Careful!' she shrieked.

'Oh, come on. You know you like it.'

She hated to admit it, but she could feel the wetness gathering between her legs.

'Here, sweet tits. Sonny will make it better.'

Shanna's nervousness increased as Sonny moved to stand behind her. She felt petite and vulnerable as she stood sandwiched between the two big men. Sonny's arms came around her, and she was trapped. His fingers dealt with the front closure of her bra, and her breasts fell into his marauding hands.

'Ah,' she sighed. His touch was rough, but it was exactly what she needed. It aroused her sexual excitement, and her uneasiness lessened. Leaving one arm draped across her head, she reached back and wrapped her hand around the back of Sonny's neck.

'Better?' he asked.

'Mm,' she sighed.

God, he knew how to work her body. Her breasts were in heaven but her pussy was in distress. Tommy was trying to jam all his fingers up her cunt. He'd managed to work two into her, but she began to struggle when he tried to force two more in at the same time.

'Shit,' he muttered.

Her clothing was in his way. He finally pulled his hand away from her and reached for her shorts. With a harsh yank, he sent them and her panties to the floor. Shanna shot him an apprehensive look when he dropped to his knees in front of her.

'You'll regret it if you're as clumsy as you were last night,' she warned when his fingers wrapped around her ankle.

'Be quiet,' Sonny snapped. 'The man just got out of the joint. He's not used to fucking a woman.'

With a tug, Tommy lifted her foot and settled her calf over his shoulder. The position left Shanna unbalanced with her sex gaping wide open. She swallowed hard. From his vantage point, nothing was hidden. He smiled at her and deliberately licked his lips.

Her eyes widened when he placed an open-mouthed kiss on the inside of her thigh. His tongue rasped across her skin, and a tingling sensation shot up her leg. It settled at her core and she squirmed with arousal and trepidation.

Tommy's mouth worked its way up her leg until only a centimetre separated him from her throbbing pussy. She flinched when the man leaned forward and buried his nose in her thatch.

'Mm,' he said, taking a big inhale of her scent. 'That's one of the things I missed most in the joint – the smell of a wet pussy.'

Shanna's heart began pounding like a big bass drum.

'Mind if I take a bite?'

He opened his mouth wide, turned his head and set his teeth into one of her swollen pussy lips. Shanna let out a shriek. The pleasure/pain was excruciating.

'No!' she yelled. 'Get off of me.'

Her words seemed to incite him. Rooting deeper between her legs, he nipped her tender flesh up one side and down the other.

Shanna was nearly delirious. The bites were merely nips, but the stinging pain had her pussy going into convulsions. When his mouth began nearing her sensitive clitoris, sweat broke out on her skin.

She couldn't take that. It would be too much.

'Aieee!' she screeched when his teeth closed around the soft nub.

Instincts overcame her, and she lashed out at him. She never even considered the consequences as she pulled her leg from his shoulder. She just had to get him off of her. Her knee connected with his chest and, in a flash, he was sent tumbling backward.

Sonny let out a roar of laughter as Tommy came up red-faced and furious.

'Hold on, Tom. Let me show you how it's done,' Sonny said as he picked her up and tossed her on the bed.

Shanna bounced once and tried to scramble away. Her loss of control over the situation made her anxious. Sonny caught her legs and settled his heavy body on to her. She was pinned.

'Come on, sweet tits. Open those long legs and show me your pussy.'

Shanna took a deep breath. Her purse and her gun were on the table behind Tommy. She glanced towards the door but knew she'd never make it. She centred a hard look on Sonny. 'Keep that asshole away from me.'

Sonny's dark eyes glittered, and she suddenly remembered what this man did for a living.

'Spread your legs,' he growled.

Shanna's heart pounded, but she'd gotten herself into this situation. She'd get herself out of it, too. Looking deep into his eyes, she slowly followed his directions. Bending her legs, she dug her heels into the mattress.

'Wider,' he snapped.

She let her knees drop open, and his hands slid under her hips. He tilted them towards him. She could only imagine the lewd picture she painted.

'Oh, that's nice. Look at that, Tommy. See that pretty pussy.'

'I see it,' Tommy grumbled. 'I was eating it a second ago.'

'You need to learn how to pet the pussy to make it purr,' Sonny said. 'Watch.'

His fingers threaded through the dark tangles between her legs, and Shanna took a deep breath. When he ground the ball of his hand against her pubic bone, she couldn't help but groan.

'See?'

Leaning closer, Sonny began to lick his way up her leg. Shanna had to admit that some of what Tommy had done had made her wet. She glanced up. The subordinate was watching his boss closely. Sonny's tongue swept along the crease at the top of her leg, and she shuddered. Just a centimetre or two to his right, and he would be at her core.

He ignored it, and she thought she might hyperventilate. Her hips swivelled towards his hot mouth but he just laughed and reversed directions. By the time he leaned back and slipped off her shoes, she was shaking with need.

'See?' Sonny said as he sat back on his heels. 'Treat the pussy right, and it will come to you.'

He was petting her again, but Shanna heard the words. He wouldn't give her what she needed until she came to him. Digging her heels into the mattress, she lifted her hips towards his mouth.

Seeing her vulnerability, Sonny swooped down and latched on to her clit. Her hips bucked. He'd zeroed in with such accuracy, she was stunned. Colour flashed behind her closed eyelids as his mouth urgently sucked the very life out of her.

'Oh, my God!' she gasped.

He had her sensitive bud captured between his lips and he'd set up such a frantic suckling, her legs gave out. His hands caught her buttocks in a tight grip and he held her up where his mouth could get at her best. It was only seconds until she was screaming in completion.

The orgasm drained the last drop of energy out of her body and Shanna sagged against the bed heavily. She saw Sonny lift his head and wipe his mouth with the back of his hand. She was too exhausted to move when he reached for his zipper.

The ringing of a cell phone stopped him just as he pulled out his enormous cock.

In horror, Shanna looked at her purse.

'Fuck, this better be good.' Sonny whipped his phone out of his jacket pocket, and Shanna settled back against the pillow. 'Yeah?' he barked.

Her ears went on the alert.

'Damn. Right now? Sonofabitch. Yeah, yeah. We'll be there.'

Tossing the phone aside, he reached for his prick. 'We've got to hurry. The deal's going down. The boss wants us to meet him there.'

The boss. He was going to meet Santos.

Shanna's eyes popped open when Sonny levered her legs wider and shoved himself into her. He was so big. Fire inflamed her pussy. She felt like he was rending her in two. 'Ah! Sonny!' she gasped.

'Sorry, sweet tits,' he said as he grabbed one. 'I'm in sort of a rush.'

'We have to get down to the docks now?' Tommy whined. He grabbed his crotch as if he were in pain. 'Sonny, you gotta let me have a go at her.'

Docks. Shanna squirmed as Sonny's cock burrowed into her, but she heard the words. Mañuel was going to be at the docks.

'Do what you want, but make it quick,' Sonny growled. His hips were pumping at a frantic pace. 'Christ, sweet tits, I think you've gotten even tighter.'

He'd lifted her hips right off the bed so he could ram into her, and Shanna's fists curled into the sheet beneath her. It felt so bad and so good at the same time, she could hardly stand it.

'I want those tits,' Tommy growled as he pushed down his pants.

He crawled on top of her, and she was disconcerted. Sonny was still pumping his thick meat into her, but she couldn't see him. Without seeing him, she couldn't prepare for his thrusts. She closed her eyes and felt him rutting deep inside of her. His hands controlled her hips, and the weight on her chest kept her pinned down.

Tommy pushed his hard cock between her breasts. With greedy hands, he plumped the heavy globes up tight against his hot shaft and began to move. The hot friction burned her sensitive skin, and she cried out. 'Find some lotion,' she begged as he plucked at her nipples.

'No time,' the thug growled.

Reaching up, she caught him with a tight grip around his throat. His windpipe wheezed as she pushed him away from her. 'Make time.'

Sonny laughed as the younger man rolled off her and bounded towards the bathroom. 'He's got a lot to learn, sweet tits.'

'You don't,' Shanna groaned when his thrusts became deeper and even harder. He was being savage with her, but she wasn't fighting him. Her clenching fingers tore a hole in the sheet. She heard the ripping sound as the tear grew across the bed. 'Oh, God, that feels so gooooood.'

Sweat was dripping off Sonny's brow as he wrapped her legs around his waist. The move changed the angle of his thrusts, and he began plunging right to the heart of her.

Tommy bounced back on to the bed, and Shanna felt thick liquid splatter across her chest. The smell of lavender hit her nostrils and they flared in appreciation. The tension in her body was mounting when he climbed back on top of her and grabbed a handful of breast with each hand.

His cock slid smoothly in her cleavage and, with each thrust, bumped against her chin. His thumbs worked the lotion into her nipples, and her hands finally left the bed. She grabbed his wrists to hold his hands right where they were.

Two men, two eager cocks, and Shanna was spiralling

out of control. Each man was working towards his own completion, and neither seemed to want to work in unison with the other. The pumping and grinding had the well-worn mattress springs screeching.

'I can't take much more,' she panted.

Tommy pinched her nipples hard, and Sonny ground into her. A thick prick bumped hard against her chin and a salty spray hit her in the face. Shanna's neck arched as her orgasm slammed into her. Her scream of completion was muffled as Tommy fell forward on to her.

Sonny's fingers were biting hard into her hips, and soon a hoarse cry erupted from somewhere deep in his chest. He reared backward as the eruption tore through him. Body shaking, he collapsed on to the bed.

Shanna pushed Tommy off of her, and the three of them lay on their backs, staring at the ceiling and gasping for air.

'Hell, how are we supposed to leave this?' Tommy moaned. 'She's hot as a firecracker.'

'Christ, tell me about it. I'm always happy to get my dick back after I've had a go at her. She grips it so hard, I'm afraid one of these times she'll pull it right off.'

'Shit,' Tommy griped. 'We've got to go.'

He rolled off the bed and reached for his jeans. Sonny struggled to sit upright, and Shanna had to smile. The one-shot wonder. He wasn't going to be of any use down at the docks.

The docks.

Adrenaline zapped through her veins. She had a time and a location. Headquarters needed this information as soon as possible.

Finally, Sonny rolled off the bed. He restored the order of his clothing before reaching for her. He gave her reddened breast a tight squeeze as he looked down at her. 'Sleep up, sweet tits. We'll be back for more later.'

Shanna ran her hand along his muscled forearm. 'I've got to get home before Joe misses me.'

Sonny's face hardened, and he looked like the dangerous criminal he was. 'That prick. He's messing things up.'

'Yeah, well, he's my husband,' Shanna said, feeling every iota of the irony. 'I suppose he has that right.'

Sonny muttered under his breath. 'As long as I get to dip my rod into your honey pot every now and then, I'll let him be.'

Shanna ran a hand through her tangled hair. She wasn't afraid of the muted threat. Between the two men, she had no doubt as to who would come out on top. 'Call me.'

His hand left her breast and slipped between her legs. 'Thanks for the fuck, sweet tits.'

'Mm,' she said, arching like a cat. She watched the two men leave. As soon as she heard their SUV leave the parking lot, she was on her feet. She dove for her purse and pawed through the contents until she found her phone.

Her hands shook as she dialled the secure number for the FBI. 'This is Agent Shanna McKay,' she said hurriedly when the dispatcher answered. 'I've got important information. Mañuel Santos and his men have a drug deal going down right now on the docks. We need to get a team in place.'

Glancing towards the bathroom, she calculated how long it would take for her to shower and get across town. She'd had plans to take Manny out on her own, but this could be just as good. If they could catch him and his team in the middle of a deal, they might be able to break the whole ring.

The key was to catch Santos himself. At this point, she didn't really care who caught the bastard, just as long as someone did.

'I should be able to be on the scene in twenty minutes,'

she said quickly. She could be there in ten, but she had to wash the come out of her hair first.

'Copy that,' the dispatcher said dispassionately. 'Hold on, Lily. I've got a message here that you're to report to headquarters.'

'Report? Now?' Her fingers clenched into fists. 'I can't come down there. Didn't you hear me? We've got solid information that Mañuel Santos is going to be at the docks!'

'I've passed the information on, and we have a team assembling. The order still stands, though. Lily, I repeat, you are to report to headquarters.'

'By order of whom?' Shanna yelled.

'Special Agent Mitchell.'

13

'Come in, Agent McKay.'

Shanna's heart sank as she stood outside Joe's office door. Correction – Special Agent Mitchell's door. There wasn't one sign of Joe, the man who'd made red-hot love to her all night long. This man ordering her into his office was cold, determined and more than a little pissed off. She could see it in the rigid line of his jaw.

With a deep breath, she stepped inside. The walls immediately started to press in on her.

'Shut the door behind you.'

Oh, God. The door closed with a click, and she stood uncertainly. She crossed her arms over her chest and instantly regretted the move. Her breasts were chafed from bumbling Tommy's sexual gymnastics. As inconspicuously as she could, she dropped her arms and clenched her hands together like an anxious schoolgirl waiting for the principal's reprimands.

Joe reached down and clicked the intercom. 'Betty, hold all calls and block the door to my office. I don't want any interruptions. I don't care if the building's on fire.'

Shanna swallowed hard. She'd never seen him like this – and she'd done a lot over the years to test his patience.

'Sit, Lily.'

It sounded like a good idea. She dropped into the chair in front of his desk and took the weight off her shaking knees. Looking up, she saw him bearing down on her from across the desk. No, sitting wasn't such a good idea. She made a move to stand, but froze when he barked, 'Stay!'

Nerves rattled, she crossed her legs. The move made her well-used pussy ache, but this time she let herself suffer.

'Where have you been?' he asked in a quiet voice that cut across the room like a sabre.

'I told you. Melanie and I –'

'Don't lie to me!' he said. 'You weren't with Melanie.'

'I was, too. We went shopping and then we visited Shawn at the hospital.'

'I called the hospital to find you. Melanie was there, but you weren't. You'd left. Where did you go?'

Shanna shifted in her seat, and the ache in her sex increased. Her mind raced for an excuse. 'I wanted to give them some time alone together, so I made myself scarce.'

'That's not what I asked.'

He'd stopped his pacing and now stood leaning over his desk with his hands planted on the tabletop. Shanna looked at those long, well-formed fingers. Now that she knew how they felt gliding over her skin, she couldn't focus.

'Where ... did ... you ... go?' he bit out.

'I had to repair the damage that was done to my relationship with Santos's men,' she said quietly.

'Damn it, I knew it!' One of those broad hands slapped the table with enough force to make the pencil lying next to it bounce. 'I ordered you to stay away from them. You weren't supposed to be working today anyway.'

The sound of the slap echoed around the room and, with it, Shanna's spine stiffened. 'I believe your order was to stay away from Tassels.'

'You know what I meant.'

'No, I guess I didn't,' she said. 'I thought I was supposed to keep my cover as a frustrated housewife looking for some attention.'

'Honey, if you're frustrated after last night, there's something seriously wrong with you.'

Shanna's face flushed, and she hurriedly glanced out the window to the main office bay. Not one iota of work was being accomplished out there. Every eye in the place was centred on the action going down in Special Agent Mitchell's office. She knew the room was soundproofed and they couldn't hear, but she wanted to die of embarrassment anyway.

'Do we have to talk about this now?' she hissed.

'Yes. We're going to talk about it now, and nobody is leaving this room until we've got a few things straightened out.' He followed her glance and walked over to close the shades. 'I screwed you last night until neither of us could walk, Shanna. Santos's men saw and heard every little sigh, groan and scream you made. What they saw last night was a husband and a wife getting back together. Don't give me some lame excuse about you trying to save your cover. It doesn't fit with what they know about you.'

Sitting in the uncomfortable wooden chair with her pussy on fire was not helping. Shanna sprang to her feet and walked over to look out the window down to the street. Pedestrians were making their way around the city like ants. Discomfited, she twisted the ring on her right hand. 'Maybe I'm a nymphomaniac.'

'In my dreams,' he said. 'I know you better than that.'

Her muscles stiffened as he walked up close behind her. She could feel the heat of his body seeping into hers.

'Last night was real,' he said quietly. 'You and I … Well, let's just say that things have been building up between us for years. Last night, the levy broke. We went at each other like a couple of horny minks, but you're no nymphomaniac. You told me yourself that you hadn't had sex in six months until this case.'

'Maybe I lied,' Shanna said in a hoarse voice. She refused to turn around and look at him. He was hitting way too close to the truth.

'I don't think so,' he said, his breath whispering close to her ear. He trailed one finger down her spine and she shivered. 'Why did you meet with Santos's men today?'

'I needed to push the pace. We needed to get things moving on this case. It's been dragging on way too long.'

'So you put yourself out on a limb.'

'Yes.'

'Why?'

'I told you. I don't like Mañuel Santos. I don't like drug dealers.'

'Why?'

'Why?' she snapped. She twirled around and bumped into him, he was standing so close. She didn't let it deter her. 'How can you ask me that? "Why?" What kind of a question is that? The man has killed people.'

'You've worked on other cases involving drug dealers. Why is this one so important?' he pressed.

He'd caught her by the waist as she knocked into him, and now he was refusing to let her go. Shanna felt the ceiling begin to push down on her. The walls had already shrunk to the point where she couldn't step sideways for fear of bumping into them. He had her effectively trapped. 'It just is,' she said, batting at his hands.

'Does it have something to do with Tassels? Did you know him when you danced there?'

The blood drained out of Shanna's body. She went absolutely numb as she stared at the golden boy. Mr Perfect. He wasn't supposed to find out about that. Her mind shot in a million different directions as she tried to think of a way out of this mess – out of this ever-shrinking room.

'I know you used to strip at that club,' he said.

Her heart thudded painfully in her chest and she tried hard to swallow past the lump in her throat. 'I don't know what you're talking about.'

His green eyes had lost their steely look but not their determination. 'Don't deny it. The bartender told me.'

Dooley. She was going to kill that big-mouthed old fool.

'That is none of your business,' she said.

'It's got an impact on this case, so it is my business,' he said. He caught her chin and made her look up at him. 'Besides, after last night, anything that has an impact on you has an impact on me.'

She tore her chin out of his grip. 'You have no claim over me.'

His eyes narrowed. 'Wanna bet?'

'I don't have to tell you about my private life.'

'Fine. I'll go back and ask the bartender.'

'Yes, I stripped at the club! Is that what you wanted me to say?' Shanna's blood pumped through her veins. By God, if he wanted the truth, he was going to get it. 'I was the best dancer that place has ever seen. When I was on stage, all eyes were on me. There wasn't a limp dick in the joint.'

A muscle moved in his jaw. 'I don't doubt that.'

'You wanted the truth,' she said, 'so there it is.'

His hands slid down to her buttocks and he pulled her into tight contact with his body. 'What's the connection with Mañuel Santos?' he asked.

The sudden change in the direction of the conversation threw her, and she tried to get her body under control. Her nipples throbbed for his ravenous mouth, and her ass tingled under the strong grip of his hands. He'd done that on purpose, she knew. He was an effective interrogator, and he knew just what buttons to push with her now that they'd been intimate.

'He hung out at the joint. I've never liked him,' she said. It wasn't a lie by any means.

'Did he do something to you? Catch you backstage one night?'

'No, he never touched me.'

'So what did he do?'

Shanna took a deep breath. 'Can we move past this, please? Have you heard what's going down at the docks? I'd like to be there.'

'No,' Joe said. He backed her up against the wall and planted a hand at each side of her head. 'I told you that we're not leaving until we straighten out a few things, one of which is why you went back to Santos's men after I expressly told you to stay away from them.'

Her eyes narrowed. 'Maybe I was just being "impulsive".'

He leaned closer until his nose brushed against hers. 'I don't think so. I think you knew exactly what you were doing. How did you get the information about the deal going down at the docks, Shanna?'

'I have ears. I listened.'

'Where were you? Where did you meet them?'

'Not at Santos's house, if that's what you're asking. We still haven't traced my way back to that yet.'

'Damn it, Shanna. Did you have sex with them? Is that how you got the inside track?'

A cold ball of fear unfurled in Shanna's stomach, but she couldn't lie. Not after he'd seen her last night with three men on her. 'Yes,' she said.

The pain in his eyes was unavoidable. 'Why?' he bit out. 'Didn't last night mean anything to you?'

'Yes! Last night was...' She swallowed as emotion overcame her. 'Last night was *everything*. Today had nothing to do with that. Nothing.'

'I can't make that distinction,' he said in a low tone. 'The thought of any of those fucking beasts touching you makes me sick. Who were you with?'

'Don't do this.'

'Who? Tell me.'

'It's not going to help.'

'Tell me,' he roared.

Shanna's heart sank. She looked for an escape route but there wasn't one. Her fingernails curled into the wall, looking for purchase. 'Sonny Fuentes and a guy named Tommy.'

'A guy named Tommy,' Joe said as he turned his head to the side.

She knew he was disgusted that she didn't even know the man's name, but she couldn't explain that it didn't really matter. What mattered was if they had caught Mañuel at the drug bust. Had there even been a drug bust? What had gone down at the docks? She was dying to know if the bastard had been caught!

'Devo just reported that they picked up a man named Tommy Larson at the site you gave us. He had five thousand dollars' worth of heroin on him. We also got the guy who was trying to buy it.'

'Santos? Did you get Santos?' she asked. She hadn't even realised she'd reached out for him, but suddenly her fingers were clenched into the material of his shirt.

Joe looked down at her hands against his chest. 'No.'

A nearly physical pain rocked through Shanna. Damn, damn, damn. She'd thought that this time they had him for sure. Tears pricked at her eyes, and her knees gave way. She sank down the wall to her haunches and covered her face with her hands. 'Sonofabitch,' she cursed at the world in general. 'Why can't we catch this bastard?'

Joe looked down at Shanna and shock rolled through him. She'd literally crumbled into a heap at the news, and it scared the living shit out of him. He'd never seen her show any weakness.

His anger evaporated. Carefully, he lowered himself until he was crouching in front of her. Her hands hid her face, but she wasn't crying. Instinct told him that she was holding on to her control by her fingertips. Gently, he laid a hand on her knee. 'I'm taking you off the case.'

He could feel the shock ripple through her body. The muscles of her thigh clenched and the tenseness ran up her arms to her fingers. Slowly, she dropped her hands from her face. Her dark eyes glistened with stunned surprise. 'You can't.'

'I can, and I am. I'm worried about you, sweetheart. You're playing fast and loose, and you're going to get hurt. I don't want that to happen.'

'You can't take me off this case. I'm the most qualified person you have. I know more about Mañuel Santos than anybody out there.'

Her hand whipped out towards the closed shades, but he ignored the gesture and keyed into her words. 'How do you know about him?'

'Damn it, we already covered that,' she shrieked. She pushed herself quickly to her feet, and he followed her. He wasn't fast enough to catch her as she slipped away from him and began frantically pacing around the room. Her arms whipped along her sides, her fingers clenched into tight fists. She took two laps before turning on him. 'Keep me on the case.'

'No.'

'Yes!' she screamed.

'No,' he said calmly. 'You're a danger to yourself and everyone else on this case.'

She spun on her heel, and her hands gestured wildly. 'I'm a danger to Santos, that's what I am,' she said.

'I need an agent who's got things under control.'

She whirled around, and he knew he'd said the wrong thing. An icy calm overcame her in that split second. 'Oh, I'm under control. I know exactly what I need to do.'

'What is that?' he said, not backing down.

'Kill the fucking sonofabitch.'

Her shocking words died away, leaving complete silence.

'Why?' he asked.

'Because he killed my sister!'

Whatever Joe had been expecting, it hadn't been that. He hadn't even known that she had a sister. The realisation rocked him back on his heels, and he didn't know what to say. She tried to storm past him but he was alert enough to reach out and catch her about the waist. She nearly ripped his arm off with her momentum, but he pulled her back hard against his chest.

For a long time, he simply held her. What in God's name could he say?

He hadn't known. Nobody had known.

Ducking his head into the crook of her neck, he concentrated on breathing and trying to figure out what to do next. 'I'm sorry,' he said.

Air shuddered into her lungs. Her head dropped and she stopped trying to get away from him.

There was the soft sound of a sniffle, and Joe realised that his rough-and-tumble Shanna was crying. The sound raked through his insides, leaving him raw. He'd never ever seen her cry, and some of their cases had left grown men bawling like babies. Carefully, he turned her in his arms.

One lone tear trailed down her face.

It nearly destroyed him.

'I'm so sorry,' he said as he drew her close. 'I didn't know.'

She didn't answer. She didn't say a word. Her arms, though, linked around his neck. She latched on to him, and Joe held her tight.

Rubbing a hand up and down her spine, he let her work it out. She'd held this secret inside for too long. It had become too much for her to bear alone. He'd gladly take the weight on to his shoulders. He'd do anything not to see her in so much pain.

Time passed, but he didn't know how long he held her in his arms. He tried saying all the right things. He kissed her forehead, her temple and the soft spot under her ear. He tried everything he could think of to give her comfort.

After a while, she shivered and pulled away. 'I'm sorry,' she mumbled. 'I don't know what I'm doing.'

'It's called taking comfort, sweetheart.'

'I'm sorry,' she repeated. She wrapped her arms around her waist. 'I shouldn't have said anything.'

'How did it happen?' he asked.

She shook her head and ran a hand through her hair. 'I don't want to drag you into this.'

'I'm already there. Tell me what he did.'

Her liquid eyes slowly looked up at him, and Joe felt his heart flip in his chest. If he'd been teetering on the edge before, the look pushed him right over.

'You'll never think of me the same again.'

'I don't think the same of you as I did a week ago.' He caught her and pulled her back into his embrace. 'What difference does that make?'

She shifted her weight as if she were uncomfortable. Although Joe felt like a total heel, the sensation of her body rubbing against his had the same old effect. He could feel himself hardening against her soft belly.

'I don't want to lose your respect,' she said softly.

She glanced away, and he knew how much that admission had cost her. Once again, he caught her by the chin. This time when he turned her to face him, he kissed her. 'You won't,' he said.

'Don't,' she said, pushing against his chest. 'I can't think when you touch me.'

'Me neither,' he admitted with a quick smile. 'My dick takes over and my brain loses the race.'

Colour flooded her face. Not wanting to lose the moment, Joe leaned down and swept her up into his arms. He carried her to his big leather chair. The old thing let up a wretched shriek when he lowered his body into it and settled her in his lap.

'Now tell me,' he said.

She sat stiffly in his arms.

'We're not going anywhere until you tell me what happened to your sister.'

'Her name was Shanille,' she said softly. 'She was a year older than me.'

'What happened to your parents?' Joe saw the ring on her right hand. He reached out and touched it. 'You told me that this was your mother's.'

She nodded. 'The nurse gave it to me after the accident. Our parents were killed in a car crash.'

'You were twelve, right? Who took care of you?'

'We were put into the foster system. We were moved around from family to family, but nobody really wanted to keep us. We were too old.'

Joe shook his head at the unfairness of it all. 'How long were you in foster care?'

'I don't know. Years.' A hazy look entered her eyes as she sank into her memories. 'We turned a little wild. We got to be too much for any foster parent to handle.'

She looked up at him. 'Can you imagine two of me?'

A jolt caught him. 'Good God, no.'

A small smile pulled at her lips. 'We were a pair. We hit the streets as teenagers and quickly learned how to survive. We never turned tricks, but we found other ways of getting by.'

Like lifting wallets, he thought. He remembered the story that Robert had told him, but he kept quiet. He'd promised not to tell.

'I got a job at Tassels, and I found out that I was a

pretty good dancer. I made great money in tips. I loved that job,' she said wistfully.

A sudden vision of Shanna humping a stripper's pole caught Joe's mind and wouldn't let go. He could see her long hair flying and her firm breasts swinging. His cock swelled against her hip. 'Dance for me sometime,' he said.

She blinked and looked up at him cautiously. When she saw he was serious, her gaze skittered away. 'OK,' she said softly.

Joe ran a hand up her body until his palm covered her breast. He massaged it gently and felt her nipple budding beneath his touch. 'Is that where you met Mañuel?'

Her body went taut, but he kept up the intimate caress.

'Yes. He was a regular at the club. Shanille worked there as a waitress for a while, and she got involved with him. That sonofabitch got her hooked on drugs.'

'So he was her dealer?'

'Her dealer and her boyfriend. I tried to get her away from him but he had this power over her. She couldn't let herself see what he was doing to her.'

Joe nodded and let his hand slip down to her waist. With a flick of his wrist, he pulled her T-shirt from her shorts. He slid his hand up along her smooth skin. Her breath caught on a hitch when he swiftly dealt with the front closure of her bra and pushed the cup to the side. The feel of her warm, naked, yielding flesh made his cock jump to attention. 'What did he do to her?'

Shanna groaned as he caught her nipple between two of his fingers and squeezed. Her reaction shuddered through her body. She shifted on his lap, trying to ease the pressure building inside of her. 'He became her obsession,' she said.

Joe gritted his teeth as she ground her buttocks over his burgeoning erection.

He knew all about obsessions.

His hand wandered from her breast. He caught the zipper of her shorts and pulled it down. Slipping his hand inside, he caught her right between her legs. He watched her as he gave her mound a determined squeeze.

'Aaahhh!' she said, her back arching.

'What happened to her? What happened to Shanille?' he asked through clenched teeth. God, just watching her squirm with his hand between her legs was going to make him come.

'Oh, God! Don't ... I can't think.' Her breathing went ragged and a low moan left her lips when he pushed the wet crotch of her panties to the side. He worked two of his fingers between her swollen pussy lips. Her hands caught his forearm, but her hips lifted and her leg dropped open to the side to give him better access.

'Joe,' she said on a high note.

Joe looked down at her and saw the very picture of eroticism. Her long hair draped across his arm as her back arched with desire. The position pushed her breasts high into the air with her nipples creating the ultimate peak. Her hips ground against his hand as he wedged another finger into her.

'Christ!' he said as her hot liquid dripped on to his hand.

He knew the door to his office wasn't locked. Sexual behaviour on FBI grounds was strictly forbidden, but he didn't give a shit. He was going to fuck this woman whether it meant his job or not. It was a small price to pay for the hot heaven he found between her thighs.

With a swift move, he lifted her out of his lap and placed her across his desk. He pulled off her shorts. They hit the floor with a whisper.

Shanna squirmed on the hard surface like a bitch in heat. 'Please,' she begged. 'I need ...'

'I've got what you need, baby,' he growled as he

yanked on his zipper and pushed down his pants. 'I'm going to give it to you.'

Her panties were still in the way, but he didn't have time to get rid of them. A bead of moisture had already gathered at the head of his cock. He knew if he didn't get it inside her soon, they'd both regret it. With a snarl, he tugged on the dainty material of her panties, but the dainty material had the strength of steel. It refused to tear, so he pushed it to the side and out of his way. The nylon lay snug against the outside of her pussy lip, but he'd cleared a path to her.

He positioned himself at her opening and heard her whimper. The sound cut straight to the centre of his brain. With a harsh growl, he thrust.

'Take it,' he demanded.

'Oh, yes,' she said. Her legs lifted around his waist, and her hips swayed as she tried to find his rhythm.

His pace was hard, fast and violent. It was the rhythm they usually found near the end of a fuck, not the beginning. Christ, if they kept this up, it was going to kill them both.

Joe didn't care. The need to fuck her was ingrained in his very DNA.

Shanna's need was so great, she was whining. He heard the distress in her voice and he rammed into her faster. She needed it hard. She needed it bad.

'Joe, please!' she begged. 'Deeper. Oh. Yes. Aaaaahhhhh.'

His hands had taken over the movement of her hips, and he'd angled her up so he could slide right down to her core. Her fingers were white as she gripped the edge of the desk above her head. Papers, files, pens and even the phone had been sent over the side as their bodies bucked and swayed.

Joe felt the tightening in his balls, and he threw his

head back as the tingling shot right up through his dick. 'Shanna!' he called as he came into her.

Her mouth opened on a silent scream, and her body convulsed. He slammed home until his dick went limp. Energy gone, he bent over his desk and let his arms take his weight. Beads of sweat dropped on to her shirt, wetting her nipples.

Looking down at her, Joe felt an overwhelming need to protect. This was his woman, damn it. She would not be going through this alone any more. He was going to take care of her.

'What happened to Shanille?' he asked one last time. He sucked air into his lungs like bellows.

'She overdosed,' Shanna said, still trying to catch her breath. 'I didn't know what to do, so I called Manny. He took her away, and I never saw her again. He told me she died, but I never even got to give her a funeral. He didn't even allow me that.'

Her body cradled his, and his softened erection was still safe inside her. Joe felt her pain, and he vowed to get vengeance for her. 'I'll get the sonofabitch for you, baby. I swear.'

'I'll get him,' she said, finally opening her eyes to look at him.

The angst was gone from the brown depths. Pleasure still glazed her eyes. Joe was bound and determined that she'd never know anything but happiness again. He knew she wouldn't like it, but he shook his head. 'You're off the case, and I'm putting you on an enforced leave of absence. I'm sending you to Robert and Annie's for some well-deserved R and R.'

'No!'

'Yes. You're leaving on the next plane.'

14

'I'll get the sonofabitch for you, baby,' Shanna mocked. 'You go take a rest.'

Her foot increased the pressure on the gas pedal and the car picked up speed. 'Rest, my ass,' she said.

Her fingers tightened around the steering wheel. The car she'd bought didn't look like much, but it had a good engine under the hood. That was what she'd wanted – a car that wouldn't catch attention but could go like a bat out of hell.

'Sorry, Robert and Annie,' she said as the wind passed through the open windows. She knew they would be disappointed, but she'd ditched them. Well, what else was she supposed to have done? Joe had taken her to the airport and made her get on that damn plane. The Haynes had met her at the airport when she'd landed, and she couldn't help but feel like she was being babysat.

'Damn you, Tiger,' she said for the hundredth time.

This was her battle to fight – not his. Just because they'd had sex a couple of times, it didn't make him her defender.

Shanna shifted on the cracked vinyl seat. All right, she admitted that it had been more than just sex. The man had gotten under her skin. She had feelings for him, but she couldn't allow herself to analyse those emotions. There was another matter that needed her attention first.

Mañuel Santos.

Damn it, *she* was going to be the one who made that bastard pay.

She'd been after him for years. Joe couldn't take this

away from her. She wouldn't let him. Vengeance was her right.

She swept back her wind-ravaged hair to rub her aching head. She couldn't believe she'd confided in him. Just a week ago, she'd barely been able to get out a complete sentence in his presence. What was happening to her? She hadn't talked about that night in years. She still couldn't talk about it, but with him it had seemed almost natural to share one of the most painful times in her life.

'You've just let it go on too long,' she told herself.

Years and years of pressure had been building up inside of her. This case had just put the squeeze on her until she'd popped. Well, that wasn't going to be the end of it. Joe might have thought he was taking care of her, but in sending her away, he'd done exactly the wrong thing.

He'd pissed her off.

Yes, she'd made mistakes on this case, and yes, she'd broken over a dozen rules. She didn't really give a rip. But to have this opportunity taken out of her hands was the ultimate slap in the face. She deserved to see Santos brought to justice, and by God, she was going to be the one to do it.

'It's just a matter of time, Manny. A matter of time.'

Letting go of the steering wheel, she looked at her watch. She could drive straight through, she knew. Physically, it wouldn't be that much of a stretch. As wired as she was, she doubted she could sleep anyway. Still, she needed to be sharp. She still had the self-discipline to realise that.

Tapping her finger on the steering wheel, she considered her options. Finally, she decided she'd drive for a few more hours and find a hotel for the night. She'd have to pay cash like she had for the car, but that wasn't a problem. The emergency stash of money she kept at Robert's house had come in handy. From this point on, nobody was going to trace her. Not Joe, not the FBI, and certainly not Mañuel Santos.

She was a renegade.

The move would surely cost her her job, but she owed it to her sister. 'For you, Shanille,' she whispered.

She was through messing around with Sonny and his band of idiots. It was time to make a move. She had three states yet to drive through, but that would give her the opportunity to think. By the time she got back to town, she would have a plan with Manual Santos's name all over it.

'I'm coming for you, you creep,' she said. 'You'll never even know what hit you.'

'Hi, doll.'

Shanna stood in the doorway to the same seedy motel room she'd shared with Sonny and Tommy. 'Hi, Weasel,' she said, struggling to keep her distaste for the man out of her tone. 'Or do you prefer "Edwin"?'

'You can call me anything you want, baby,' he said in that scratchy voice that made her skin crawl.

He stepped aside to give her room to enter. She brushed past him, intentionally allowing her body to caress his. A shiver of revulsion trickled down her spine, but she ignored it. She had a plan, and nothing was going to sway her from it.

'We've been wondering where you've been,' Weasel said casually. 'You haven't been home.'

'Really?' she said, turning on her heel to face the man. His beady eyes were focused on her face, and she fought the impulse to back away. She'd never been alone with him. In fact, she'd done everything she could to avoid it. There was just something about him – something dark dangerous and intimidating. Her nerve faltered, but the memory of her sister bolstered her. 'Have you been watching me, Weasel?'

'You know I have.'

The low whisper crossed the room and rasped across her skin like sandpaper. He had been watching. He'd watched almost every time Sonny had touched her. In fact, that had been half of the sick attraction he held for her.

'My husband and I have been fighting again,' she lied. 'I had to get away for a while.'

'So you come back to town, and the first person you call is me.' Myers ran one bony finger along his jaw line. 'Interesting.'

Shanna paused. This man was borderline genius. She could see that now. Why had she wasted so much time concentrating on Sonny?

Taking a deep breath, she gathered her nerves. There was no going back. With a casual move, she dropped her purse on the bedside table. She shot a sultry glance at the man who made her cringe. 'I'm impulsive like that sometimes,' she said smoothly.

One of Myers's eyebrows rose, and a smirk settled on his lips. He set his briefcase on the small table by the window and crossed the room. He stopped less than a foot away from her. 'Sonny isn't happy with you.'

Myers's height matched her own, and Shanna held his gaze. 'Why? Because I called and asked for you?'

'That's one reason.'

He reached out and skimmed a finger across her collarbone. Her skin rebelled at the touch, but her nipples beaded tightly. She stood absolutely still as that deadly finger ran slowly across her chest to the rigid peak. He pressed his nail against her. Her aching nipple swelled even more in a rapid response, and she choked back a strangled gasp.

'He's also upset because he thinks you ratted out him and Tommy. He really wanted to come down and talk to you about that.' Myers ran his finger around her puckered aureole in a slow, tight circle. 'I told him I'd take care of it.'

Shanna felt heat spreading from her breasts down to her belly. Her pussy clenched with a combination of excitement and dread. There was a veiled threat in his words. 'Ratted him out to whom?' she asked, thinking quickly. 'My husband? I swear, I didn't even know he followed me to Tassels the other night. I'm sorry about the scene he made.'

'Not at Tassels,' Myers said calmly. His gaze still held hers, but his hand wandered down and slipped between her legs. He palmed her tightly, and she went straight up on to her tiptoes. 'We had a deal go south after he and Tommy left you the other night. Sonny thinks you might have blabbed what you heard. You wouldn't blab, now, would you, doll?'

The hand between her legs squeezed tighter, and Shanna's eyes drifted shut. Even through her leather pants, this man's touch could do strange, powerful things to her. She couldn't really define her reaction as good or bad, but it was intense. Everything about him was intense.

Forcing her eyes open, she looked him in the eye again. She had to be very, very careful how she played this. 'I don't even know what you do. Sonny didn't get in trouble, did he?'

A hard look crossed Myers's face. 'He barely made it out of there. Tommy wasn't so lucky.'

'I swear, I didn't have anything to do with it.' Fighting her repulsion, Shanna reached out and laid her hands on Myers's chest. He was thin and wiry, just like he looked. There was strength there, though. She'd always known this man was the most dangerous of the bunch. She needed to gain his trust. 'I couldn't do anything like that to Sonny.'

'Like his big prick that much?'

Myers's beady eyes glinted with a hint of anger. He'd seen the two of them. She couldn't lie about it. 'Yes.'

The hand that had been holding her pussy moved to her ass. He pulled her closer and forced his thigh between hers. 'How am I supposed to believe you?' he said. 'You fuck the two of them, and within hours police are surrounding them.'

'Police?' she said. 'I never called the police.'

'No? How did they find out about the deal?'

'I don't know. I don't know anything about any so-called deal.'

'Sonny doesn't believe that, and neither does Manny.'

Adrenaline pumped through Shanna's veins. 'Who's Manny?'

'Shit,' Myers snapped, obviously embarrassed at the slip. 'He's our boss.'

'Well, take me to him, and I'll explain that I had nothing to do with this.'

The challenge made every muscle in Weasel's body go taut. Shanna forced her breaths to remain even, but she worried that she'd pushed him too far.

'I think there's a lot going on in that head of yours, doll,' he said quietly. 'I don't like not knowing what you're thinking.'

Her breasts were tight against his chest and his nose touched hers as he spoke. Shanna knew that she had to do something quickly to get him off the subject. Asking to see Mañuel had been a mistake. 'Don't you like a woman with brains, Weasel?'

'On the contrary. It turns me on.'

'You turn me on,' she whispered. Giving in to a need she never would have admitted, she leaned her head forward and kissed him.

Her reaction to the touch of his lips caught her by surprise. Myers held her in an unbreakable embrace, and waves of fear alternated with an undertow of desire somewhere deep in her chest. His tongue forced itself into her mouth, and she met him halfway in a sensual battle. Their tongues swirled, clung and tasted each other. His hand tightened on her ass, and when he broke the kiss they were both gasping for air.

'I told you once that it would just be you and me. I'm tired of waiting.'

'So am I,' she said.

'Then let's fuck.'

An element of steel had entered his voice and something within Shanna shifted. She couldn't explain the effect he had on her. It was as if he embodied her every dark forbidden wish. In her head, she knew she shouldn't want him, but her body desperately craved the depraved things she knew he would do to her.

He let go of her, and she took a small step back.

'Get rid of that shirt,' he said. 'Do it slowly.'

Her hands trembled as she reached for the hem of her black tank top. *The plan*, she thought. *Remember the plan.*

She was here to seduce the man. Once she had his trust, she'd convince him to take her to Mañuel. Defending her part in Tommy's arrest was a convenient excuse that had just been laid in her lap. She'd use it. The plan was simple, but Myers was a smart man. She had to make this convincing.

Bunching the soft cotton in both hands, she pulled it upward. Cool air hit her, and she flinched when Weasel reached out and trailed his fingers lightly across her belly.

'Keep going,' he said.

She pulled the shirt over the swell of her breasts and immediately felt the heat of his gaze. She tugged the top over her head quickly, not trusting him enough to keep him out of her vision for even a split second. Her air came a little too quickly as she dropped her clothing to the floor.

'Nice,' Myers said. His hand reached for her again, and Shanna shivered. His fingertip barely brushed her skin as he traced the edge of the lace bra. 'Take it off for me, doll. Let me see those beautiful titties. Sonny likes them best, you know.'

'Do you?' Reaching up, she released the front clasp of the bra. The cups sagged, but for the most part kept her covered. He didn't like that, she could see immediately. Shrugging her shoulders, she availed herself to his dark probing gaze. His cool hands came up to cup her, and she sighed as he took the heavy weight of her breasts in his hands.

'They're very sexy,' he said as his thumbs moved to play with her red stiffened peaks. 'But I'm partial to that gorgeous ass of yours.'

His dark gaze met hers as he said the words, and a dark vibe settled in the cheap motel room.

'I want to touch it.'

Shanna swallowed hard. Suddenly, the air in the room had become thick. Her fingers trembled as she reached for the side tab of her leather pants. The rasp of the zipper seemed to ring off the walls of the small room. When she leaned down to pull off her boots, an unexpected caress on her backside caught her by surprise.

'Easy,' Myers whispered. 'Nice and easy.'

Her nipples perked up under the sudden chill in the room, and Shanna blinked to clear her head. She couldn't determine if it was hot or cold. She felt both.

'Continue.'

Taking another deep breath, she leaned down to quickly rid herself of the other boot. This time, she expected Myers's caress – only he chose to fondle a swinging breast instead. It swelled to his touch.

'You're doing well,' he told her.

She reached for her pants. The leather was warm and supple. She started to pull it over her hips, but he stopped her. With those cool, guiding hands, he moved her thumbs inside the waistband of her silk panties.

'I thought you wanted me to do this slow,' she said in a hoarse voice.

'I'm getting impatient,' he admitted.

The look he gave her was challenging, and for a moment Shanna felt a volt of fear. It was a strong aphrodisiac. She had a plan, but she wanted this. She wanted him to screw her brains out.

Determinedly, she pushed the rest of her clothing down. When she stepped out of the encumbrances of her clothes, she realised how vulnerable she was. She was stark naked, and he was fully dressed. Suddenly, she realised she'd never seen him any other way. Was he going to fuck her with his clothes on? He'd have to at least open his zipper, wouldn't he?

A shiver of fear and excitement ran down her spine. Maybe he wasn't planning on fucking her with his dick. Maybe he had something else in mind.

'Give Weasel a kiss,' he said, licking his thin lips.

Shanna gave herself over to the delicious dark feeling that had caught her in its grip. His lips came down on hers as he pulled her against him. His clothing abraded her bare skin, and the effect on her body was strange. It was as if every nerve-ending came to attention.

He started backing her across the room, but he was heading away from the bed. Confused, Shanna pulled away.

'Keep kissing me,' he ordered.

She complied. His tongue swept through her mouth and she didn't complain when the edge of the table pressed tightly against her ass. The sound of him opening his briefcase, though, made her break the kiss.

'What are you doing?' she asked, suddenly suspicious.

Looking over her shoulder, she saw him pull a latex glove out of one of the briefcase's many compartments. Nervously, she took a step to the side, but the circle of his arms kept her firmly in place.

'I want your tongue in my mouth *now*,' he said in a tone that was hardly louder than a whisper.

The order whipped through the air, and she leaned forward. Closing her eyes, she touched her lips against his and pressed her tongue deep. There was the snapping sound of the glove being pulled on and then a slurp. A jumble of emotions caught Shanna smack-dab in the middle of her chest. She knew without a doubt what he was going to do to her, and it shocked her.

It also excited her.

Myers spread one hand against her lower back and pulled her tightly against him. It was he who finally broke the erotic battle of their mouths. 'Spread your legs, doll. I need better access.'

Shanna slowly widened her stance. Goose bumps popped up on her skin. Her breath caught as one of Myers's latex-covered fingers wormed its way between the cheeks of her ass. Like a mindless creature going to ground, it soon found a dark tiny hidey-hole and began to wiggle its way inside.

A sharp gasp left Shanna's lips at the feel of the foreign penetration. Even though Myers's finger was slick with lubricant, the sensation was uncomfortable. The pressure increased as his long cool finger worked its way up inside her.

'You know what I'm going to do to you,' he said, his hot eyes intent on her face.

'I – *Oh!*' she gasped in surprise.

He'd pulled the finger back, and she'd begun to relax. When he'd returned with two, she hadn't been prepared.

The added thickness of a second finger spread her open even wider. The pressure was disturbing, and she squirmed as he pressed harder, forcing his wriggling digits up into her.

'Oh, yeah,' he said. 'You're really tight. This will be hot.'

Hot. Yes, she felt incredibly hot. The burning sensation radiating from her ravaged anus was spreading across her buttocks. The heat crawled forward to her pussy, and she was embarrassed to find herself nearly dripping.

'You've never taken it up the ass,' he said.

'No,' she answered. She bit her lower lip as he began working his fingers harder into her. In and out. In and out. She lifted herself on to her tiptoes to try to get away from those marauding fingers, but Weasel only chuckled. Using both hands, he spread her cheeks wider apart. He pushed his fingers deep and began scissoring them.

'This will help,' he whispered into her ear. 'I'm not as big as Sonny, but you'll feel me back here.'

'Please,' Shanna said. She didn't know if it was a plea for mercy or a plea for more. Not even Dooley had gone this far.

'Are you begging me, doll?'

His dark side was becoming more and more apparent. With every second, Shanna felt the pull of his sinister attraction becoming stronger and stronger. Every breath of the hot heavy air filled her with a craving for his repellent touch. Those insidious fingers of his tickled every nerve-ending inside her secret passage, bringing it to fiery awareness.

He was going to fuck her there. The thought terrified and thrilled her.

His slick, coated fingers found a home deep, deep inside her.

'Give me a kiss,' he said. 'A nice, hot, long one.'

Oh, God, she was so turned on. She knew she shouldn't be. Any good girl would be horrified. She should be kicking this man's butt, or at the least, screaming for help. She did neither. Instead, she lifted her chin and felt his mouth come down hard against hers, pressing her swollen lips against her teeth.

His free hand slid under her and made its way to her pussy. The move pulled her even tighter against him, and she wound her arms around the freakish man's neck. His fingers brushed against her pussy lips, and he felt the moisture that had already coated her bush.

'You're ready,' he said, pulling back from the kiss. 'Get on the bed. On all fours.'

He jerked his fingers out of her so abruptly, the friction left a burning trail. Shanna groaned out loud. Losing the penetration was almost as bad as taking it. Her legs wobbled as she turned obediently towards the bed. A quick smack on her butt cheeks made her screech and move faster.

'That's more like it. I want to see you eager for Weasel's weenie.'

Her hands shook as she turned down the bed. The sheets were crisp but she knew they wouldn't stay that way for long. A thin sheen of sweat already covered her body. Her heart was pounding like a racehorse's.

She didn't know why she'd let things come this far, but she needed this. She wasn't a good girl. She'd been a bad girl for the better part of her life, and she liked being bad.

She couldn't do this with Joe.

The thought crept into her mind, but she quickly shut the doors to her brain. Tonight wasn't about thinking. Tonight was about doing what she wanted to do, and she had several things to cross off her list.

She crawled on to the bed and assumed the position

Myers had ordered. She loved this sexual position, but she had a feeling it was about to become even more special. A shiver of forbidden delight ran across her skin.

'Hurry, Weasel,' she whispered.

He came up alongside the bed. 'You don't hurry this, doll. This is something to be savoured. We're going to take our time.'

Oh, God. He was going to ride her. Shanna's arms buckled, and she went down on her elbows.

'That's a pretty picture,' he said in that raspy voice that sent a new shiver down her spine.

She held the position as he stacked pillows under her belly. He found more in the closet, and soon her body was gently supported on a pile of feathers. His touch brushed against her occasionally as he arranged her into the position he wanted. Every time he ran that gloved hand down the crack of her ass, she flinched.

'You're responsive,' he said. 'That's good. Now reach up and grab the headboard like you did with Sonny. That made me hard.'

Shanna reached forward and wrapped her fingers around a thick wooden spindle. The move stretched her forward and emphasised the erotic lift of her hips. The hard cool wood felt almost alive under her touch, and she caressed the furniture like it was Myers's cock.

God, she wished he would hurry.

He retrieved his briefcase and set it beside her on the bed. She quivered, wondering what sort of playthings he kept in there. Before she could figure out what he intended to do, he whipped out a long silk scarf. He was wiry, he was quick and he was strong. She realised his intention to tie her, but in her position, she didn't have enough leverage to stop him. Soon, her hands were tied to the wooden headboard and she was left immobile.

Shanna's nerves faltered. This was a mistake. She

shouldn't have let him bind her. She couldn't get to her gun. She couldn't use any of her hand-to-hand skills. She was too vulnerable, and she didn't like it.

The snap of a latex glove made her flinch, and the soft cool touch of Myers' bare finger running down her spine made her back bow. She struggled against her ties, and a sharp rap on her backside made her rear upward. It was followed by another stinging blow, and she gasped in pain.

'What are you doing?' she yelled. 'Stop that!'

'Did you go to the cops, Lily? Did you tell them about the deal that was going down?'

Oh, God. She hadn't expected him to use this tactic. She'd thought he'd given up on the subject. Fool. She should have realised that he'd been convinced too easily. Another swift smack made her toes clench.

'No,' she panted. 'I told you I didn't.'

'I don't know if I believe you.'

He stood at the side of the bed, still fully dressed, and she saw him lift his hand. She'd been spanked before, and although she wouldn't exactly choose it, it was a sexual stimulant for her. She had no doubt he knew that as his punishing hand moved lower around the curve of her buttocks. Every sharp rap sent a pulse through her pussy, and she closed her eyes as a dark deep wanting started to rise within her.

'How much information did you give them, Lily?'

'None,' she said. The feelings were becoming over-whelming. 'I told you I didn't do anything.'

A series of sharp slaps on her tender ass made her cry out.

'The boss wants to know who did.'

'Then take me to him,' she screamed. 'Maybe he'll believe me when I tell him it wasn't me.'

His hand came down harder still and her body trem-bled. He stopped to caress her burning skin, and she moaned. She was so sensitive, she could barely stand his gentle touch.

A raspy chuckle filled the air. 'You'll eventually tell me the truth.'

Myers reached into his box of treasures and Shanna looked on with a combination of excitement and dread. She could feel her pulse in her throbbing buttocks. It was as if her heart had dropped and taken residence there. His hand came away with something and she strained to see it. Her eyes widened when she saw a nipple clip approaching her dangling breast.

'No,' she said. The plea ended on a high note as Myers let the clip close anyway. The sharp pain sent dark waves through Shanna's brain, and she closed her eyes only to see flashes of red. Myers's devious hand brushed against her other tender breast, and she pulled hard at her bindings.

He fondled her mercilessly. This time her 'no' was less forceful. The pain wasn't punishing, she realised. If anything, it only pushed her to the brink of sexual awareness. Her breasts and her buttocks were on fire.

Her pussy naturally responded.

The second clip took hold, and she let out a high-pitched whine. Her forehead dropped against the cool sheets and she took in deep gulps of air.

'Did you betray us, doll?'

Her hair had swung forward to curtain her, but the question was whispered directly into her ear. The intimacy made her shiver. 'No,' she said in a hoarse voice.

She felt Myers step back and heard the rustle of clothing. She turned her head to watch, but her hair blocked her view. When he reached out to brush it away, she found his cock inches from her face.

'Take a good look, because in a few seconds you won't be able to see it any more.' The smile on his face was almost maniacal. 'But you'll feel it.'

Shanna's eyes widened, and she swallowed hard. She was tempted to laugh, but she couldn't. She knew precisely what that tool was going to do, and it was well suited for the purpose.

'Oh, God,' she said.

Weasel's prick looked like a long thin pencil. A rock-hard pencil. No wonder he'd never brought it out in Sonny's presence. He had to feel inadequate around his well-hung friend.

Still, she felt a drip of moisture spill from her pussy. He was incredibly long. Compared to his prick, his fingers had barely entered her. She was going to feel thoroughly invaded.

'It's time.'

She tensed. It was time. It had been time for quite a while now, and her body was ready for him. Her breasts had swelled to what seemed to be twice their normal size, and even the cool air in the motel room was uncomfortable on her red-hot buttocks.

Weasel reached into his briefcase. He found the tube of ointment he'd used before and squeezed out a good portion into the palm of his hand. He intentionally stood where she could see his actions. She couldn't help but watch as his hands oiled up his long skinny cock.

Her long-time revulsion for the man surged inside her as she watched him. He was short. He was so thin, the outline of his ribcage showed clearly. His prick, so much like the rest of him, stood upright like a bony finger.

'I hate you,' she said truthfully.

'But you want me.'

'Yes.'

The confession finally spurred him into action, and the mattress shifted as he climbed on to the bed behind her. A cool dollop of lubrication dropped on to her responsive flesh, and she flinched. She was soon squirming as Myers worked the slick ointment around the tight ring of her anus. Every now and then, one of his fingers would push inside her.

By the time his slick hands clamped down on her hips, she was clawing at the headboard. He positioned the knobby head of his cock against her tightly clenched opening, and her pulse thundered through her veins.

'Blow out a long breath,' he said.

She was gulping air as fast as she could get it, but she tried. As she let out a long hot breath, the pressure increased. Her muscles fought him, but he was inexorable. He rocked against her until he gained entrance. Once inside, his cock moved up her tight passageway with less resistance.

The pressure was more than Shanna had expected, and she couldn't keep her breaths controlled, no matter how hard she tried. Sharp gasps of air hit her lungs. 'Weasel,' she begged.

His knees bumped against hers and spread her legs wider. The open position gave him better access to her, and she felt the muscles in his thighs clench.

'Oh, God,' she said.

He thrust and forced her to take more of that long cock. He was unstoppable as he moved towards his goal. She was tight, but he wasn't accepting any excuses. His fingers bit into her hips, and he ground into her. 'Take it,' he growled.

'I can't!'

'You can.'

'No, I –'

'Arch,' he demanded.

The familiar order sent waves of dark pleasure spiralling through her chest. She automatically fell into the position he wanted, and he pressed two more inches inside of her. 'Yes,' she sighed.

His penetration was slow and thorough. He moved up, up inside her until she didn't think she could take any more.

He showed her she could.

When his pubic hair scratched against her sensitive ass, she felt a wicked delight. His tiny hard balls bumped against her, and her fascination bloomed. Pain radiated through her, but she took pleasure in it.

And when he began to move . . . She dissolved.

'That's my doll,' Myers said, panting as he began thrusting.

The friction of his cock burned her virginal passage. Shanna's pulse pounded in her ears until she could barely hear the filthy things he was saying to her. Her sexual excitement was nearly unbearable. It threatened to overwhelm her.

Myers pumped in a deep steady rhythm, and his arms came around her. She ground her forehead against the sheets. It was too much – the discomfort and the exhilaration. Sensations pulsed through her but she just couldn't reach that top peak.

'My clit. Please,' she begged. 'Please play with it. I can't come.'

'In time,' Weasel said.

He pulled out of her, and Shanna cried out. She was so close. He wasn't going to stop now. He couldn't! 'Oh, please, please,' she said. 'Don't stop. Finish it, I'm begging you.'

She looked frantically over her shoulder and saw that Myers had only withdrawn to lube up again. A smirk crossed his hard face. 'I knew you'd be a natural. You like it nasty.'

'Yes!' she screamed. 'Put it back in.'

'All right,' he said with a harsh chuckle. 'Hold on.'

When he thrust into her this time, he did it quickly and roughly. Shanna screamed at the hot bold penetration. It was still new to her, but her training time had apparently come and gone.

Weasel began fucking her with no regard for her comfort. He thrust that hard skinny dick so deep into her, his balls banged against her backside. The tension inside her increased as his stimulation pushed her to limits she'd never reached before.

She was unprepared when his hands circled her and removed the nipple clips from her swinging breasts.

'Aaahhh!' she screamed.

Hot darts of pain shot through her as circulation returned to her delicate peaks. One of Myers's hands covered her throbbing breast as the other dove between her legs. He finally fingered her trigger, and she shot to her crest.

The orgasm was intense. Another followed hot on its heels as he continued to butt-fuck her. Shanna lost count of how many times she peaked before she felt him ejaculate inside her.

Myers fell forward, and she was pressed harder against the pillows and the mattress. Both of them gasped for oxygen. It was a long while until Shanna's world righted. When she regained her senses, her skin crawled. Weasel's air rasped against her ear, and she shivered from revulsion.

He felt her shiver, and he grunted. 'Good, huh?'

'Yes,' she said.

They lay there for a long while until she began to feel uncomfortable. 'Could you take it out?' she asked.

'I thought you liked it there.'

'When it's hard. It feels like a big soft worm now. Take it out.'

'Maybe I'll just leave it there until it gets hard again,' he threatened.

And that was exactly what he did. He fucked her in the ass over and over again until he ran out of lubrication. Shanna was spent by the time he finally rolled off the bed and headed to the bathroom to clean himself up. By that time, he'd loosened the constraints on her arms.

That had been his vital mistake.

The moment the bathroom door closed, she was up and moving. The unfamiliar ache in her backside made her flinch as she stood, but she hurriedly tugged on her clothes. She was fully dressed by the time Myers came back into the room.

'That was fast,' he said.

The light from the bathroom lit him from behind, making him look even more pathetic. His skinny frame hardly filled the doorway, and his long dick hung limp between his legs.

She shrugged casually. 'You and your boss seem very concerned about me. I thought you could take me to him so I could talk to him.'

One of Myers's eyebrows lifted, and the glint in his eye would normally have made her shiver. 'That's not such a good idea,' he said in a cool voice.

'Why not? You all seem so suspicious of me. I think I should have the opportunity to defend myself.'

He folded his arms over his chest. 'I'll tell him you didn't do it. If you had, you would have broken down and told me. You're not a snitch; you're just a horny bitch.'

'Now that's where you're wrong,' Shanna said, her patience evaporating. Plan A was not working. It was time to go to Plan B. Her voice went ice cold. 'Get dressed.'

'Why?' he said with a smirk.

'Because we're making a trip.' She pulled her nine-millimetre Glock from the small of her back and aimed it between his beady eyes. 'You're taking me to Mañuel.'

15

'Think, Robert!' Joe barked into the phone. 'Did she give you any clues where she was going?'

'I'm telling you, Joe. We brought her home from the airport, and Annie made dinner. Shanna just poked at it. I've never seen her so stressed.'

The muscles in Joe's jaw tightened. That was due to him. 'Did she give you any indication what she was going to do?'

'Hell, no. She's a pro. She excused herself from the table and went to the guest room. By the time Annie went looking for her, she was long gone.'

'She couldn't have just disappeared into thin air.'

'Yes, she could,' Robert said matter-of-factly. 'If she were to go to ground, you would never find her.'

'Shit,' Joe said, muffling the telephone receiver against his chest. He glanced at the clock hanging on the wall. It was late, but he hadn't left his office in three days. Ever since Robert had first called and told him that Shanna had given him the slip, he hadn't been able to rest. 'She's out there somewhere. With all the agents I've got looking for her, somebody's bound to stumble across her.'

'If she doesn't want you to find her, you won't. She lived that life for too long. She knows how to disappear.'

'With all the technology we have –'

'She knows how to get around every bit of it.'

Joe raked a hand through his hair. He had a sick feeling in his stomach. No matter how good she was, she was out there alone. After what she'd told him, he wasn't sure she was in a good state of mind. 'I'm worried about what she's going to do. She's ready to snap.'

'You don't sound so good yourself.'

'I made a mistake. I never should have sent her away, but I was just trying to protect her. I couldn't . . .'

'You don't have to tell me, son,' Robert said quietly. 'I know how you feel about her.'

For a moment, Joe was taken aback. He'd never talked to his old partner about his feelings for Shanna. Had she said something? His heart took off at a frantic pace.

'You don't call her "Lily" any more,' Robert explained.

His kick-started heart lurched to a stop. Of course she hadn't said anything. She wouldn't say anything. 'Yeah, well, we worked together pretty closely on this case,' he mumbled.

'You two actually had to have conversations?' Robert teased. 'Hell, the two of you have always been like lions in a cage. You were always tip-toeing around, but you couldn't take your eyes off each other.'

'Well, I'd like to clap eyes on her again,' Joe said, bringing the conversation safely back to the present. Right now, he'd give his right arm just to see her safe and sound.

'If I had to guess,' Robert said, 'I'd bet she's after that Santos character.'

'That's the one thing I know for certain. The problem is that we don't know where he is.'

'How would she find him?'

Joe shifted his weight uncomfortably. He was still more than a little touchy about the way she'd infiltrated Santos's group. 'She's gained the trust of Santos's men. I can't use that route.'

Silence on the other end indicated that Robert was thinking. That was good. Joe had run out of thoughts of his own. He felt like he was grasping at straws.

'Hasn't your investigation come up with anything?' Robert asked, starting at the beginning.

Joe rubbed a hand across his chest. That tight feeling had returned. 'No, the man's like a fucking ghost.'

'Would Shanna's partner have any ideas?'

'He's still out on medical leave. The doctors let him out of the hospital a day or two ago. He . . .' A blinding flash of insight finally hit Joe. 'Damn it, that's it.'

'That's what?' Robert asked sharply.

'There was a tape! Shanna gave it to one of the women in the lab to analyse. She turned on her tape recorder the last time Santos's men took her to his place.'

'A tape? She's actually been there before? Why didn't she just sketch out the route for you?'

Joe took a slow breath. There were a lot of details that Robert didn't know. There were even more that he could never know. 'She was blindfolded,' he said slowly.

'Sonofabitch,' Robert growled. There was more silence before his voice came sharply back on the line. 'Well, why haven't you used this goddamned tape before now?'

'The lab is still working on it.'

'Then how the hell is it going to help you?'

'I've got motivation on my side,' Joe said firmly. For the first time in days, there was a light of hope at the end of the tunnel. 'I've got to go, Robert. Give my love to Annie.'

'Call us as soon as you find her.'

'I'll get her back, Robert. You can count on that.'

'Give them a warning and you'll regret it,' Shanna said in an ice-cold voice. Her gun was steady as she pointed it at the back of Edwin Myers's head. They were at the gate outside Santos's country home. This time, she'd been able to watch the entire trip and determine the house's location.

Weasel reached out and pushed the button on the security box. 'Myers,' he said into the intercom.

The gate opened slowly and he drove up the bumpy road. Adrenaline poured through Shanna's veins. She'd waited years for this. Years. The SUV crept up the long driveway until Myers parked in front of the main door to the house.

'Get out slowly,' she said as she slipped out of the vehicle. She'd ridden in the back seat to keep herself hidden and Myers under control. She left the SUV's door open so no observant ears would catch the sound of two doors closing.

Myers stepped down from the tall vehicle and she put one hand on his shoulder. Her eyes darted in every direction, looking for any sign of possible danger. At this point, it was going to take an act of nature to stop her from going through the front door of that house.

As her gaze swept the grounds, she felt Myers' muscles tense. Before he could take a step away from her, she grabbed his wrist and twisted his arm high behind his back. 'That was a mistake,' she hissed into his ear.

His mouth opened to call for help, but his voice died in his throat when he heard the soft click of the hammer of her gun.

'Follow my orders and you won't get hurt,' she said. 'Now, we're going to march up those front steps nice and easy. You're going to knock on the door, and if anybody asks who it is, you say your name. Nothing more, nothing less. Got it?'

Myers had gone an unhealthy shade of white. He swallowed hard and nodded.

'OK, let's do it.'

She kept a strong grip on the man's twisted arm. His steps seemed unsteady as they rounded the front of the vehicle. She didn't blame him. She was using him as a human shield.

She evaluated the house closely. There still hadn't been any signs of attention from inside. The place was well lit. She knew somebody was home.

Her breaths came steadily but her muscles were poised for action. Control had settled over her. She'd been preparing herself for this moment for longer than she could remember. There was no time or place for nerves now.

'Ring the doorbell,' she said when they'd climbed the steps and stood on the front stoop.

Myers's bony hand shook as he reached out and pressed the button. The delicate tinkling of the bell inside the house seemed incongruous. Shanna shook off the feeling as her senses focused on the front door.

Footsteps approached from the inside of the house.

Her grip on her gun tightened as she lifted it.

The door handle twisted without question. Manny was getting careless.

Shanna's finger tightened on the trigger as the door swung open.

It was Sonny.

'Hey, Weasel.' Sonny's dark eyes quickly took in the situation, and he reached for his gun.

'Stop right there,' Shanna said sharply. Using her hip, she pushed Myers against the doorjamb and turned her gun on the bodyguard. 'Pull it out with two fingers and drop it at your feet.'

For a split second, humour lit Sonny's eyes. It vanished quickly. The gun she had pointed at him didn't waver, and Myers's helplessness was hard to miss. Slowly, he followed her orders.

'Kick it over here.'

The gun slid across the hard wood floor. Watching the men closely, Shanna reached down and tossed the weapon into the darkness behind her. 'On your knees. Both of you.'

She could sense that the two thugs hated being bested

by a woman, but they knew better than to challenge the accuracy of her gun. Slowly, they lowered themselves to the floor. 'Hands behind your head,' she said.

Her control was icy as she positioned herself behind them. With the wall at her back, she let her gaze swiftly scour the living room.

He was here. She could feel the evil in the house.

'Santos,' she yelled, calling him out.

Quick footsteps sounded down the hallway, and her pulse leapt. She had him. This time, she really had him.

A man turned around the hallway corner and a wave of hatred nearly knocked Shanna over. It was him! He'd changed, but the evil in his eyes would be there until the day he died.

He dressed better. His clothes were expensive but he was still gaudy enough to wear his shirt open to display the gold necklaces around his neck. Rings weighted down his fingers. She was looking for a gun, and he didn't have one.

'What the fuck is this?' he snapped.

She'd heard that voice in her nightmares.

Her own voice shook, but her gun was rock steady as she aimed it at him. 'The end, you bastard. You're under arrest.'

'For what?' he laughed. 'You haven't got anything on me.'

'Take your pick,' she said. 'There's drug dealing, assault of an FBI agent, and ...'

Her voice cracked.

'Who are you?' he asked, his eyes narrowing. 'You look familiar.'

'I should, you sonofabitch. I'm –'

'Shanna!'

The voice on the staircase made her spin to her left. Her attention was split between Santos, his men and the new threat. She looked up.

And saw a ghost.

'Shanna,' the woman repeated weakly.

Shanna froze.

'Shanille?' she said. Suddenly air didn't seem to want to go in her windpipe.

Her sister. Alive. With Manny.

Her thoughts jumbled into a tangled mess as she stood helplessly in the middle of the room.

Myers saw her distraction and used it. His hand whipped out and knocked the gun from her grip. It tumbled across the floor, but she had no time to reach for it as his elbow caught her in the stomach.

Shanna doubled over in pain but managed to weave away from his next swinging punch. He missed, and she caught him off balance. Grabbing him by the shoulders, she pulled him down as her knee came up. A groan split the air, and she pushed him away.

'You bitch,' he roared as his arms came up around her. Her knees buckled under his weight and he dragged her to the floor.

All the training she'd ever experienced as an FBI agent came into play when she realised she was in a fight for her life. Her hand fisted and she caught Myers sharply on the chin. His head snapped back, but behind him she saw Sonny coming to his feet.

Her heart surged. She couldn't fight him.

Sonny thudded across the room and reached down to grab her hair. She squirmed away from him just as another dark body came charging through the open door. The blurry figure put down his shoulder and tackled Fuentes in the chest. The two went rolling across the floor with fists flying.

'Joe!' Shanna screamed.

The two men went at each other taking furniture, draperies and trinkets with them. Grunts filled the air as they pummelled each other. She heard the crunch of a fist against someone's jaw but her attention quickly returned to Myers.

He was coming to. She hit him again, putting her weight behind the punch.

'You touched her,' Joe growled from the other side of the room. 'Your filthy hands touched her.'

A surge of emotion caught her in the chest but she didn't have time to analyse it. Instead, she dove for her gun.

It was already in Shanille's hands.

Everything suddenly screeched to slow-motion speed.

Shanna hesitated. She really didn't know anything about the woman standing in front of her. Was this still her sister? What had happened in the years since she'd last seen her?

'Shanille, let's go,' Mañuel said. He stretched his hand out to her. 'Now!'

Shanille seemed dazed as she looked at the sleek, cold weapon in her hands. Her eyes lifted but Shanna couldn't read what was behind them.

'He told me you were dead,' she said in a hoarse voice.

'We've got to get out of here,' Mañuel yelled. 'They know where we live.'

'Not any more,' Shanille said in an eerie voice.

The gun lifted, and Shanna's heart stopped.

'No!' she screamed as her sister pulled off three rounds.

16

Shanna walked slowly down the hallway of the FBI building. She'd been summoned for a meeting. She didn't know what it was about but it couldn't be good. She'd been suspended for the last two weeks. Obviously, some decision had been made as to her fate.

The echoing of her footsteps off the empty corridor's walls sounded like a ticking time bomb, and she stopped to compose herself. The Bureau had been trying to sort things out on the case, but she didn't know how much the internal investigators had learned. A lot of it depended on what Joe had told them.

Straight-shooting, by-the-book, Special Agent Tiger Mitchell.

She took a deep breath as her nerves got the better of her. She dreaded facing him. She hadn't seen him since the night Shanille had shot Mañuel.

A door down the hallway swooshed open, and Shanna jumped.

'Lily, you're back!'

'Melanie,' she said in surprise.

A look of concern crossed the cute blonde's face and she hurried towards her. 'Are you OK? Shawn and I have been worried.'

Even with her nerves pulled to the breaking point, Shanna found reason to smile. '"Shawn and I". I take it that things are going well?'

Melanie blushed right up to the roots of her hair. 'Very well,' she said.

'That's great,' Shanna said, truly meaning it. She

was happy that these two people had found one another.

Melanie glanced down the hall and lowered her voice. 'I need to apologise to you. I'm sorry I gave that audiotape to Special Agent Mitchell. I know you wanted to keep that confidential but he ordered me to give it to him.'

Shanna bit her lower lip. So that was how Joe had found her. She'd been wondering about that. It also explained his mood that night – he'd heard the tape. No wonder he'd gone ballistic on Sonny. 'It's all right,' she said weakly. 'I needed back-up. You might have helped save my life.'

'Are you sure?'

'I'm sure.' She nodded towards the offices. 'How are things in there?'

'Busy.' Melanie hooked her hair behind her ear and Shanna noticed that she no longer wore it in a bun. Come to think of it, her glasses were missing, too. 'They need you back.'

But would they let her come back? Somehow, Shanna didn't think so.

Fear, cold and dark, wrapped around her heart. Her job had been her salvation. Without it, she wouldn't know who she was. What would she do? Where would she go?

'Well, I guess I should bite the bullet,' she said softly. Her spine straightened and she lifted her chin. She'd never been a coward. Whatever happened, she would find a way to survive. 'Wish me luck.'

Shawn spotted her the moment she walked through the door. So did a dozen other agents, but she couldn't deal with them right now. Her eyes were immediately drawn to Joe's office. The blinds were closed.

It wasn't a good sign.

She headed to Coberley's desk and was relieved to see that the bruises had faded from his handsome face. 'Hey, partner,' she said softly.

'Hey, yourself,' he said.

He rounded his desk and pulled her into a tight hug. She held back. 'How are your ribs?' she asked.

'They're fine.'

He pulled her closer, and she gave in. With a sigh, she dropped her forehead on to his shoulder. She'd missed him so much. 'Oh, Shawn,' she whispered. 'How much trouble am I in this time?'

He looked down at her and his face tightened with concern. Quickly, he settled her into a chair and pulled another one close. 'The case is coming together really well,' he confided. 'That's a huge plus on your side.'

The news was comforting. With her suspension, she'd been cut off from everything. 'The information Shanille gave you helped?'

He nodded quickly. 'We found stashes of heroin at every location she gave us. We're talking about hundreds of thousands of dollars in confiscated drugs.'

Some of the weight lifted from Shanna's shoulders. That was good. That was very good.

'The case is air-tight,' he said firmly. 'We're just waiting for Santos to recover from his injuries.'

'He'll be able to stand trial?'

Something in her voice made Shawn reach out and squeeze her shoulder. 'Your sister isn't as good with that Glock as you are,' he said solemnly.

Shanna swallowed hard. She didn't know if she'd ever get over the look she'd seen in Shanille's eyes when she'd turned on Mañuel.

'How's Tiger?' she finally dared to ask. The question was hardly louder than a whisper by the time she managed to force it between her lips.

Coberley rolled his shoulders and sat back in his chair. 'Meaner than a man-eater looking for his next meal.'

It wasn't the answer she'd expected, and she looked at him sharply.

'He's been in a rotten mood ever since you left. He nearly ripped Devo's head off over a typo yesterday. We've all been trying to stay out of his way.'

Shanna's heart sank. She'd be lucky if she stepped out of that office alive.

'Lily?'

She looked over her shoulder to see Betty Simpcox.

'Welcome back, dear,' the woman said as she laid her gentle hands on Shanna's shoulders. 'Special Agent Mitchell is waiting for you.'

Shanna shuddered, but summoned her nerve. It wasn't going to be pleasant but she might as well get it over with. With one last glance at Shawn for support, she stood and crossed the room to Joe's office door.

'Come in,' he said when she knocked.

She entered and found him standing in the middle of the room waiting for her. Electricity practically crackled in the air.

'Close the door,' he said.

She flinched, but her claustrophobia was the least of her worries. Turning, she shut the door and heard the latch click.

'Lock it.'

This time her stomach somersaulted. She glanced quickly over her shoulder. He crossed his arms over his chest and stood firm. 'Just do it, Shanna.'

Oh, God, why did he have to go and do that? Why did he have to call her by her name? Why couldn't they keep things as impersonal as possible?

Sweat broke out on her palms as she turned the deadbolt. She turned to face him, but her legs didn't feel solid underneath her. She leaned back against the door for support. Joe ran a hand through his hair, and she realised he looked as uncomfortable as she felt. No doubt this had been hard on him, too. She wondered how much trouble he'd gotten into as a result of her actions.

'How's your sister?' he asked.

The question threw her as much as it touched her. 'Better,' she said quietly. 'Robert and Annie have taken her under their wing.'

He nodded as if that were the best thing for her. 'Will she be able to testify at the trial?'

'Her doctors think it will be cathartic for her.'

In a way, the last two weeks had been cathartic for Shanna. She and her sister had been inseparable. They'd spent every minute trying to catch up on each other's lives. Although she still hated Mañuel Santos with every fibre of her being, she'd been relieved to hear that he'd done his best to be good to her sister. He'd even gotten her off the drugs. In his own twisted way, he loved her.

'How are you?' Joe asked.

The soft question cut straight to her heart. She'd regained a sister, but the rest of her life was in a state of chaos.

Suddenly, Shanna couldn't bear it any more – this tip-toeing around the real subject. She didn't want him to be nice to her. She didn't want him to be considerate before he lowered the boom. 'Are you firing me?' she blurted.

His green eyes flashed. 'What?' he said.

'I know you've spent a lot of time with Internal Affairs this week.' She put a hand to her rolling stomach. 'Are they recommending that I be let go?'

'Shanna...'

'I'd understand,' she said, not letting him finish. 'I know that I deserve it. I wouldn't hold it against you.'

He moved quickly towards her but she held him off by holding up a hand. She couldn't deal with him touching her. She just wanted him to do it quick and clean. It would be less painful that way.

'You're a part of us, Lily,' he said. His gaze ran across her face. 'There's no way I'd fire one of my best agents.'

Best. He'd said *best*. The praise touched her deeply but

she tried not to take too much hope in the word. After all, the decision wouldn't be solely his. The Bureau had rules and guidelines. She'd tromped all over them in her haste to get revenge on Mañuel Santos. 'I was impulsive and out of control,' she admitted.

'Yes, you were, but there were extenuating circumstances.'

'I went there to kill him,' she said, cutting to the heart of the matter.

Joe's head snapped up, and his face went hard. 'No, you didn't. I heard you try to arrest him.'

Parts of that night were still hazy to her. Everything had happened so fast. 'I did?' she asked hesitantly.

'Yes, you did,' he said, taking another step towards her. He reached out and caught her chin. 'That was when I knew that you weren't as bad as you seem to think you are. You've got a soul and a conscience, sweetheart. You've also got feelings that run a mile deep.'

Shanna shook her head, not wanting to accept his words. His touch sent off fireworks in her system but she fought her reaction. She had to take responsibility for her actions. 'I disobeyed your orders. You took me off the case but I came back anyway. I was a renegade agent.'

He folded his arms over his chest and rocked back on his heels. 'That's why you're being punished with two more weeks of leave and then a month of desk duty.'

'But Joe, my ... tactics.' She hated to even bring up the subject, but she couldn't let it go unsaid. She'd fucked Santos's men. She'd done it willingly and intentionally. Internal Affairs had to have had a heyday with that information.

'Nobody knows but me.'

A muscle moved in his jaw, but that was the only indication he gave as to how much he hated the lengths to which she'd gone. He hated it, but he was willing to keep quiet about it to protect her.

'Joe . . .'

'Nobody needs to know.' His tone was final.

'Thank you,' she said.

He took a final step closer, invading her space. Nervously, she ran a hand through her hair. She couldn't think when he got close. Her body had been crying out for him for two weeks. Being cooped up in this tiny office was almost too much for her to handle.

His gaze focused on her unconscious motion and he suddenly reached out to catch her hand. 'You're still wearing your ring.'

Shanna glanced down at her left hand, and the wedding ring glittered under the fluorescent lights. She hadn't been able to bear the thought of taking it off. Gritting her teeth, she reached to pull it from her finger. 'The props department probably needs it back.'

His hand covered hers to stop her. 'It's not a fake, Shanna.'

Her eyes flew up to his. 'What do you mean?'

He crowded her right up against the door. 'I bought it for you. Those diamonds are real.'

Her jaw dropped, and she looked with astonishment at her hand. 'But why?'

'I liked the idea of you wearing my ring.' His hand fisted in her hair, and for added emphasis, he nudged his crotch against her. He was hard as a brick. 'I told you that what was between us was real.'

Suddenly, the air in the room was too thick to breathe. 'I . . . I . . .' she stuttered.

'Maybe this will convince you,' he said.

He pulled her to stand in front of him and wrapped both arms around her. Shanna struggled to ignore the feeling of his hard cock pushing at her buttocks and focus on whatever he was trying to show her.

'We were meant to be together,' he whispered in her ear.

He nodded towards his desk, and she gasped. Huge vases of fresh flowers took up practically the entire room. The display of colour was shockingly beautiful. She looked closer, and her chest tightened when she realised what they were.

The blooms were tiger lilies.

Her heart began to pound inside her chest and she struggled for something to say.

'If those don't convince you, take a look at these,' Joe said harshly. He'd obviously interpreted her silence as a refusal. He grabbed a videocassette from the top of a file cabinet and shoved it in front of her face.

'What is it?' she asked in a raspy voice.

'A surveillance tape from the safe house. Watch it and then try to tell me that we aren't good together.'

Her knees went weak, and her hungry pussy clenched. 'Evidence?' she asked.

'Hell, no,' he barked, spinning her around in his arms. 'They're for us.'

'Us?' she asked, daring to hope.

'Us,' he said firmly as his head swooped down towards hers.

His mouth covered hers and Shanna heard a roaring in her ears. His lips were hard against hers as he established his possession. When his tongue ran across the seam of her lips, she shuddered with need. They were both breathless when they came up for air.

'I've missed you like hell,' he said gruffly.

His hands went to her suit jacket and hurriedly began unbuttoning it. He pushed it off her shoulders and she let it drop to the floor. His impatient desire lit a corresponding flame deep in her belly. Her toes curled when his lips found a sensitive spot on the side of her neck.

'I missed you more,' she said as she reached up to undo his tie.

'Then why didn't you call me?' His quick hands found

the zipper at the back of her skirt. It soon went skimming down her thighs and on to the floor.

'I didn't know what to say. I thought you were upset with me.'

'I was,' he said grumpily. 'But I still missed the sound of your voice.'

His hand slid up to cup her breast. The heat made her knees turn to jelly. 'You could have called me,' she said breathlessly.

'I started to about a hundred times. Then I'd convince myself you needed time.'

'I needed *you*,' she whispered. She tugged off his shirt, and her hands went immediately to his belt buckle. In her haste, she brushed her fingers against his swollen cock.

'God, I missed this,' he said. 'These past two weeks have felt longer than the past five years.'

'I know,' she said urgently. There had been times she couldn't sleep for wanting him.

His hands tugged her chemise over her head. He tossed it to the side and went absolutely still when he saw the white teddy she wore underneath it all. 'Holy hell,' he hissed.

She'd worn the lingerie as a good-luck charm.

'Oh, baby,' he groaned. Reaching out, he caught her by the waist. His thumbs moved against her but he seemed caught in a trance as he looked at her body.

'I bought this the same day you put that ring on my finger, but my plans didn't work out the way I'd hoped,' she said.

'They're working out now,' he said roughly. He attacked his own clothing and she watched with mounting excitement as his incredible body was uncovered before her eyes.

He reached for her, and she gasped as her world tilted. She held his shoulders tightly as he carried her to the big leather chair behind his desk. That chair – God, she'd had fantasies about that chair. It let out a loud squeak as it took their combined weight.

He adjusted her until she was on her knees straddling his hips, and his hands moved to her breasts. The snug-fitting cups of the teddy had them locked into place, but he squeezed them even tighter. Shanna groaned with need as her nipples swelled against the lace. Impatiently, she wiggled her shoulders, trying to dislodge the straps.

'Leave it,' he whispered against her lips. 'I like it.'

His arm wrapped around her back, and his head dropped. Gentle kisses traced a path from her neck down her collarbone to a straining nipple. When his teeth closed over the peak, her body bucked.

'More,' she begged. Leaning back over his supporting arm, she offered herself up to him. His teeth nipped at her until she was squirming in his arms. The racket sent up by the squeaky chair was nearly deafening.

'God, I can't wait much longer,' he said when her hips twisted and rubbed against his straining dick. 'Two weeks was too long. Get up here.'

Shanna lifted herself on her haunches, and he began tugging at the teddy, trying to get it off of her.

'Wait,' she said, covering his impatient hands. She looked him in the eye and smiled. 'This is the best part.'

She caught his hand and led it between her legs. His eyes widened when he found the open crotch. Watching her reaction, he let his fingers circle her wet opening. When her eyelids drifted shut with pleasure, he began probing her.

'Joe,' she gasped. The things he could do to her with such a simple touch were incredible. 'Oh, fuck me. I've missed you so much. Please fuck me.'

'Anything you want, baby,' he said.

He quickly positioned himself against her and thrust.

His hot cock went deep, and her body arched with over-whelming pleasure.

'I love you.'

Shanna froze when she realised that the words had slipped from her lips. She slowly opened her eyes, and his gaze captured hers. The look on his face was one of total possessiveness.

'I love you, too,' he said as he gave another hard thrust. He shot straight up into her, embedding himself deeply inside her. 'You're mine.'

A long groan left Shanna's lips and her forehead dropped against his.

'All mine,' he snarled.

'All yours,' she said. Reaching down, she caught his hands and lifted them up beside his head. She twined her fingers through his and let her body sink down hard.

'Mm,' she whimpered. He felt so good.

Their pubic hair tangled, and his hard drawn-up balls pressed against her pussy lips. She looked at him, and a glint from the diamond ring caught her attention. A slow smile spread across her face. 'And you're mine, Tiger. For ever.'

Their knuckles turned white as their palms sealed face to face. Shanna began plunging up and down on Joe's burning-hot erection, out of control. He met each of her downward plunges with an upward thrust of his hips. With each move, the chair responded with a loud screech.

Their bodies slapped together with the lace material of her teddy creating an erotic barrier. It held her tight as his big cock stretched and probed her. The chair's creaking and groaning became faster and louder as their actions became more frenzied.

Shanna's orgasm thundered towards her. She arched backward, squeezing Joe's hands tightly. His hips rose off the chair and ground into her. He thrust so hard, he lifted her knees completely off the chair and impaled her on his cock. She screamed, and his mouth came down on hers to muffle the sound. His body strained and bucked until one final thrust buried him at her core.

'Shanna,' he groaned. His muscles shuddered as he collapsed into the old chair. Her limp body sagged against his, and their sweaty skin clung. The quiet was broken only by the sound of their heavy breaths.

The startling silence made Shanna smile. 'When are you going to oil this damn chair?' she asked.

'Never,' Joe said firmly. He groaned and laid his head back against the supple leather. His lungs worked hard, but he found enough breath to give a soft chuckle. 'Absolutely never.'

LOOK OUT FOR THE ALL-NEW BLACK LACE BOOKS – AVAILABLE NOW!

All books priced £6.99 in the UK. Please note publication dates apply to the UK only. For other territories, please contact your retailer.

KING'S PAWN
Ruth Fox
ISBN O 352 33684 6

Cassie is consumed by a need to explore the intriguing world of SM – a world of bondage, domination and her submission. She agrees to give herself to the inscrutable Mr King for a day, to sample the pleasures of his complete control over her. Cassie finds herself hooked on the curious games they play. Her lesbian lover, Becky, is shocked, but agrees to Cassie visiting Mr King once more. It is then that she is initiated into the debauched Chessmen Club, where she is expected to go much further than she thought. **A refreshingly honest story of a woman's introduction to SM. Written by a genuine scene-player.**

COOKING UP A STORM
Emma Holly
ISBN O 352 33686 2

The Coates Inn Restaurant in Cape Cod is about to go belly up when its attractive owner, Abby, jumps at a stranger's offer to help her – both in her kitchen and her bed. The handsome chef claims to have an aphrodisiac menu that her patrons won't be able to resist. Can this playboy chef really save the day when Abby's body means more to him than her feelings? He has charmed the pants off her and she's now behaving like a wild woman. Can Abby tear herself away from her new lover for long enough to realise that he might be trying to steal the restaurant from under her nose? **Beautifully written and evocative story of love, lust and haute cuisine.**

Coming in May 2002

SLAVE TO SUCCESS
Kimberley Raines
ISBN 0 352 33687 0

Eugene, born poor but grown-up handsome, answers an ad to be a sex
slave for a year. He assumes his role will be that of a gigolo, and thinks
he will easily make the million dollars he needs to break into Hollywood.
On arrival at a secret destination he discovers his tasks are somewhat
more demanding. He will be a pleasure slave to the mistress Olanthé – a
demanding woman with high expectations who will put Eugene through
some exacting physical punishments and pleasures. He is in for the
shock of his life. **An exotic tale of female domination over a beautiful
but arrogant young man.**

FULL EXPOSURE
Robyn Russell
ISBN 0 352 33688 9

Attractive but stern Boston academic, Donatella di'Bianchi, is in Arezzo,
Italy, to investigate the affairs of the *Collegio Toscana*, a school of visual
arts. Donatella's probe is hampered by one man, the director, Stewart
Temple-Clarke. She is also sexually attracted by an English artist on the
faculty, the alluring but mysterious Ian Ramsey. In the course of her
inquiry Donatella is attacked, but receives help from two new friends –
Kiki Lee and Francesca Antinori. As the trio investigates the menacing
mysteries surrounding the college, these two young women open
Donatella's eyes to a world of sexual adventure with artists, students,
and even the local *carabinieri*. **A stylishly sensual erotic thriller set in the
languid heat of an Italian summer.**

STRIPPED TO THE BONE
Jasmine Stone
ISBN 0 352 33463 0

Annie has always been a rebel. While her sister settled down in Middle America, Annie blazed a trail of fast living on the West Coast, constantly seeking thrills. She is motivated by a hungry sexuality and a mission to keep changing her life. Her capacity for experimental sex games means she's never short of partners, and she keeps her lovers in a spin of erotic confusion. Every man she encounters is determined to discover what makes her tick, yet no one can get a hold of Annie long enough to find out. Maybe the Russian Ilmar can unlock the secret. However, by succumbing to his charms, is Annie stepping into territory too dangerous even for her? **By popular demand, this is a special reprint of a free-wheeling story of lust and trouble in a fast world.**

Coming in June 2002

WICKED WORDS 6
A Black Lace short story collection
ISBN 0 352 33590 0

Deliciously daring and hugely popular, the *Wicked Words* collections are the freshest and most entertaining volumes of women's erotica to be found anywhere in the world. The diversity of themes and styles reflects the multi-faceted nature of the female sexual imagination. Combining humour, warmth and attitude with fun, filthy, imaginative writing, these stories sizzle with horny action. Only the most arousing fiction makes it into a *Wicked Words* volume. **This is the best in fun, cutting-edge erotica from the UK and USA.**

MANHATTAN PASSION
Antoinette Powell
ISBN O 352 33691 9

Julia is an art conservator at a prestigious museum in New York. She lives
a life of designer luxury with her Wall Street millionaire husband until,
that is, she discovers the dark and criminal side to his twilight activities –
and storms out, leaving her high-fashion wardrobe behind her. Staying
with her best friends Zoë and Jack, Julia is initiated into a hedonist circle
of New York's most beautiful and sexually interesting people.
Meanwhile, David, her husband, has disappeared with all their wealth.
What transpires is a high-octane manhunt – from loft apartments to
sleazy drinking holes; from the trendiest nightclubs to the criminal
underworld. **A stunning debut from an author who knows how to
entertain her audience.**

HARD CORPS
Claire Thompson
ISBN O 352 33491 6

This is the story of Remy Harris, a bright young woman starting out as an
army cadet at military college in the US. Enduring all the usual trials
of boot-camp discipline and rigorous exercise, she's ready for any
challenge – that is until she meets Jacob, who recognises her true
sexuality. Initiated into the Hard Corps – a secret society within the
barracks – Remy soon becomes absorbed by this clandestine world of
ritual punishment. It's only when Jacob takes things too far that she
rebels, and begins to plot her revenge. **Strict sergeants and rebellious
cadets come together in this unusual and highly entertaining story of
military discipline with a twist.**

Black Lace Booklist

Information is correct at time of printing. To avoid disappointment check availability before ordering. Go to www.blacklace-books.co.uk. All books are priced £6.99 unless another price is given.

BLACK LACE BOOKS WITH A CONTEMPORARY SETTING

☐ THE TOP OF HER GAME Emma Holly	ISBN O 352 33337 5	£5.99
☐ IN THE FLESH Emma Holly	ISBN O 352 34498 3	£5.99
☐ A PRIVATE VIEW Crystalle Valentino	ISBN O 352 33308 1	£5.99
☐ SHAMELESS Stella Black	ISBN O 352 34485 1	£5.99
☐ INTENSE BLUE Lyn Wood	ISBN O 352 34496 7	£5.99
☐ THE NAKED TRUTH Natasha Rostova	ISBN O 352 34497 5	£5.99
☐ ANIMAL PASSIONS Martine Marquand	ISBN O 352 34499 1	£5.99
☐ A SPORTING CHANCE Susie Raymond	ISBN O 352 33501 7	£5.99
☐ TAKING LIBERTIES Susie Raymond	ISBN O 352 33357 X	£5.99
☐ A SCANDALOUS AFFAIR Holly Graham	ISBN O 352 33523 8	£5.99
☐ THE NAKED FLAME Crystalle Valentino	ISBN O 352 33528 9	£5.99
☐ CRASH COURSE Juliet Hastings	ISBN O 352 33018 X	£5.99
☐ ON THE EDGE Laura Hamilton	ISBN O 352 33534 3	£5.99
☐ LURED BY LUST Tania Picarda	ISBN O 352 33533 5	£5.99
☐ THE HOTTEST PLACE Tabitha Flyte	ISBN O 352 33536 X	£5.99
☐ THE NINETY DAYS OF GENEVIEVE Lucinda Carrington	ISBN O 352 33070 8	£5.99
☐ EARTHY DELIGHTS Tesni Morgan	ISBN O 352 33548 3	£5.99
☐ MAN HUNT Cathleen Ross	ISBN O 352 33583 1	
☐ MÉNAGE Emma Holly	ISBN O 352 33231 X	
☐ DREAMING SPIRES Juliet Hastings	ISBN O 352 33584 X	
☐ THE TRANSFORMATION Natasha Rostova	ISBN O 352 33311 1	
☐ STELLA DOES HOLLYWOOD Stella Black	ISBN O 352 33588 2	
☐ SIN.NET Helena Ravenscroft	ISBN O 352 33598 X	
☐ HOTBED Portia Da Costa	ISBN O 352 33614 5	
☐ TWO WEEKS IN TANGIER Annabel Lee	ISBN O 352 33599 8	
☐ HIGHLAND FLING Jane Justine	ISBN O 352 33616 1	

☐ PLEASURE'S DAUGHTER Sedalia Johnson	ISBN O 352 33237 9
☐ JULIET RISING Cleo Cordell	ISBN O 352 32938 6
☐ DEMON'S DARE Melissa MacNeal	ISBN O 352 33683 8
☐ ELENA'S CONQUEST Lisette Allen	ISBN O 352 32950 5

BLACK LACE ANTHOLOGIES

☐ CRUEL ENCHANTMENT Erotic Fairy Stories Janine Ashbless	ISBN O 352 33483 5	£5.99
☐ MORE WICKED WORDS Various	ISBN O 352 33487 8	£5.99
☐ WICKED WORDS 4 Various	ISBN O 352 33603 X	
☐ WICKED WORDS 5 Various	ISBN O 352 33642 0	

BLACK LACE NON-FICTION

☐ THE BLACK LACE BOOK OF WOMEN'S SEXUAL FANTASIES Ed. Kerri Sharp	ISBN O 352 33346 4	£5.99

To find out the latest information about Black Lace titles, check out the website: www.blacklace-books.co.uk or send for a booklist with complete synopses by writing to:

> Black Lace Booklist, Virgin Books Ltd
> Thames Wharf Studios
> Rainville Road
> London W6 9HA

Please include an SAE of decent size. Please note only British stamps are valid.

Our privacy policy
We will not disclose information you supply us to any other parties. We will not disclose any information which identifies you personally to any person without your express consent.

From time to time we may send out information about Black Lace books and special offers. Please tick here if you do <u>not</u> wish to receive Black Lace information.   ☐

Please send me the books I have ticked above.

Name ....

Address ....

....

....

....

Post Code ....

Send to: Cash Sales, Black Lace Books, Thames Wharf Studios, Rainville Road, London W6 9HA.

US customers: for prices and details of how to order books for delivery by mail, call 1-800-343-4499.

Please enclose a cheque or postal order, made payable to Virgin Books Ltd, to the value of the books you have ordered plus postage and packing costs as follows:

UK and BFPO – £1.00 for the first book, 50p for each subsequent book.

Overseas (including Republic of Ireland) – £2.00 for the first book, £1.00 for each subsequent book.

If you would prefer to pay by VISA, ACCESS/MASTERCARD, DINERS CLUB, AMEX or SWITCH, please write your card number and expiry date here:

....

Signature ....

Please allow up to 28 days for delivery.